THE
DANGER
IN BOHEMIA

H. E. KOLLEF

Published by

DREAMSPINNER PRESS

5032 Capital Circle SW, Suite 2, PMB# 279, Tallahassee, FL 32305-7886 USA
www.dreamspinnerpress.com

The Danger in Bohemia

Cover Art
http://www.breearcher.com
Cover content is for illustrative purposes only and any person depicted on the cover is a model.

ISBN: 978-1-63477-141-2
Digital ISBN: 978-1-63477-142-9
Library of Congress Control Number: 2015920896
Published March 2016
v. 1.0

Printed in the United States of America
∞
This paper meets the requirements of
ANSI/NISO Z39.48-1992 (Permanence of Paper).

ACKNOWLEDGMENTS

Thank you to my long-standing editor, Tricia.

AUTHOR'S NOTE

EAGLE-EYED READERS may recognize some of these characters and locations from my previous short story, "One Cold Night in Prague," published in the *Random Acts of Kindness* anthology. Both stories take place in Prague, where I lived for a few months' shy of two years. Prague has a special place in my heart—I hope you enjoy exploring it as much as I did.

PROLOGUE

WILL MRACEK, twenty-seven and newly in love, hesitated at the door to the private office in the lower floor of Jean Claude's—*no, their*—penthouse apartment. It was his first day living with Jean Claude, and he'd thought a surprise lunch date a good way to celebrate.

Feeling nervous, he reached up to shove a stray lock of hair out of his face, wishing for the umpteenth time that his wavy chestnut hair wasn't so damned unruly. As he did so, he saw with dismay that he'd missed a smear of brown binding glue on the back of his hand when he cleaned up before leaving his workshop that morning. He sighed, trying in vain to rub it away. It was bad enough that he wore silver-rimmed glasses and all his clothes made him look like Professor Plum without absentminded stains to complete the picture. He needed to get out more too. Hiding away at his desk was not doing any favors for his olive-tinged complexion.

Even now, Will wasn't sure what a powerful businessman like Jean Claude saw in him, a quiet book restorer. He remembered the first time Jean Claude had walked into his shop, a priceless first edition of *Madame Bovary* in his hand. He could still feel, even now, the way his stomach had clenched at the sight of such handsome, powerful elegance, at the gray eyes that had pierced him so deeply. He'd never felt such instant attraction before, and it had made him clumsy, awkward.

But Jean Claude had smiled, seemingly charmed. And the next day he'd returned—this time with a bouquet of flowers and an invitation to dinner, which Will had instantly accepted. Three months later, he'd told Jean Claude he loved him. Caught in the throes of such powerful feelings, he hadn't been able to say no when Jean Claude asked him to move in, despite their short courtship.

Now he wondered if he'd made a mistake. Just standing in the expensive penthouse in uptown Manhattan made Will nervous. He hoped a lunch date would remind him why he'd come here, who he'd come for.

Clearing his throat, Will raised his hand to knock, then hesitated when he heard voices just inside the door. He frowned, still too unsure of his place to know if an interruption would be welcome.

The door—made of heavy, polished walnut—stood open just a crack. It was enough that he could see Jean Claude inside at his desk, talking to a bald man dressed in a black business suit who stood on the other side with hands clasped at his waist. Will still felt a little jolt when he saw Jean Claude. The Frenchman was so handsome, with his silver-black hair and aquiline nose, pale as winter skin, and piercing gray eyes. Adelaide, his gorgeous Amazonian assistant, took notes in the corner.

Will should have left. Later, he would wish he had.

"…Operation was successful," the bald man said. Even from the distance, Will could see the sweat gleaming on his forehead. Intrigued—he'd always been cursed with an overabundance of curiosity—he leaned forward, straining his ears to hear. "The goods made their way across the border with no suspicions."

"Good." Jean Claude's voice was colder than Will had ever heard it, almost bored. "Any difficulties?"

"A few Iraqi border guards stuck their hands in the bags. We took care of them. The usual procedure. We were discreet, sir."

Will paled. Goods? Borders? What was he talking about?

"Are you sure?" Jean Claude's voice dropped to a dangerous murmur.

The man in front of him fidgeted nervously. "Sir?"

"Are you sure you were discreet?"

"Uh, yes. No witnesses."

"Then what do you call this?" There was a hiss as Jean Claude slid a manila folder across the polished wood of his desk.

The man in black cringed and reached out to flick open the folder with a shaking hand. When he saw what was inside, he stepped back as if he'd been slapped. "Sir, I—I don't know how—"

"That is a report from US Military Intelligence," Jean Claude said. "From a small boy in Nippur who saw men dressed in black gun down the guards at the National Museum. Men wearing uniforms with the Graywater logo."

Silence.

"I'll take care of it," the man said after a long moment. He was short of breath, and Will heard a palpable fear in his voice. "I'll—"

"You can't clear this up," Jean Claude said. "This isn't the FBI—I don't have any sway with military courts. There's only one choice here." In one fluid motion, Jean Claude reached into his jacket and pulled out a gun. There was a click, the sound too quiet for what it was, and the man crumbled onto the carpet with a heavy thud.

Will slammed his hands over his mouth to stifle a scream.

"Take him to the Midtown office." Jean Claude's voice was silky smooth. He stood and walked over to the body. Bending, he pulled a handkerchief from his pocket and wiped the gun clean. Holding it with the white cloth, he slid it carefully into the dead man's fingers. "Make sure the note takes full responsibility."

"Shall I alert our contacts at the FBI?" Adelaide asked.

Jean Claude was silent a moment, looking down at the dead man. Then, standing, he shook his head. "The NYPD, I think. If and when the FBI gets to it, they'll know not to involve me. I want all traces of the Nippur operation to lead back to him."

"Understood, sir."

Outside the door, Will felt nauseated. Panic threatened to overtake him as he listened to Jean Claude coldly determine how to dispose of a dead body. He must have made some noise because Jean Claude suddenly looked over, meeting his eyes with a cold gray stare through the crack in the door. Surprise ran across his face.

"William?"

Will didn't wait for him to take action. Instinct took over, sending him running back to the elevator, his heart thumping as he jumped inside and jammed the button for the first floor. It closed on Adelaide's menacing form at the end of the hallway, nostrils flared, and a dangerous glint in her eyes.

He rode the elevator forty floors with his heart in his throat, sure that at any moment it would stop, that Adelaide would be there, forcing the doors open, bringing that gun up, ready to—

The elevator stopped at the ground floor with a quiet ping. He stepped into the apartment's gold-and-marble lobby, breath held, and made a beeline for the revolving doors that led outside.

Keep walking. Don't look back.

He forced himself to smile at the doorman, to walk, not run, into the busy streets of New York outside. He knew it would be easier to find him if he stood out from the crowd, so he bowed his shoulders and kept his head down. Will slipped into the stream of drab New Yorkers on their way to lunch, moving around the dog walkers with their small leashed packs and the occasional bike messenger who dared to ride amongst the pedestrians. Only when he was a dozen blocks away did he let himself step into an alleyway and fall to his knees, his breath coming fast.

What was he going to do?

He ran through the possibilities, forcing the fear down. His workshop in the Village—but no, that would be the first place Jean Claude would look. He didn't have any close friends or family in the area either, not since his father had died the year before.

Suddenly his phone rang. Will took it from his pocket, saw Jean Claude's picture blinking on the screen, and hesitated a long moment before answering. "Hello?"

"William." His voice sent shivers down Will's spine. "Love, you've seen something shocking, I know. But I can explain. Please, come home. I'm worried about you."

"Worried about me? You just shot a man," Will hissed into the phone. His eyes widened as he looked up at the mouth of the alleyway, making sure he was still alone. Saying it aloud made it all the more true. "You're a... a murderer."

"Will, I love you, and you love me. Isn't that worth listening to what I have to say? I promise, I don't want to hurt you."

Will saw again his hand snap out, the cool disinterest with which he pulled the trigger, cleaned the gun, and placed it into the man's hand—framing him as a suicide. "I trusted you," he whispered. His heart ached in his chest, and tension sent pain ratcheting through his head, mixing with his panic. "I'm going to the police. Homeland Security!"

4

"Don't be ridiculous. There's no need for hysterics. Just come home. I can send Adelaide with the car for you—you're on 85th and Park, *non?*"

Will looked up, his heart skipping a beat as he saw Jean Claude was right. How did he know? "No, I—I need time to think. To decide what to do," Will stalled, looking around like a cornered animal.

There was a cold silence. When Jean Claude spoke, there was a hard edge in his voice. "Come home now, Will. Or there will be trouble. Don't make me come after you, my love."

Fear curdled Will's blood as Jean Claude's words struck him through the phone. *Don't make me come after you.* Panicked, Will slammed on the End Call icon and watched the call minimize. Still on the first wave of adrenaline, he stared at his phone, then realized what had happened.

The GPS locator. Jean Claude was tracking him.

Riding that adrenaline, Will dropped his phone on the ground and stomped on it till the screen cracked and flaked off. That done, he took a deep breath and tried to make his brain work again. He would only have a few minutes before Jean Claude came for him. He needed a plan, and quickly.

If Jean Claude found him again, assurances or not, he was going to kill him. Will knew it like he knew his own name. Nor could he go to the police, not with the way Jean Claude had talked about them, about their ties. He had only one choice if he wanted to survive: he had to disappear.

He pulled out his battered brown wallet, hoping something in it would spark an idea, the faintest hint of a plan. He took a quick inventory—a debit card, driver's license, Antiquarian Book Society membership, twenty dollars, and a few old business cards. Then he saw the corner of some dirty cardboard sticking out from the back of his wallet. He pulled it out, the memory coming to him in a flash as he read the business card, the international number carefully printed by hand on the back, his cousin John's name scrawled on the bottom.

It had been raining the day he gave it to Will.

"I'm done with the Marines. Thought I'd try going to Prague to teach English," John had said, sounding embarrassed. They'd been close as children, and in the brief time John spent in New York while recovering from a battle wound, had regained some of their old friendship. "If you ever have business in Europe, give me a call. You know you're the only family I've got left that I actually like, right?"

Will had laughed and taken the card, promising to use it but doubtful he'd ever leave the continent. He'd seen John off at the airport with a quiet wave, wishing he were brave enough to set out on such an adventure.

Maybe now was the time.

Heart pounding, he hurried out of the alleyway and down the street. First, he'd run—far away from here, disappear into the city. Then he'd buy a disposable phone and make that call.

And then?

He swallowed hard and let his mind blank as he dove into the crowd of people hurrying down the street.

CHAPTER 1

Prague, February 2nd, 2016

"CHRIST, DAMNED snow," Hadrian Walls growled, stamping his feet and reminding himself, again, to get his worn soles repaired before he broke his neck on the ice. The ancient cobblestones outside were beautiful, yes, but traitorous when buried beneath half a foot of snow and counting. He snarled again, shrugging snow off his back before pushing open the door to the subterranean pub U Medvídků.

The staircase down was dark and winding. He stomped down the wood, not paying attention to the old plaster walls or the beer advertisements that hung on them, and finally emerged into the quiet warmth of the pub. There was still half an hour until they officially opened, and the pub was empty save for a massive white dog that trotted up to him with a canine grin.

"All right there, Vaclav," he said, giving the dog's velvet ears a good rub. "Having a nice Friday?"

The dog whined and nudged Hadrian's hip with his cold nose before walking back to the fireplace and settling down.

"Right. Work," Hadrian muttered to himself.

Windows, set high in the walls at street level, let some cold winter light into the room. The rest came from yellow antique lamps and the fireplace opposite the bar. It gave the pub a medieval feel enhanced by scarred wooden tables and chairs, all Czech craftsmanship and as old as the pub itself. The walls, made of more stone and yellowed plaster, held metal signs advertising Czech beers and framed copies of important newspapers. Hadrian's favorite, from the day Václav Havel was declared president and the Czechs abolished communism, hung at the end of the bar beneath a giant stuffed moose head.

His ice-blue eyes adjusting to the dim light, Hadrian took a last look at the snoozing dog before moving to duck around the gleaming wooden bar. After hanging his leather jacket on the wall, he brushed stray lint off the black sweater he wore above tight, faded jeans. He rubbed his head once, hand running over the ash-brown hair he still kept military short. There was a small electric kettle beneath the bar, and Hadrian shook it, checking to make sure it actually held water, before flicking it on. As he did so, he caught a glimpse of himself reflected in the waxed wood.

His contoured face, all sharp angles and too-big nose and ears that stuck out just a little, should have been cartoonish. Instead, he had an angry grace, a compelling *something* that could have made him a movie star in another life. Or so he'd been told by one of his numerous exes. Maybe it had been a one-night stand. Who could keep track?

"*Ahoj*, Hadrian" came a booming voice from behind him.

Hadrian turned to see a giant, balding man with a big belly and more tattoos than skin coming toward him. He relaxed a little. Despite Ivan's tough appearance, he was a kind man with an infectious laugh. The son of a Russian businessman of questionable morals, he'd lived all over the world before choosing Prague to settle down and start his restaurant—a fact Hadrian was grateful for every time he walked into U Medvídků.

"Hullo, Ivan," Hadrian said. He leaned on the gleaming wood. "How was lunch?"

"Slow, my friend," Ivan said. "The snow keeps them away. But I do not worry—they will come when they are hungry. I have boar goulash for tonight's special. Fresh from Moravia." He winked, the gesture so ridiculous on such a man that Hadrian had to smile.

"Save me a bowl, would you?" Hadrian asked, his Northern English accent thickening.

"*Prosím*, Hadrian. Of course. I must feed my best bartender."

Hadrian snorted. "Your only bartender. Where's Jitka?"

Ivan shrugged. "She will come soon." Clapping Hadrian on the back, he turned to head back to his kitchen, his true passion.

Alone, Hadrian sighed and checked the progress of the kettle. Finding the water boiled, he grabbed a mug, cracked open a packet of instant coffee, and poured it and the water into the mug before giving the concoction a quick stir with a handy spoon. He let his mind go quiet as heat seeped from the mug to his skin. The pub, still warm and dry, stretched out in front of him. From outside he could just hear the faint whistles of the wind, blowing more ice and snow about above their heads.

He brought the mug to his mouth and took a sip. Too sweet, but at least it was warm and caffeinated.

His thoughts drifted, but not too far. Not into the dark places. Instead, he thought of what he'd done that day—a late morning after the closing shift the night before, a walk through the city before the snow had begun to fall. He'd avoided the tourist-dense Wenceslas Square and kept to the edges of his city, vetoing a trip to tree-lined Petřín Hill in exchange for a wander through the older, grittier neighborhood of Žižkov, where he kept his small flat. He'd found a used bookstore and added a few more paperbacks to his collection. It had been a good day.

Until the snow, and then more of the snow. And a bit of snow on top of that.

He felt the scowl creeping back on his face as the bell rang on the door upstairs. It deepened as he heard the unmistakable giggles and excited "Oh my *Gods*!" of young American tourists. Hadrian had been in the Czech Republic long enough to have absorbed the Czech predilection for politeness and quiet conversation in public. Sighing, he put down his coffee and set a few hefty glasses on the bar in front of him, ready to serve.

There was a crash and shattering from the stairs. In the silence after, he heard a small, nervous "Oops."

He gritted his teeth. It was going to be a long night.

A FEW hours later, dinner guests in search of boar packed the pub, just as Ivan had predicted. Jitka, their pretty blonde waitress, had showed up only twenty minutes late, a new record. There were enough people in the pub that she was kept busy, and Hadrian poured a decent number of pints and a few of the harder drinks. The air smelled like cigarette smoke and earthy goulash.

"*Tři* Staropramen, Hadrek," Jitka said, coming around the bar with a tired smile.

"*Ano*," he said and, pulling the glasses down, began to pour. "How are you, Jitka?"

She bit her lip. "Ah… I be good. *Ne*, I am fine," she corrected herself, and Hadrian grunted with approval as she held out her tray and took the beer from him. "*Díky*," she said, winking. She put an extra sashay in her hips as she walked away.

Hadrian watched, thoughtful. Though he was fluent in Czech, Jitka had recently asked Hadrian to speak to her only in English to help her practice. It was a pretty common request, and most of his Czech acquaintances liked to practice with him when they could. But he had the feeling she was looking for a little more than English practice. It was too bad—he wasn't in the market for complications at the moment.

"She's cute," said a familiar voice down the bar.

Hadrian looked up to see his American friend, John, pulling out a stool. Snow melted in his sandy hair, and every muscle in his compact frame seemed to be slumped with barely restrained exhaustion. Hadrian snorted and reached out to pull a pint of Kozel. "Not my type."

"Your type?" John said, eyebrow raised. "I've seen you with more partners than I've got fingers since I moved here, and none of them looked the same."

"Didn't say it had anything to do with looks," Hadrian said, as the glass filled with amber liquid, a foamy head forming at the top.

John rolled his eyes but couldn't hide a small, amused smile.

"Where's your better half, then?" Hadrian asked, turning off the tap and setting the pint in front of John. He leaned against the wood as John took a long, grateful sip.

"Karel'll be here soon," John finally said, setting his glass down with a heavy clink. He stared at the amber liquid, amusement falling away as he became lost in some thought. The frown lines around his mouth, usually faint, were deep tonight.

Hadrian felt himself frown in response. While not the most talkative guy, usually John had some conversation for him. They'd grown friendly in the past year, ever since John had begun dating Karel, one of Hadrian's friends and a regular at U Medvídků. They'd bonded over past military experiences, though he'd only told John a fraction of what he'd been through, and he was positive John was holding back at least that much. John didn't know about what Hadrian had seen, and in return Hadrian respected the ghosts hiding in his eyes. One warrior to another.

"Trouble?" he prompted after a long silence, turning his piercing blue eyes on John.

"I... well," John said. He ran a hand through his hair. "Stress at work," he went on waving his hand in the air. "We've got a batch of new English teaching recruits at Foxrod," he said, referencing one of the best teacher-training schools in Prague, where John worked as a course director. There, groups of trainee teachers would receive guidance in making lesson plans, teaching adults and children, and essential grammar and teaching philosophies. Every day they'd spend between one to three hours teaching real live classes. It was stressful, especially for the trainers, but it worked. And word in the city was that Foxrod produced some of the most capable language teachers in Prague.

"Where are they from this time?"

"Two from the UK, one from South Africa, two Americans."

"*Tch*, Americans," Hadrian said. "You lot. Always loud. Drive me up the bleedin' walls," he said, as John rolled his eyes.

"Because the Northern English are paragons of good behavior," John shot back, raising an eyebrow.

"Compared to y'all, yeah," Hadrian said, cracking a hint of a smile, and John returned it.

"*Prosím*," said a voice down the bar.

Hadrian turned to see a woman leaning against the wood, waiting for him. He nodded at John. "Duty calls, mate."

John waved him off and returned to his beer.

As Hadrian took the woman's order and poured her beer, he eyed John, who had returned to his grim mood. Hadrian didn't believe his story for a second. His slightly too-big nose had been honed to find trouble, and often his life had depended on it. John was a man with some serious trouble on his back.

But he respected John's privacy. His, after all, was of utmost importance to him. Shrugging, he finished helping the woman, turned to the handlebar-mustachioed man behind her, and poured him a shot of cheap whiskey. Every man had his troubles. And he wasn't getting involved.

CHAPTER 2

MAX KNIGHT sighed in relief as the clock hit five. Around him, his four fellow teacher trainees were laughing with one another and closing their notebooks in relief. It was the Friday of their first week of English teacher training, and between three hours of live English teaching in the mornings and five hours of grammar, theory, and lesson preparation practice in the afternoons, it was grueling. Harder than that was remembering who he was supposed to be every day, at least for Max. His old life—and his old name—had been left behind on the streets of New York, and it took half his attention just to keep his story straight.

He was Max Knight now. American, English major, Europe traveler, and aspiring TEFL teacher.

Maybe if he could get some sleep at night, things would be easier. But every night he relived the murder in his dreams and woke up in a cold sweat. Sometimes the dream ended there, watching Jean Claude pulling the trigger. More frequently it ended with him on the other end of Jean Claude's gun.

His flight from New York all those months ago had left him thin and weak, and only sheer luck had saved him. Max hadn't realized just how much John could help him when he'd placed that call. John, it turned out, hadn't just been a Marine—he'd been deep in the military police, in a position secret enough to prevent him from telling his family what he'd really been up to. Until the mortar that had shattered his femur and sent him home, John had worked with the best the Marines had to offer and built up the necessary black-ops skills to keep himself, and his fellow soldiers, alive. He'd put all those skills to use helping Max, getting him a new name, passport, and Czech visa, and finally getting in contact with an ex-colleague in the States, who had kept Max alive until he could be smuggled out of the country. It had been months of hiding, of homeless shelters and bus stations and cheap motels. But it had done the job. Max was still alive, after all.

Now John was helping him once again—by welcoming Max into the home he shared with his boyfriend, Karel, and finding ways to make him feel comfortable. Max had spent most of November and December locked in his room, the trauma of what he'd gone through keeping him weak and too afraid to leave the apartment. But the gentle warmth of Karel and the quiet, bumbling affection of John had worked to help him heal. In January he'd left his room for the first time, taking in the fresh air, the rich beauty Prague had to offer. It had helped to heal him, to give him hope for the first time that he'd truly escaped Jean Claude.

Foxrod was the next stage of his recovery and their best plan for keeping Max hidden in the long term.

Max would be less noticeable, John said, the more he blended in. And blending in meant becoming another English teacher looking to have fun and get the European experience. The faster he could melt into the rest of the expat community, the better.

"Tough today," said Maggie, his tablemate, in her Midwestern drawl. She scrunched up her face, wrinkling her pert nose and round cheeks the color of warm amber. Though she looked about eighteen in her T-shirt and jeans, Max knew she was closer to thirty than him. "Think I actually fell asleep in that last grammar session."

Max laughed as she reached her arms up and stretched, revealing surprisingly strong biceps. "You did," he said, with a half smile.

Maggie rolled her eyes and shoved him playfully in the shoulder. "You can give me your notes, then," she said, flipping her dark hair over her shoulder.

In response, Max rolled his eyes and pushed his notebook over to her before pulling his glasses off to polish them on the edge of his shirt.

"Max?" said a voice over his shoulder.

Max jumped in his seat, almost dropping his glasses. Turning, he saw a blurry version of Christopher, his English classmate, standing with his hands in the air and an amused smile on his face. On the first day of class, Max had been struck by his handsome face, the smoothness of his midnight-dark skin, the way he held himself.

"Jumpy much?" Christopher laughed.

Max chuckled weakly and settled his glasses back on his face. "Sorry. Uh, what's up?"

"Well…," Christopher started, sticking his hands in his pockets and rocking back on his heels. "I was wondering if tonight was the night you'd come out with us and have some fun? It is Friday, after all, and you missed all our precourse bonding sessions. You're kind of obligated to get drunk and have fun." He flashed Max a charming grin, full of bright white teeth that contrasted handsomely with his dark skin.

Max bit his lip, trying to decide what to say. It would be strange if he said no—going to bars, drinking, it was all expected here. But the idea of going to a crowded pub, dark and smoky and full of strangers, terrified him. Anyone could be lurking there, spying on him. It was still too dangerous. "Sorry," he said, wincing at the disappointment in Christopher's eyes. "I, uh… I've got a lesson Monday, and I still need to do some prep."

"You're kidding, right?" Christopher said, grinning. He flicked one of the papers on Max's desk, sending it skittering a few inches. "Plenty of time for work later. How long can it take?"

Max raised an eyebrow, thinking of their instructor's vehement warnings earlier that day about their coursework. "I'm pretty sure we were told it would take 'hours of pain and suffering' to finish this essay, if you remember."

Christopher rolled his eyes. "They're just trying to scare us. We've all passed uni. This'll be a piece of cake. Anyway, no one said you had to go on a rager. How about one beer? I promise I'll make it fun. All kinds of sober things we can get up to." He winked, the innuendo clear enough to send a light blush to Max's cheeks.

Max shook his head. "Ahhh, no, I'm sorry."

"All right, all right," Christopher said, nodding. "I know, Mr. Bookworm, gotta get your stuff done. But this weekend you're coming out. No excuses."

Max watched him walk away to join the others, who were waiting by the door to the classroom. He sighed.

"He's got a point," Maggie said, pulling his attention back to her. She stared at him with narrowed eyes, a probing look on her face. "I know for a fact that you've got your lesson plans done. And Christopher is hot as hell. So… what's up?"

Max bit his lip.

Something flashed across Maggie's face, and she sat back, nodding to herself. "Ah, okay. I get it. Not interested, huh?"

"Not in anyone," Max reassured her. "Really. Just… not in the market."

"I understand," she said, face softening. She leaned forward, looked like she was going to say something else, then caught herself. Shaking her head a little, she stood and ruffled his mess of dark hair. "I'll see you later, okay?" she said, smiling. "And remember… you don't have to be looking to get laid to go out. It can be fun, and very platonic," she added, with a half smile that Max returned.

He watched as she left the room, leaving him alone in the classroom. He took a deep breath, sat back, and let his eyes wander. The room was painted white all over, with a drab carpet and fluorescent lights, but that didn't rob it of a kind of cheerfulness. There were English teacher cartoons painted on the walls, and a bulletin board with thank-you notes from former and current students.

Just that morning, the room had been full of English students for the trainee teachers to practice on, ranging from sixteen to sixty-seven. He'd been surprised to learn he'd mostly be teaching adults in Prague, and even more surprised to see the diversity in the classrooms. He'd been expecting Czechs, but not the mix of Russians, Koreans, Ghanaians, Poles… the list went on. He even had one student from Columbia. All united by a common goal: to learn English. Or, perhaps better said, to improve their lives. Most of his students already spoke at least two other languages, and several knew more than four. He was constantly amazed at their kindness as well. He'd never taught before, never had designs on working with or, especially, in front of people, but somehow it was coming together.

He took a deep breath, inhaling the smell of whiteboard markers and old paper. It was so different from what he'd been used to. He'd spent his college days fixing antique books, binding new ones, and turning the irreparable ones into art. He sighed, remembering the feel of working with those pages, the sharp smell of book glue, the quiet rustling of the pages. Even better were the times he could devote to creation, merging the fine arts with books in gilded pages, lace cut-out illustrations, and bindings of leather made to look antique.

It was his passion. And he missed it with an ache that hadn't gotten any easier in the months since he'd fled his workshop.

"Get over it," he told himself, sitting back up with a sharp exhalation. That was behind him now. He couldn't do that kind of work here—not without raising flags, dangerous ones that might be picked up by one of Jean Claude's people. Even buying the supplies he needed would be too risky; they were rare. People noticed when strangers came to town looking for unusual things.

He took a deep breath and looked at the empty room around him. This was as it should be—stay alone, stay quiet. It was safer that way, for him and the people around him.

Shrugging his massive peacoat on, Max grabbed his bag and made for the door. Outside, he saw Christopher and a few others having a cigarette by the entrance to the building. He waved but didn't stop to say hello, instead turning into the cold wind and making his way to the subway ahead.

CHAPTER 3

SOMETHING VERY loud, and very annoying, tapped on Hadrian's window. Growling, he turned over in his bed, pulling the thick white comforter with him. When that didn't work, he grabbed a pillow and slammed it over his ears. He took a deep breath, trying to find that nice, sleepy place he'd been in only moments before. He'd been having a dream. There was a cabin and it had snowed and, inside, a fire and someone warm was waiting for him—

Tap. Tap. Tap.

"Christ's bloody sake!" he snapped, throwing the pillow to turn and glare at the window.

A pigeon sat there, winter fat beneath mottled gray feathers, and slowly tapped the window again with its beak. He stared at it a long moment. It stared back. Then, without warning, it flew off into the morning, leaving a long furrow in the snow gathered on the sill.

His apartment was on a hill in Žižkov, and from it Hadrian could see the heart of Prague laid out before him. He took in the sun rising behind orange-tiled roofs frosted white with snow, the pastel houses and apartments beneath them, all set against a lightening sky. In the far distance, the great Prague Castle watched over the city from its perch above the Vltava River. Even Petřín Hill was noble this morning, frosted as it was with fresh snow. Another morning he might have lingered beside the view, but it was too early to appreciate it today.

Hadrian glanced at his bedside table. The clock read 7:00 a.m., far too early to be awake on his Sunday off. Especially when he'd been cleaning up at U Medvídků till two o'clock the night before. He briefly contemplated going back to sleep, then shook his head. Wouldn't work. He was too well trained to reach instant alertness at the hint of a problem. No way he'd calm that adrenaline rush now.

17

Sitting up, he let the covers slide down his chest and bunch at his lean waist. His morning wood bulged uncomfortably between his legs after his dream. He closed his eyes, trying to call it back.

He'd been in a cabin. He recognized it—it was the one he rented in Český ráj, a beautiful natural park only a few hours from the city. It had been covered in snow, white drifting up the sides, along the tops of the trees. Inside, there'd been a fire. He hadn't been alone. Reaching down, he took himself in his warm, callused hand, closing his fingers around his throbbing cock.

The cabin was as it was in reality: the walls made of heavy logs, the floor of hard wood with a thick woven carpet to keep feet warm. There was a fireplace, and in front of it, reclining on his trim stomach, was a man. Hadrian couldn't see his face, but he could tell he was young, late twenties at most, with thick dark hair and smooth, gentle hands....

He squeezed, pulling up and down, his body framed in the sunlight coming through the window as he threw his head back and remembered what that dream man had done to him. Hadrian had knelt before him on the rug, the fire hot on the side of his face. Lifted the younger man to his knees and kissed him, gently. The other had sighed as Hadrian wove his fingers in his dark hair, pulled him closer, and rubbed their cocks together. And then the younger man had pulled away, and soft lips had closed around him, and Hadrian held him close as he sucked, and the fire roared behind them—

"Ahh!"

He came with a final shuddering stroke, his back bowed, scarred skin gleaming with sweat in the morning light. The air chilled on his damp skin, raising goose bumps along muscles lean with years of hard work.

After a few moments had passed, he reached over to the bedside table and grabbed a tissue from the box. He cleaned himself quickly, then crumpled the tissue and sent it into the wastebasket with an easy throw.

He was definitely awake now.

He got out of bed, his movements quiet, nimble. The wood floor was cool under his feet as he padded across the room, trying to decide what to do with his day.

He lived in the attic of an old Czech townhouse. Like many of the buildings in Prague, it had been preserved in its original glory, which meant high-beamed wooden ceilings with plaster running between and golden, gleaming floors. Only the bathroom was in a separate room. The rest was sparse, neat, and full of interesting lines, like Hadrian himself. A functional pine bed from IKEA took the corner on the left end of the attic. On the other corners were his bathroom and small kitchen, all wood and white plaster. Beneath the high ceilings, every piece seemed to be on display.

But the biggest piece in the room, and arguably its only decoration, was the massive oak bookshelf that filled the entire wall between the kitchen and his bed. It was crammed with paperbacks, hardbacks, and rare antiques alike, all jumbled together. In front of it, positioned in just the right place to catch the rays coming from a large skylight, was an antique armchair. It was covered in red velvet that had worn thin on the arms, showing the many hours of elbows resting there. Beside it was another round table, beautifully carved with scalloped edges and just the right height for resting a cup of coffee.

He stopped in front of it, frowning. A stack of science-fiction novels spanning two hundred years of writing was lazily distributed around his reading chair. Some of them were actually quite valuable, and definitely suffering at his hands. He winced at a first-edition copy of *Brave New World*, spine cracked and jacket torn at the edges, lying on the chair itself.

"Right," he said aloud, rubbing his chin. "That needs fixing."

It was still new to him, the business of having things that needed taking care of. One didn't carry possessions around in the Royal Air Force, and especially not in the UN. Peacekeepers needed to travel light when genocidal rebels were watching their every move.

A pair of eyes, white and yellowed at the edges, flashed out at him from some dark recess in his mind.

"Not today," he told himself. He clenched his fists, nails digging into his palm. The image vanished from his mind. It was too beautiful a Sunday to be wallowing in the dark.

Shaking his head again, he headed for the shower. Time to be up, early hour or not. A shower, a fresh coffee, and he'd finish that book. A walk later, and he'd see about repairing his valuables.

It was his life now. He had things to care for. And he'd be damned if he didn't do it right.

CHAPTER 4

MAX WAS having a very different dream.

He stood a ghost in his own past, lucid enough to know he was dreaming but unable to control it. He was back in New York City, in the apartment he'd taken above his book repair studio. It looked just the same, with the bare wood floors and faded white walls, no bigger than his bedroom as a child. A metal-framed bed tucked in a corner, a small table, no chairs. In the dream it was empty, only a faint trace of oil paint in the air reminding him of the messy, beautiful canvases he'd accumulated and worked on late into the night.

And in another corner, a small sampling of what had become his greatest passion: a table laid out with his first book press, a simple two-board device he'd made himself; a pile of cloth waiting to be cut and carefully glued onto board, to craft the covers he designed; needles for sewing up bindings; pots of glue and stains and brushes....

In the dream-he-knew-was-a-dream, he felt a flash of yearning. He'd loved this place, loved everything it represented, but he hadn't realized how much it meant to him. And now it was too late. He could never go back.

He heard a lock click, saw himself enter the apartment, younger, hair pulled back in a loose ponytail, wearing the only suit he had. He looked nervous, face flushed.

"This is it," he watched himself say as he stepped into the room. "My place. Not much, I'm sure, compared to what you're used to...."

"It is perfect." Jean Claude, in one of his fine gray suits, came in behind him. There was the hint of French in that voice, of glittering cities and, most importantly, power. "Your work...?" he asked, stepping over to Max's desk. He ran his fingers over a leather-bound copy of *Le Morte d'Arthur* that Max had completed just the night before. "It is lovely, William."

"It's not bad," he'd said, shrugging uncomfortably.

"No. It is a masterpiece," Jean Claude said. He turned to him. "You feel the souls of these books. Bring them back to glorious life. You are not an artist, *cher*. You're a healer."

He fixed Max with eyes that glowed like metal. Now, watching the scene replay, Max saw the danger there, the ruthlessness that wouldn't let law or human life stand in his way. But his younger self only blushed and held still as Jean Claude came up to him and took his chin in his hand.

"You have rare talent," he said. "Never let anyone tell you otherwise." Jean Claude kissed him—mouth taking, controlling, fitting over Max's like a vise.

And he'd let him.

Suddenly the room changed. They weren't in Max's bedroom anymore. They stood in Jean Claude's office, a room full of oak and glass and gray silk wallpaper. Max stepped forward, and the carpet squelched beneath his foot. He looked down to see it stained in sticky red.

"Your turn, *mon cher*," Jean Claude said in his silky voice.

Max turned just in time to see Jean Claude point his gun and pull the trigger. He screamed, fell back as a cannonball thundered into his chest, felt the carpet sag beneath him, then hot liquid flowing over and around him, submerging him in red, filling the sky, the air, his lungs—

"No!"

Max sat up in bed, his real bed, sweat pouring down his back. It took him a long moment to remember where he was. There—the smell of old wood and dried pine branches. The dark wood bed, the handmade quilt he slept under. His room was small and messy, with discarded clothes draping the chairs and old books lining the bookshelf across the room, but it was his. On the wall, a painting of the Charles Bridge, which Karel had bought him as a welcome present, greeted him and reminded him of where he was.

"Okay," he said to himself, wiping away the sweat from his forehead. "Okay, Max. You're okay."

He reached for his glasses and settled them on his face as his mind wandered to the face in his dreams. Jean Claude la Bête—*the Beast*—head and owner of Graywater security, a sleek vision in bespoke suits and perfect hair. Who could have said no to that? Not him, much to his regret.

Max had fallen quickly, and hard. The sex had been great—Jesus, that was putting it mildly—but it had really been the intimacy. Jean Claude had had a way of making you feel like you were the only person in his world that mattered.

He'd bought it hook, line, and sinker.

There came a knock at the door. "Max?" The wood muffled John's voice. "You okay?"

"Fine," he shouted back.

"All right. Karel's got breakfast on when you're ready."

He waited until John's footsteps faded before pushing himself to his feet, still shivering from the chill in his dream. He walked over to the simple pine dresser that held all the things he'd had on him when he'd fled Jean Claude. It wasn't much: an antique bronze-and-leather watch he'd inherited from his father, his wallet, a few family photos he'd had stuffed into the billfold, and the paperback he'd bought on the plane to try to distract himself.

All he had left of his old life. It seemed kind of pathetic in the morning light.

Feeling melancholy, he pulled out clean clothes. He dressed quickly and warmly, trying to dispel the cold that lingered from his dream. He tugged on a pair of jeans and pulled on one of Karel's borrowed sweaters, a green turtleneck at least two sizes too big. Catching himself in the small mirror above his dresser, he sighed. It was getting ridiculous, having to rely on Karel and John for everything. He couldn't wait to start making his own way again.

Back in NYC, he'd had his own business and his own place before the fateful move to Jean Claude's penthouse. He'd enjoyed that independence and looked forward to reclaiming it. But for the moment, unable to access his US bank account for fear of it being traced, he was entirely reliant on John. It stung, but there was nothing to do.

His room opened into a small hallway connecting the kitchen, front door, and Karel and John's bedroom. He heard Karel's cheerful tones coming from the kitchen. Wandering inside, he grinned at the scene before him.

John, dressed neatly in jeans and a polo, sat at the table, his expression grumpy but determined. A brown box the size of a loaf of bread waited unopened at his elbow. Karel was grinning by the kitchen counter, hot coffee in hand. He wore a T-shirt with a violently bloody zombie on the front and battered jeans.

Max had to hide a smile. They made a bit of an odd pair: his stiff, compact cousin with his neat fashion sense, blond hair never out of place, and the tall, relaxed Karel with his chestnut ponytail and weird T-shirt collection. They'd met in Prague on a snowy night and moved in together barely two months after that. The English teacher and the game designer. And anyone could see they were in love. Max had known it, with a soft pang of jealousy, from the moment John had brought him home.

Despite everything he'd been through, watching Karel and John gave Max hope. Sometimes things did work out. The world wasn't all blood and horror; there was goodness too.

"*Miliju tě*," Karel was saying as Max stepped inside. He spoke slowly, carefully enunciating every syllable.

"Me-lu-jeee ta," John said in return, tanned face crinkled with concentration.

Karel winced. "No, John, your Czech is still terrible," he complained.

"There's a lot of difficult sounds," John said, defensive. "You don't use enough vowels."

Karel rolled his eyes and took a long sip of coffee. Seeing Max at the doorway, he held out his cup. "Coffee?" he asked.

"Sure, thanks. I mean, *díky*," he said. Max was making an effort to use more Czech when he was with Karel. It seemed unfair to make him speak English all the time without making some effort himself.

"Look at that," Karel said. He grabbed the coffee pot and poured a mug for Max. "Those are manners. Max, *mluvíte česky*?"

"*Mohl byste mluvit pomaleji, prosím*?" Max said in perfect Czech, accepting the black coffee Karel held out for him.

"You're making me look bad!" John grumbled.

Max surprised himself with a laugh. "All I did was ask him to speak slowly," he said, smiling as he sipped his coffee. "C'mon, Jingles. How do I know more Czech than you and you've been here a year already?"

"God, not that old nickname again," John groaned.

Max's grin widened. Unfortunately for John, his parents had a very bad sense of humor and the already ridiculous last name of Jingleheimer. No one had been able to stop them naming their firstborn John-Jacob, dooming him to a lot of childhood trauma. And in his sometimes role of John's little brother, Max had always taken pleasure in teasing his older cousin.

"Anyway, I'm a very busy man," John went on, sniffing importantly. "Can't expect miracles."

"Busy. I think that is not the word you meant," Karel said with a sly grin. "Maybe 'lazy' is more correct?"

"Who's the English teacher here?"

"Soon to be Max," Karel said. John rolled his eyes. Turning to Max, Karel went on, "What are you doing today? It is Sunday. Must you work? All day yesterday you were in your room. It is not healthy."

Max shrugged. "Might take a walk. There's so much of Prague to see."

And I need to clear my head, he thought. *After that horrible dream this morning.*

Karel nodded, leaning his long frame back against the cabinets. "Very good. But it is Sunday, and tonight I will cook fish. So you must be home. Yes?"

"Yeah," John added. "Family dinner. No excuses."

"I promise," Max said.

Karel, looking satisfied, walked over to John, and planted a kiss on the top of his head. "I'm off to the shops," he said. Max smiled to himself, knowing that Karel's "shops" meant the comic book store and the specialty delicatessen down the road. "I'll see you both later."

"Bye, Karel," Max said. When he was gone, Max sat and pulled over the plate of rough brown bread Karel had left out for them. He grabbed a slice and bit down on the rich crust. It was one thing the Czechs definitely had over Americans. He'd never had such hearty bread before coming to Prague.

"Anyway," John grunted. "I was going to ask you, how are things at Foxrod?"

It had been John's idea that Max train as an English teacher, and he'd been the one to secure his place on the course. It was the same course John had done when he'd first come to Prague and was currently one of his employers.

Max shrugged. "Better than I'd thought. You were right, the students are very forgiving."

"Told you they would be. And I knew you'd be good at this. It's not a bad life," he said, gently. "After all this… well, after things are more settled, it's something to consider."

A frown crossed over Max's face. "I can't say it was by choice. Not that I'm not grateful. But… I miss my workshop. My life was in those tools, those books." He sighed. "I'm sorry. I know I sound ungrateful."

"Not at all," John said. "I understand. But for better or worse, this is what you've got, at least right now. And I have to say it's been nice having you around. I feel like this is kind of a second chance for us. I just want you to know you're welcome. Extenuating circumstances aside."

"Extenuating circumstances." He snorted. "Yeah. That's a nice way to describe fleeing for your life."

"Hey—Jean Claude is scum." The gentleness fell from John's voice to be replaced with steel. Max felt he was glimpsing the soldier John had been, the man who guarded Pentagon officials and Shi'ite tribesmen alike in the deserts of Iraq. "I'm not letting that piece of shit get anywhere near you. Understand?"

Max looked at him, saw the weather-beaten lines from years in the desert, the echoes of lost friends. "I'm putting you in danger," he said, meeting John's brown eyes.

John shrugged. "Life's full of dangers. I know what I signed on for. So does Karel. I don't hide anything from him. Besides, I picked up a little insurance this morning." He patted the box on the table, his face careful.

Max looked at it, then back at John. He had a strange feeling in his stomach. The box was just the right size for a handgun. "Is that…."

"I have a license. Got it when you first called, just in case. Seemed prudent."

"John, that's dangerous."

"Not in my hands. Not unless I want it to be." He shrugged. "Look, I don't want you to be afraid. I don't think I'll ever need this. But I want to be able to protect you, and Karel, if the time comes. And this weekend I'll take you out and show you how to use it."

"No," Max said, backing away. His mind flashed. Again he saw the man fall to the ground, the spreading stain of his blood. Could almost smell it, a hint of copper in the air. "I can't, I—"

25

"Okay!" John said. He got up and stood in front of Max but didn't touch him. "Hey, come back. You're okay."

Max took a deep breath. The memory faded, leaving him looking into John's concerned face. He took another deep breath, focusing on the familiar eyes in front of him. "I can't use that," Max said again, nodding toward the box.

John watched him a long moment, then nodded. "No. We'll find you something else, though. Maybe a Taser."

Max felt his hands shake, but there was nothing he could say.

They fell silent, the room's tension melting slowly. Self-loathing rolled through Max. It was his fault any of them were in this position—his fault for falling in love with that false face.

"I've got to go," he said abruptly. He turned and hurried toward the door.

"Don't miss dinner. You'll break Karel's heart," John said from behind him.

Max paused in the doorway to nod. "I'll be here."

CHAPTER 5

HADRIAN AMBLED down one of the streets of Prague, head hunched into his scarf, ears sticking out from under a knit red beanie. As he walked, he passed the time thinking of increasingly creative curses to hurl against the foot of snow trampled into slush along the sidewalks.

It was too cold. Unnaturally cold. Why had he left his apartment, again?

As he huddled closer into his jacket, he glared at the buildings that challenged him with their beauty. Sure, they were gorgeous—structures that had stood and housed people and shops for hundreds of years. Their façades, a fascinating blend of Neo-Renaissance and Art Nouveau, alternated pastel stucco fronts with white trim and gothic stone buildings with stags above the entrances and doors twice as tall and just as narrow as the average man. Even the ugly, flat communist-era buildings, scattered amongst the beauty, had a kind of presence. Between them and the cobblestoned streets, it was a losing battle not to be charmed.

But Hadrian was stubborn and very good at fighting losing battles.

To prove it, he scoffed when he reached a particularly gaudy building, covered in baby-pink stucco with ornate, scrolling white designs around the windows and curling metal vines caging the roof. There were a few stucco sculptures in the vein of Venus de Milo molded in sharp relief between the windows. One, a particularly simpering cherub, peered down at him from beneath a little cap of snow.

"Trying too hard, lad," he muttered and kicked some slush at the wall as he passed. He much preferred the quiet buildings, the ones that still held some dignity even with crumbling bricks covered in interesting graffiti.

Luckily his destination was close by. He could see the painted wood sign for Čapek's in the distance, proclaiming in Czech and English that they sold used foreign books. He hurried forward, eager to be out of the cold. Small windows with little overhanging roofs framed either side of the door. Nestled inside were rows of deep-discount paperbacks in a mix of French, English, and German, their covers ripped and worn and inviting.

He pushed inside. A cheerful bell announced his entrance, and the first thing he felt was a burst of warm air redolent of dusty pages and old wood. Hadrian wiped his feet on a small rug before closing the door behind him. Taking a deep breath, he felt some of the tension ebb from his shoulders as he took in the crowded, cluttered shop. The front room was deceptively small, with every wall covered in bookshelves, along with a low table in the center of the room and a stack of discount paperbacks pushed up against the clerk's table in the back corner. There, a bored-looking blonde with a psychology textbook in her hands was almost obscured by yet more books stacked on top of the counter itself.

"Andrea," Hadrian said, nodding at the woman.

She glanced up over the top of her book and lifted an eyebrow. "Hadrian. You are always so early. Can't you see I am studying?" She smiled as she said it, an old joke of theirs.

Hadrian smiled. "I won't keep you. Is Honza in? I have something for him to look at." He held up his bag.

She shrugged. "I do not know. I have not seen him, but perhaps he was earlier than both of us. Check upstairs in the staff room."

"Thanks." He nodded.

She waved him off and returned to her book, and he wandered away, fingers trailing along the bookshelves around him.

Like the fabled Strand in New York City, Čapek's was a temple to the book, and it had the largest collection of foreign-language books in the Czech Republic. Beyond the front room stretched half a dozen additional rooms, each devoted to a different genre and crammed with more shelves. Čapek's crammed collection ranged from the mundane, like history and romance, to such obscurities as ornithology and parapsychology.

Hadrian stepped into the maze and took a right through the romance, western, and fiction rooms, then hooked left to where they housed medical textbooks and the science-fiction section. Usually he'd stop here and make himself comfortable somewhere between Asimov and Huxley, but today he had a mission.

The staircase leading upstairs was at the very back of the shop, next to a pile of coverless bibles. Its black iron gleamed under the dim incandescent light, and Hadrian smiled to himself as he stepped over the *Nevstupovat*!/No Entrance! sign strung across the bottom.

His boots clanked on the metal as he climbed, soon reaching the second floor where Honza repaired the antique books they received. He was about to keep climbing when he heard someone moving at the end of the hall. Thinking it was Honza, he stepped into the hallway and made his way down to Honza's shop.

Honza kept things neater here than downstairs. A red floor rug dominated the room, with shelves of leather books encased in glass on either side. At the far end, beneath a double bay window that let in the winter sunlight, was a heavy wooden desk covered in repair paraphernalia. An old printing press sat against the wall beside it.

As he stepped away from the staircase and into the binding room, he said, "Honza, I've got something I'd like you to look at…." He frowned. There was a short man hunched over Honza's desk, looking at something intently. "Hey!" Hadrian barked. He knew everyone who worked here, and this man certainly didn't. "What the hell are you doing?"

The stranger jerked at the sound of his voice, turning with guilty speed. He was a slight man with olive-tinged skin, younger than Hadrian's own age of thirty-five and completely swamped by the black peacoat he wore. He had dark hair swept to the side of his face, which held an angled nose, dark brows, and full lips frozen in an embarrassed grimace. Big, dark eyes sized him up from behind silver-framed glasses like a deer caught in headlights. "You speak English?" he blurted out, then blushed. "Um. Obviously. Look, I'm sorry, I just got curious and I wandered up here, and…."

"Well, you can wander back down, like," Hadrian said, glaring, as the man lowered his hands to his sides.

The blush grew stronger. "I wasn't doing anything. I love books. I thought there were more up here, and then I just wanted to see…."

"What?" Hadrian snapped. Despite the grumbling, he could feel himself beginning to soften. There was a fragility to the man, one that made it even more surprising when he lifted his chin and glared back at him.

"There wasn't a sign or anything, okay?" he said, jamming his hands in his pockets. "How was I supposed to know?"

"There was on the stairs," Hadrian said, folding his arms. "No Entrance. *Nezadávejte*. Funny, claiming to love books and all. Doesn't seem like you're much for reading."

The blush became an angry flush that rose to the top of his cheekbones.

Hadrian had to bite back a small smile. Teasing him was unexpectedly fun. He had a lot of spirit for someone so small.

"How do I know you're allowed up here, then?"

Hadrian raised an eyebrow. "You taking the piss, mate?"

"I… I… sorry," he ground out. He took a deep breath, and Hadrian felt a small laugh bubble up in his chest as the stranger's nostrils actually flared. "I won't make the same mistake twice. Excuse me." He stomped out of the room, pushing past Hadrian to clomp his way downstairs.

Hadrian watched him go, amused. Well. That had been a surprise.

Because he wasn't a fool, he did step farther inside, checking to make sure everything was where it was meant to be. It was. The man had been telling the truth. But there was something more to it. In the few seconds before surprising him, he'd seen a powerful longing on his face, the kind of look a man gives a picture of his missing wife.

He'd been looking at the repair equipment. A book lay open on the table, spine cracked, leather cover chewed through, likely by a dog. Hadrian ran a finger along its edge now, feeling the old paper rub against the whirls of his skin. What had so captivated him? Why had he looked like someone who'd lost a child? And that combination of vulnerability and defiance was dangerous. Hadrian had a weakness for underdogs, especially those that kept on fighting.

"Hadrian?"

He turned to see Andrea in the doorway, looking in.

"I just got a call from Honza. He has broken hand, cannot fix your book today."

"Ah, poor sod," Hadrian said, frowning. "My luck today, eh?"

She rolled her eyes. "His luck, you mean."

"Yeah," Hadrian said. He glanced back at the desk. "He say how long he'd be out?"

Andrea frowned and shrugged. Worry crept across her face. Selling used books was, unsurprisingly, not that lucrative. Most of the money made in Čapek's came from a trade in rare antique books as well as book repair.

"Well. Hope it heals up soon," Hadrian said.

Andrea nodded, then shook her head as if to clear it from such dark thoughts. "We have new order of science fiction," she said, tilting her head. She smiled. "I have saved it for you. First look."

"You're a keen businesswoman, Andrea," Hadrian said, walking over to her. "Lead the way, love."

"JERK!" MAX complained under his breath. He was too angry and embarrassed to stop downstairs and browse the books as he'd intended. He gritted his teeth as he stepped into the cold, the icy slap of the air cooling his cheeks. Taking a deep breath, he set off north toward the center of the city. There the streets grew wider, and cars zipped through lights, narrowly dodging the tramlines that ran like arteries through the busy city and splashing snow as they passed. It was louder and busier, and Max felt himself blending into the comings and goings of the Czech capital.

As he walked, the weather cooled his temper and embarrassment replaced anger. There *had* been a sign at the bottom of the stairs. He must have stepped over it on his way up, too intrigued by the promise of more books to notice it. But that had always been his problem—he was too curious for his own good. And once he'd found that room, it was doubtful anything but the stranger could have gotten him out of it.

It was as if Prague had heard his prayers and answered. The beautiful old wood, redolent with the smells of books and bindings and old leather, smells he'd forgotten, smells he'd desperately missed. Seeing the book on the table, spine cracked, pages ripped, he'd almost cried. He knew exactly how to fix it. He hadn't been able to help himself from touching it, examining it with a professional eye.

And then that man…!

Replaying their conversation, Max realized the other man had been more amused than angry. There'd been a crook to his frown that Max would have seen immediately had he not been blinded by embarrassment. And he'd had such a striking face. All cheekbones and deep-set blue eyes, like chips of ice off a deep glacier. His nose should have been too big, but it was sharp and proud, and it gave him a kind of angry dignity. He'd been tall too, adding to the sense of quiet presence he had about him.

He should have scared Max, considering the charisma of the man he'd fled. Instead, Max had had the strangest feeling in that room, like he was safe. It didn't make any sense.

Max shook his head, trying to banish the stranger from it. He had more than enough to worry about without mooning over strange men he'd never see again.

"Knock it off, Max," he muttered to himself, pushing through a snowy patch of sidewalk as a tram rattled down the road to his left. Up ahead, a car horn blasted through the streets. He looked up, caught sight of a distant church spire, and made his way toward it.

CHAPTER 6

PRAGUE AT night was a sight to be seen.

After the Christmas season, there were still plenty of bright fairy lights hanging in shop windows, which only enhanced the sense of mystery that filled the city. A fresh snowstorm had left a new layer of white on top of the previous week's slush, turning everything crisp and clean. A perfect canvas for the sodium streetlights and the laughter bouncing out from pub windows and old oak doors.

It was a night to be inside with friends and lovers, drinking to keep warm, with hearty, steaming food meant to be eaten before glowing fires.

Almost a week had passed since his adventure in the bookshop, and Max had tried hard to put it out of his mind. When he'd returned home that night to a lovely dinner with Karel and John, he'd made a kind of pact with himself. He couldn't keep living in the shadows. John had stressed that he try to behave normally while in Prague, to blend in rather than hide.

Well, all he'd done so far was hide. Maybe, like with the teacher training, it was time to come out of his shell. He couldn't keep locking himself away.

He'd told John and Karel over their fish. Karel had clapped his hands, glad. John smiled, but there was an edge to it.

"I'll still be careful," Max promised. "Surely, though, we would have heard something by now? It's been five months."

John nodded but looked just a bit reluctant. "None of my contacts have heard anything, and there's been no sign that he's found you, not here. You'll be as safe as any other tourist. Still…."

"I know," Max said, taking a deep breath. "I'll be careful. Believe me, I would rather curl up into a ball and never go out. But I can't live like that, not forever. I need to get out before I suffocate."

John had clapped Max on the back. "I know." Then he'd taken him into the living room, handed him a Taser, and made sure he knew how

33

to use it. "And once he's on the ground, you run," John said, pressing the Taser into Max's hands. "Run like hell. Don't stop until you reach a crowd, and then stay there and call me."

"Yeah," Max said, holding the square metal gingerly before slipping it into his pocket.

Which was how Max had ended up squashed into a corner at U Medvídků, an untouched soda in his hand. The pub was crowded, air full of cigarette smoke, and a little too warm between the winter heat and the press of bodies. It was a handsome place—Max could see that beneath all the people, but they were his first problem.

When they'd walked in and he'd seen the crowd, he'd almost turned to leave. There were too many. It was risky. But Maggie had pulled him down the steps by his arm, and he'd seen the bar's owner—a huge, heavily tattooed man named Ivan whom Karel and John spoke of fondly—and he hadn't turned around.

Maggie had squealed with delight when he'd said he would join them for their weekly pub night, which had seemed the best choice for his first outing. His cousin was friendly with everyone who worked at U Medvídků, as was Karel. Surely there he'd be safe.

"Come on, Max! Being here and sulking in your drink is as bad as not coming," Maggie muttered, elbowing him in the side.

He looked up to see the rest of his classmates chatting around him. They'd found a broad wooden table in the corner, and Max was sandwiched between Maggie and the wall. Across from him, Christopher was laughing at something Debbie, the lone South African of their group, had said.

"Okay, okay." Debbie turned to the rest of them, her blonde hair braided around her head in a crown, and a faded hemp sweater draped across her shoulders. She pounded on the table a few times to get everyone's attention. When they were looking at her, she went on. "We've done all the getting to know you blah, blah, blah. Now for the real shit, eh?"

"Real shit? If you want to see a real shit, you should stop by the men's room," barked Donovan, the oldest teacher trainee at fifty-four, as well as the lewdest.

Max winced as Maggie rolled her eyes, but the rest of them laughed. It was hard not to with Donovan. He was rotund, unapologetically English, balding, and never able to take anything seriously.

Debbie rolled her eyes. "Yeah, okay, so. Real *stuff*, that better?"

Donovan grinned. "Sure, luv. Tons."

"Aaaaanyways," Debbie went on, "I want to know something about you all. Something secret. Fastest way to true bonding," she said, nodding. "Reveal the inner soul and all that."

Max shifted in his seat, not liking the sound of this new game. He took a deep breath, willed himself to be calm. He'd just make something up, that was all. Out of the corner of his eye, he thought he saw Maggie grimace. But when he turned to look at her, she seemed perfectly at ease.

"All right, I'll have a go," Christopher said, grinning. He glanced across the table, catching Max's eye. "My secret is…."

"Well?" asked Donovan, when Christopher paused.

"My secret is that I'm amazing in bed," he said, grin widening to show every one of his perfect teeth. He turned to Max, and the grin shifted, becoming an invitation. "And I'm happy to prove it."

Max swallowed hard as the others laughed, then forced himself to laugh along. Christopher was just being a ham, and if he wasn't… well, Max would deal with that when and if it came up.

"That's not a real secret," Debbie whined, pulling at the peace beads wrapped around her wrist. "I mean a *real* real secret."

"I've got one," Maggie spoke up suddenly. She grinned at them.

"Oh?" Debbie asked, leaning forward.

"Yeah," Maggie said, shaking her dark hair with a little laugh. "Um. Well, you know I studied biology in school? The truth is… I only did it because the TA was hot."

"And?" Debbie asked, grinning.

Maggie squeezed her eyes shut, nodded. "We fucked! And she was amazing. So worth it." She sat back, smiling wide, as the table burst into laughter around her.

Max, unsure what to do, patted her shoulder.

"Nice, Maggie," Donovan said. "Knew you were a bit wild."

Maggie glanced at Donovan and shrugged. "Thanks."

"That was a proper secret," Debbie said, nodding. "Who's next? How about… Max?"

"Uh—" he said, choking on the sip of beer he'd just taken. Four faces turned eagerly to him. His mind raced as he tried to think of something to say, something innocuous that wouldn't give him away but sounded scandalous enough that they'd leave him be.

"Yes, you're always so quiet," Donovan said. "What's your story, eh? You on the run from the law or something?"

Christopher grinned. "Maybe Max isn't his real name. Perhaps he's a spy!"

Max froze, his mind stuttering to a halt as his veins filled with ice. Christopher looked at him, obviously kidding, waiting for Max to join the joke. But he couldn't force a laugh.

They don't know. How could they? They don't know.

"I, uh… well, it's kind of…."

"C'mon, then, out with it." Donovan grinned. "Which acronym're you working for—CIA? FBI?" He laughed heartily, but Debbie was giving Max a strange look.

Max felt the blood drain from his face, and he took a gulp of soda to try to hide it. His heart sped up. He was supposed to be anonymous. He was supposed to blend in. How could they have guessed—?

"Oh, please," Maggie suddenly said, rolling her eyes. She shifted on the bench, somehow becoming larger as she did so. Max watched, grateful, as the attention shifted off him and onto her. "Max is the most obvious guy I've ever met. No offense," she added, winking at him.

"Hah, that's me," Max said, weakly. To his relief the others laughed, and some of the tension drained from the air.

"All right, enough of the secret game," Christopher said, rubbing his hands together briskly. "Bit too middle school for us grownups, really. What are we doing this weekend?"

"I was thinking of going to the castle, actually…."

As the conversation tilted to other things, Max took a deep breath, willing his pulse to calm down.

"You're pale as paper," Maggie murmured, when the others had drifted back to their own conversations. Debbie was still looking Max out the corner of her eye with something like suspicion.

Max inhaled, trying to force color back into his face. "I don't like attention," he said, pasting a smile on his face. Suddenly the noisy pub was too loud, too crowded.

"You do fine in class," Maggie pressed.

"Different." There was something heavy on his chest. His lungs wouldn't fill. "Not talking about me, then." He rubbed a hand above his heart, breathing slow and deep. It wasn't helping.

"Hey," Maggie suddenly said, putting her hand on his arm. "Come outside with me for a second? Feel like a bit of fresh air."

He met her eyes and saw the understanding there. He nodded. "Yeah. Sure."

They made their way out of the bar, Maggie leading and Max close on her heels. They climbed the steps and pushed open the door to the outside, a blast of icy winter air hitting Max with refreshing coolness. He let the cold fill his lungs and banish the smell of cigarette smoke.

Maggie shut the door behind them, cutting off the last of the sounds from below. Now they were alone. The snow had been pushed from the sidewalk to make heaps along the edges of the road. Around them, gold light from pubs and corner shops spilled onto the streets. In the building across from them, a house party sent laughter and faint music into the air, but it was a pleasant, cheerful sound.

"That's better," Maggie said. Her cheeks dimpled as she looked up at the sky, breath fogging in front of her.

"Thanks," Max said. His pulse slowed in the cold. Snow and the starlit sky replaced his nerves, filling him with calm.

"I get them too. Panic attacks, I mean." She leaned back against the bricks, hands stuffed into the pockets of her jacket. "Besides, the bar thing isn't always my thing. Too many people, you know? Hard to have a conversation. And people get weird in groups."

Max half smiled and went over to stand beside her. "I didn't know you were so wise."

A startled laugh burst from her, and she elbowed him gently. "Wiseass, maybe. Wise? Wouldn't go that far." She coughed and shrugged. "Anyway. What did you do last weekend? You never finished telling me about that bookstore."

"Oh, God, that was embarrassing," Max said. He pulled his jacket closer and frowned. "All I wanted to do was see if there were more books upstairs. I maintain that the sign was obscured," he added, sniffing.

"Sure thing." Maggie smiled.

"I went upstairs and I found this room. I guess it's where they fix old books." He looked away, hiding his face. "It was so peaceful, and... I was just looking. Then this guy walks in—this giant British guy."

"What flavor Brit?"

"English. I think. Strange accent. Next thing I know, he starts demanding I explain myself. I tried to apologize, and he walked all over me. Like he owned the place! He's not even Czech. How can he own a bookshop?"

"I hate to break it to you, but there are ways," Maggie said through a laugh.

"I guess," Max muttered. "The point is, he was an asshole. Very smug."

"What did he look like?"

Max shrugged. "I don't know. Tall. Thin. He had a long face," he went on, voice almost resentful. "And really blue eyes. Nothing special," he added quickly when she raised an eyebrow. "Lots of people have blue eyes. Plenty of nonjerks, I could add."

"Well, it sounds less like he was being a jerk and more like he was messing with you," she pointed out.

"Maybe," Max said, sighing. The fight drained out of him in one big whoosh. "I just wanted to... it doesn't matter." He shrugged.

They were silent a moment, letting the quiet street noises and winter wind fill the air around them.

"You know, if you ever need help with anything...," Maggie said. She turned and met his eyes. There was an odd look in hers that Max didn't quite understand. "Any kind of trouble. You can ask me."

Max frowned. "I... I mean, sure thing, Maggie. You too."

"I mean it, Max. Anything at all. I've got your back, okay?"

"All right," Max said again. He had the feeling she was trying to tell him something, but whatever it was, he couldn't understand. "Thank you. Really."

Maggie gave him a tight smile and relaxed back against the wall.

Before he could think about it further, the door to the pub opened, spilling sound and light into the snow. Out stumbled their classmates.

Debbie saw Max and Maggie and, biting her lip, came over to them. "Max, I'm sorry about that," she said. "Me and my big mouth. It was only supposed to be fun. I didn't mean to make you feel weird or whatever."

"Hey, it's okay," he said with an awkward laugh. "I was just a little dizzy. Too much smoke," he said shrugging.

She smiled. "Okay, great. I was worried you were pissed at me. Hah!"

"Who could be mad at you, Debra?" Christopher said. He came over and slung his arm around Debbie's pixie-sized shoulders. "You're a light in the dark. A vision in hemp!"

"Oh, shuddup," she giggled, swatting at his arm.

Max found himself laughing with them. Probing questions aside, they were good people, funny and kind. Christopher caught him laughing and gave him another wide grin. Max felt himself returning it.

He was surprised to realize he really liked his classmates. It was strange to think of these people as friends after going without for so long. But it felt good.

"So, we're thinking of heading to another pub," Christopher said. "The Bar—I went there last week and it was quieter than here. And no smoking. What do you think?"

Max glanced at Maggie, who shrugged. Ball in his court. "No smoking?"

"None. And no drinks if you don't want—I'll buy you a Coke myself," Christopher coaxed.

Max glanced at him and his charming grin, and a heel-bopping Debbie, and Donovan laughing uproariously behind them. He was on another continent. Anonymous, hidden—and what better place to hide than in a crowd, surrounded by friends? He told himself he was only going to keep up his cover. But in reality he was just so sick of being alone. "Okay," he surprised himself by saying. "Yeah, let's go."

"Really?" Christopher's grin stretched wide. "I mean, yeah. Okay."

Together they started out into the snow. As they left U Medvídků behind, Maggie slipped her arm into his and smiled up at him. The wind picked up, washing cold and bright across his face.

He had a good feeling about this. Maybe this was the next step he needed to take—not to keeping safe, but to keeping *himself*.

After all, what was the worst that could happen?

CHAPTER 7

"KOFOLA, *PROSÍM*." Hadrian leaned on the bar as he ordered, his black jeans, jacket, and cowboy boots a swathe of lean darkness against the old wood. He ran a hand over his short hair as the bartender, dressed in an old-fashioned three-piece suit and newspaper cap, gave him an odd look.

"Kaflao? *Prosím*?" he asked, frowning.

Hadrian sighed. "Kofola," he said again, louder to be heard over the music. "Soda, Kofola? No booze."

The bartender raised an eyebrow before nodding and turned to get a bottle of the cola-like Czech soda.

Hadrian eyed his back a moment, then let it go. He wasn't the first person to take issue with Hadrian's not drinking. He wouldn't be the last.

"Hello," said a high-pitched voice to his left.

He looked over to see a tall, doughy man a few stools down smiling at him. Clearly a tourist, if his tight pants and "I <3 Praha" T-shirt were to be believed, and probably on his first trip to Europe. He clutched a martini and eyed Hadrian with what he probably thought was a seductive expression.

"Not tonight, friend," Hadrian said, turning away.

"Let me buy you a drink. Come on."

He winced at the whine in the man's voice and glared at him.

The man cringed back and turned away. "Just being friendly," the stranger muttered.

Hadrian sighed and turned to contemplate the rest of the room. The Bar buzzed with conversation and the chinks of glasses, all flooded over a background of postrock music that came from speakers around the room. The noise, combined with the blue-tinged lights, gave the place a surreal feeling.

Adding to the strangeness were the curiosities that hung from the ceiling and sent strange shadows dancing across the walls. Old perfume bottles crowded shelves and hung from hooks on the walls, along with chipped records, model airplanes, army-issued tin cups, and a handful of old violin bows. Interspersed among them were yellowing photos of silent film actors and baby-faced sailors, all grinning out at the crowd, sharing their not-so-secret secret. Here tourists mixed with locals, enjoying a relative freedom that would be met with disapproving stares and frowns were it above ground.

For all those there to find love, there were just as many catching up with friends. The Bar was a haven for the Prague gay community, and Czech mingled with English, Russian, and German.

"Kofola, *prosím,*" the bartender said, sliding a tall mug over to Hadrian.

He leaned back and took it with a "ta" of thanks. A careful sip confirmed it—the black drink was cold soda. *Good.*

It had been a hard couple of days. U Medvídků, always popular with locals, had been host to more than a few birthday parties and football matches during the week. Ivan had also started a Wednesday night Pub Quiz, in Czech, which had become very popular very quickly. The flip side was that the odd scheduling had given him an extra night off. He needed it.

Hadrian took another sip of his drink, eyeing the crowds in front of him. He didn't come here very often. For the most part, he was perfectly happy keeping to himself and his books. Since he'd stopped drinking a few years back, he'd also cut down on the rest of his vices. And for the most part, that included the many men and the occasional women he'd had a habit of taking home with him. But tonight he'd felt the need for some company.

He'd had the cabin dream every night for the past week, and every time he'd woken with a throbbing hard-on. There were only so many nights he could take care of himself before he ached for another to do it.

Unbidden, a face popped into his mind. The man from the bookshop—that loose black hair, eyes snapping in a face full of vulnerability and defiance. Hadrian chuckled into his soda, remembering their interaction, how he'd gone from embarrassed to angry to indignant and stormed out with his head held high.

Still smiling, he turned back to scoping out the bar. It seemed like he might strike out tonight. Everyone seemed to be paired up already, save for a few loners nursing beers in the corner booths. One caught his attention, but not for the right reasons. He was in the back, in a corner by himself, hunched over a barely touched drink. There wasn't anything obviously wrong—his short hair was neatly combed, as was his trim beard, and nothing about the sweater he wore gave off bad signs—but still....

Senses trained in civil wars and guerilla-patrolled jungles marked him as dangerous. There was something in his expression. Eyes a bit too wide, lips pursed, too tight, as if to hold back a snarl, a slight tremble in the cigarette he brought to his mouth.

"Who is that?" Hadrian asked the bartender, nodding at the quiet man in the corner.

The bartender looked up and shrugged. "I don't know," he said, his accent thick but clear. "He is new. I have not seen him before."

"Ta." Hadrian took another long look at the man, watched him blink and take out a paperback. Hadrian snorted into his drink. It was clear he was just another lonely man, wanting company, not knowing how to ask for it. Jesus, he was paranoid. This was Prague, safe enough if one stayed away from the dealers and watched one's pockets. And there'd be nothing heavier at The Bar than marijuana. Most people coming here had a vested interest in staying under the radar. "Not in the jungle anymore," Hadrian muttered to himself, turning away from the stranger. Now if he could just find someone who looked interesting, worth his time.

"*Sakra turisté*," he heard the bartender mutter behind him.

Looking up, Hadrian nearly choked on his Kofola. There, coming down the steps, was the man from the bookshop. He was with a small group led by a handsome man with dark skin and a tiny woman dressed like the worst of the hippies on Wenceslas Square. A woman with dark hair and lovely round cheeks walked beside him, an older man with a pale ruddy face just behind.

English teachers and new ones. He could smell their enthusiasm from the bar. And he was sure he'd served them at U Medvídků—all but the bookstore man. He seemed shy here. He lacked the defiance, the blushing anger he'd shown Hadrian. Now he hunched into his oversized coat, looking nervously around the room but smiling through it.

Quickly, Hadrian turned, leaving his back to the party coming down the stairs. A strip of polished copper had been nailed to the wall behind the bar. He watched the teachers in it, watched as his—what? Friend? Acquaintance? That was too familiar—followed them to a table in the corner and sat. One, the handsome man with flashing white teeth, stood. Hadrian strained to hear them over the music.

"All right, Kozel for everyone?" He had a strong voice, with laughter in every syllable.

The bookstore man spoke, but his voice was too quiet to be heard over the music.

"No problem, Max. Kofola coming up."

Max! So that was his name.

Hadrian leaned forward, studying the group in the copper reflection as they ordered their drinks, chatted, hung out. He took in their details by habit—even now, years later, he couldn't stop seeing the people around him, assessing them, looking for dangers and tells and weaknesses. But his eyes barely left Max.

What was it about Max that drew him? Hadrian couldn't decide. There was a boyish charm to him, with his tousled hair, his hidden grin. Hadrian watched as he ducked his head at something the older man said, smiling with a cringe that told him he was embarrassed.

He was cute.

Hadrian caught the thought and scowled at himself. Cute? *Cute*? Since when was he into cute? Or anything more than a night's fix, for that matter?

The thought snapped him out of whatever strange mood had kept him watching the group in the copper. As he glared into his Kofola, annoyed at himself and for some reason a little sad, he felt someone move up next to him.

"What are you, stalking me now?"

He turned to see Max, arms crossed, glaring up at him. He was as slim as Hadrian remembered, but now he could see his eyelashes were long and curling behind his silver glasses. Hadrian raised his eyebrows. "Caught me, have you?" he said, straightening. He saw Max's eyes widen, just for a moment, before he coughed and tightened his arms. *Interesting.*

"Yeah. I did. You're not so subtle, okay? What do you want from me? You following me around?"

Hadrian raised his eyebrow a little higher. Maybe he'd read this man wrong. There was some genuine fear in his voice beneath the bravado. "Hadrian Walls," he said instead, holding out his hand.

Max glared at it like it was some kind of snake.

"Come on, lad. I'm not going to bite."

"You didn't answer my question."

"Look, I was in here having a pint." He sighed and let his hand fall back to his side. "You lot showed up, and yeah, I was curious to see more of my favorite trespasser." He shrugged, letting the hint of a smile show as Max blushed. "No harm meant. Promise."

Max studied him a moment longer, those eyes still wary over the burning cheeks.

"You got a name?" Hadrian pressed.

"W—Max," he said quickly.

Hadrian tucked that away for future reference. He'd been about to say something else, and judging by the flustered look on his face, it had been a close call. "Okay, Max. Nice to meet you. Again." He nodded at the group back at the table, all of who were watching very closely. "How d'you know that lot, then?"

"We're English teachers," Max said, voice cautious. "Well, in training."

"Course ya are. City's lousy with you these days."

"Yeah, well. It's a job." Max stuck his hands in his pockets and shrugged.

"We've all got to work, aye," Hadrian said. "And Prague's a pretty place for it."

"She is," Max said, still reluctant. He looked away, then back at some point above Hadrian's shoulder. "And you? I assume you're not an English teacher."

Hadrian grinned. "Haven't the patience for it, I'm afraid. No, I fill the other expat role—bartending. Pays the bills."

"I thought maybe you worked at that bookstore," Max said, then blushed again. "In that repair area…."

"Nah, I'm just a lowly reader," Hadrian said. "Haven't the patience for that work either." Hadrian eyed Max, read the line of his body, the way he'd turned from his friends completely to face him. He'd always been good at body language, and Max read "reluctant interest." Maybe he was about to have a change in his luck. "You know, you say you're a teacher, but I'd have pegged you for something different." Hadrian lifted an eyebrow and smiled, unable to stop himself flirting. "Something more artistic. You were looking at that old repair equipment like a drowning man looks at a plank of wood."

He wasn't prepared for Max's reaction. He paled and stepped back, eyes wide, terror written clear on his face. Tension snapped through his body, his chest heaving, leaving Hadrian confused as hell.

What just happened?

"Hey, no harm meant," Hadrian said, holding up a hand. "Sorry, sensitive subject? I—"

"Stay the hell away from me," Max interrupted, hand going for his back pocket in a way that told Hadrian he had some kind of weapon.

He watched as Max hurried back to his friends, glancing over his shoulder, panic written in every muscle. The tall one was standing and glaring at Hadrian. He put his arm around Max as he came back to the table. Jealousy, surprising and a little disturbing, seared through Hadrian at the gesture. It pacified slightly as Max shrugged the arm off, making some hurried excuse before running out of the bar alone. The dark-haired girl stood and made as if to follow him. The handsome man put his hand on her arm before she could move.

Hadrian turned away, trying to give himself a moment to think. He'd stepped on something there. Something important. His first feelings had been right: there was more going on with this man than Hadrian had realized. A mystery wanting to be solved. And Hadrian felt it sinking its teeth deep into him.

He fought it. Hard. He'd had enough mysteries in his life, and they'd all ended badly. Leave the other to it. It was none of his business, the life of this strange, and strangely compelling, man.

He'd just about convinced himself to let it go when someone brushed past him. He turned around, ready to tell that chubby tourist where he could put his hands.

It wasn't the tourist. It was the strange man from before, the one he'd pegged as dangerous. He hurried through the crowd, eyes fixed on the door where Max had just fled.

Hadrian recognized the man's movements from a lifetime of danger of his own.

The stranger was hunting.

"Mother of Christ," Hadrian cursed, and set down his drink with a thud. Slipping between people, he hurried out of the bar into the waiting night.

CHAPTER 8

"I'VE GOTTA go," Max choked out, shrugging Christopher's arm off and pushing back from the table. Glancing over his shoulder, he saw Hadrian at the bar, staring into his drink. If that really was one of Jean Claude's people, nowhere would be safe. But why hadn't he killed him already? Maybe he was waiting for a better opportunity.

"That jerk bothering you? We can go somewhere else," Christopher said, stepping forward.

Max shook his head, then looked at his friends in growing horror. He had to get away or put them at risk too. Anyone working for Jean Claude wouldn't allow witnesses. "I... sorry," he half shouted, not sure what to say. He ran from the table, pushing through the crowd to race up the stairs into the street, not sure exactly where he was going but knowing he needed to get away.

Once outside, he ran, slipping and almost falling a few times on the slick streets, only panic keeping him upright. Fear, cold and vicious, had his nerves dancing beneath his skin. After some time—he didn't know how long—he started to feel the cold where it stung his cheeks, shaking him out of his panicked fog. He slowed, checking behind him, looking for dark shapes creeping where the streetlights didn't touch.

There was nothing.

"Okay," he said to himself. "You're overreacting. It's just a guy. He's not... not... one of them."

But he'd seemed to know him. How did he guess about the book repairing? And to find him again, here....

Maybe he was being paranoid. But he had good reason to be.

Logic began overriding the fear-flight sense that had overtaken him. First, he had to get to his cousin. John would know what to do, and he was far from a civilian.

Max turned a corner. There was a well-lit area up ahead, in front of a *potraviny* with a bright storefront and a few people milling about.

He angled toward it, reaching into his pocket for his phone as he did so. He'd go inside and browse around in public where it was safe while he called John.

Just as he reached for the phone, he felt someone come up behind him. A pinprick at his back made him freeze as a heavy hand clamped down on his shoulder.

"Don't move, faggot," his attacker snarled, flooding Max's senses with the scent of rotting onions. "Scream and I push this in." He pressed harder on the knife at Max's back. He had a British accent, intelligible through the hoarse croak of a smoker.

"What do you want?" Max asked, trying to keep his voice even. As he spoke, he took in his surroundings with the quick instincts of the hunted. The *potraviny* was close, but not so close they'd hear him if he screamed. This patch of road was dark, and there was an alley not too far to his right. Behind him, the man twisted the knife. Max felt it cut into the felt of his coat.

That was bad.

"What do you think I want?" the man sneered as he pulled him toward the mouth of the alley. "Yer fucking money, asshole."

"I don't have much," Max said, trying to stay calm, not fighting the man. He had the Taser John had given him in his back pocket. If he could just reach it….

They were almost in the alley now. The man was breathing hard, like he was sick. He didn't notice Max move his hand into his pocket. *There!* His fingers brushed plastic. He grabbed it, ready to pull it out—

"What the fuck are you doing?" snarled his attacker.

In a whirl of violence, Max found himself shoved up against the wall inside the alley. He didn't see the fist coming until it had already slammed into him, sending his glasses flying and a dull ache radiating through his right cheek. The world faded into a blur of shapes and impressions. Then the knife was at his throat and his attacker just inches away, teeth bared.

"This can go real smooth if you don't fuck around," the man said. He flung open Max's coat with one hand, looking for inside pockets.

Max closed his eyes.

"Lovely night, eh, lads?"

A familiar voice suddenly broke through the tension. Max felt the knife at his throat loosen as they both turned toward the mouth of the alley. He could tell who it was even through the blurring of his vision. The cocky posture alone would have cued him in.

Hadrian Walls.

Annoyance, mixed with shock, broke through Max's fear for just a moment. Was this guy insane? There he was, all long and lean in black jeans and leather, his hands stuffed in his pockets. He was in the mouth of the alley, distant light hiding some of his face, but even without his glasses, Max knew he'd be smiling.

"Fuck off or you'll get it too," his attacker spit.

Hadrian shrugged. "No way to talk on a fine snowy night like tonight."

"I'll stick you!"

"No, you won't. Here's what's going to happen. You're going to let the lad go. And then you're going to drop your knife and put your hands on your head and wait with me for the *policie* to come and pick you up like the good little cockroach you are."

"Fuck you," he spat, repositioning the knife against Max's throat.

Max held his breath as the blade pressed against him, unwilling even to swallow. A kind of numbness spread through him, an inability to move, to think, as he felt the very real danger of that weapon upon him. *Not tonight. Not like this, after everything...!*

"I warned you," Hadrian said, voice quiet with menace.

After that, Max wasn't sure exactly what happened.

One moment, his attacker was screaming, spittle flying, knife shoved up against his Adam's apple. Then the lean dark blur that was Hadrian barreled into him, grabbing his wrist and sending the knife clattering to the frozen ground, shoving the mugger deeper into the alley.

"Get back!" Hadrian shouted at Max, who found he couldn't move. Then Hadrian was attacking again, knocking the mugger down to the ground. He pushed the fight farther into the alley, where the shadows were deeper. All Max could see were dark shapes tussling against the cold blue snow. "For fuck's sake," Hadrian growled, followed by a loud *thwack* as something meaty hit something hard. There was another *thwack* and more cursing.

One shape came out of the darkness, barreling past Max and out of the alley. Hadrian cursed and ran after, then stopped at the mouth, pausing. A moment later Hadrian was standing in front of him, and then he was handing Max his glasses.

Max slipped them on with hands that trembled. The world snapped back into focus, showing Hadrian, breathing hard, peering into his face with concern.

"You all right, lad?"

"I don't know," Max said, voice shaking. He couldn't stop shaking.

"Hey—it's okay," Hadrian said, reaching forward to take Max's chin gently in his fingers. They were so warm on Max's skin. He let Hadrian tilt his head back to peer at his neck. Hadrian grunted, satisfied. "Neck's fine. Did he get you anywhere else?"

"I don't know, maybe on my back...."

"Turn around." There was something clinical, impartial, about Hadrian's tone. It was strangely comforting—the voice you'd want to hear from a doctor.

Max turned around and let Hadrian gently lift his coat and his shirt. Cool fingers spread along his back near where he'd felt the knife.

"Didn't cut the skin." Hadrian took his hand away and let the coat fall to cover Max. "No need to go to the hospital."

"Good. Uh.... Jesus," he said, and then just as suddenly, he was laughing, his whole body shaking with it. He felt Hadrian guide him out of the alley, into the street, to sit on a low ledge brushed free of snow. "I... sorry... can't stop," Max burst out between giggles. The laughter was a heady, unstoppable thing.

"Bit of hysteria. It'll pass," Hadrian said, standing in front of him. He looked up at the sky and sighed.

Max watched the tilt of his head, outlined with stars. "Still think you might be stalking me," he added as the giggles slowed. In their place flowed exhaustion and an odd kind of relief. If Hadrian were one of Jean Claude's men, he wouldn't have saved him. And Jean Claude would have been caught dead before employing one such as the man in the alley.

They hadn't found him. He was still safe.

The thought made him start laughing again, his breath coming fast and wild.

"Ah, Jesus. Look. Calm down. You're all right." Hadrian's face creased with concern. "Fucking muggers are like vermin in this city. You just caught the eyes of a bad one, that's all. Wish he hadn't gotten away," he added, glaring at the street as if he'd like to chase the mugger down.

Max just shook his head and reached into his pocket to pull out his phone. He pressed the button that would put him through to his cousin, fingers trembling, a few wild laughs still escaping.

"You can call the police, not a bad idea," Hadrian said. "Might not catch him, though. Don't get your hopes up."

"No, no way," Max said, freezing over the phone. He looked up at Hadrian with wide eyes. "Don't call the police. I don't want any trouble."

"You running from something?" Hadrian asked quietly, staring Max down.

"Please." Max held Hadrian's stare a long moment, pleading with those icy blue eyes to listen to him. Then his awareness snapped to his phone as he heard his cousin's voice pick up.

"Max? Hey, you okay?" John sounded worried.

Max took a deep breath, not sure how to say what had happened. "John, I—" He couldn't go on. The line grew very quiet.

"Are you in trouble?"

"Yes. No. I was mugged."

"What! Where are you?" John barked.

Max looked around, trying to find a street sign, some landmark he could give him.

"You're a block east from Jiřího z Poděbrad," Hadrian said, naming one of the metro stations, and Max repeated that over the phone.

"Who's that?"

"Some guy, saved my ass," Max said. "Hadrian got the mugger off me, then—"

"Hadrian?"

Something in John's tone gave Max pause. He looked up at Hadrian, who was staring down at him too, confusion written large on his face.

"Tall guy, skinny, British? Looks like he shaved his head himself?"

"Yes, how'd you know?"

"For fuck's sake," John snapped. "How… I… look, just stay there. I'll be there in ten minutes. You're not too far. And don't move!"

With that John hung up, leaving Max, shaking and confused, staring up at his rescuer.

"Huh" was all Max could say. Hadrian glanced down at him, his brow furrowed. Max swallowed hard, then leaned his head back against the brick. "Life is strange."

"Hmm."

He shifted over as Hadrian came and sat beside him.

"Someone coming to get you?"

"Yeah, my cousin," Max said, and almost started to laugh again. "And apparently you know him. John-Jacob Jingleheimer?"

"Fuck off," Hadrian said, starting. "Christ, I guess it must be. Only bloke I ever met with a name more ridiculous than mine."

"Guess you're not a stalker after all," Max said and sighed. The street fell silent around them, the snow and cold making a safe, intimate space around the two almost-strangers. It was funny. Not twenty minutes ago, he was convinced Hadrian would try to kill him. The switch from attacker to savior should have been disorienting, but instead it only felt right.

He glanced at a frowning Hadrian out of the corner of his eye. Sitting, they were almost the same height, letting Max examine his face for the first time. He had a strong profile against the yellow lamplight, his nose proud, bold. There was nobility to him, beneath the roughness. An edge of kindness.

Strangest of all, Max felt no danger from him. Instead, there was warmth.

"Hey, thanks," Max said, pulling his coat closer around him. "For the save, I mean."

"Anytime," Hadrian returned. His voice was gruff, and he shifted on the hard stone ledge, brushing Max's shoulder with his own. Max had a sudden urge to lean on the taller man, and squashed it with difficulty. "You really ought to carry something, you know. If you're trying to be... cautious."

Max winced. "I was," he said, pulling the Taser from his back pocket. A wave of embarrassment swept over him, at his own uselessness, his inability to keep himself safe. "Fat lot of good it did me."

Hadrian glanced at it, raised an eyebrow. "Keep it in your front pocket next time. Closer to hand, like."

"I will." Max put it away—in the front, this time.

They were silent awhile before Hadrian broke the quiet. "You going to tell me where you came from?"

"No," Max said, but he didn't feel it. In his mind he already knew it was a "not yet."

CHAPTER 9

JEAN CLAUDE la Bête made a striking figure against the New York skyline. His dove-colored suit spoke of the deceptively simple elegance that only large amounts of money could attain. He was thin and tall, with a patrician face that burned from beneath a steel-gray widow's peak. Everything about him—the way he leaned against his powerful oaken desk, the city laid out in the glass wall behind him, the panther-like muscles bunching beneath the silk of his suit—spoke of intense control in all things.

It was his greatest strength. And, consequently, weakness.

Before him, CNN danced silently on the flat screen mounted to his office wall. They were running blurred pictures of a man in a black suit, his head covered by a bloodstained sheet. Police walked past the body, cordoning it off with yellow tape.

Jean Claude lifted the remote and turned on the volume.

"New updates today in the suicide of Robert Kingston, head of external security for the Graywater security firm," a female anchor said. The picture shifted, showing a desert city with military vehicles riding through the streets outside a dusty museum from the seventies. "The FBI has released a statement naming him the head of a multibillion-dollar smuggling operation in Iraq. Sources say that he acted alone, anticipating—"

Jean Claude grunted in approval and switched off the television. Good. That, at least, had gone as planned, freeing him from scrutiny so he could begin moving a shipment of rare manuscripts he'd obtained in Afghanistan. He'd make a public apology, of course. Perhaps arrange a donation to the families of those Iraqi soldiers killed in the operation. But he, and Graywater, were in the clear.

There was a knock. Irene, one of his many secretaries, stood in the door with a manila file in her hand. She was neatly dressed, the picture of a sleek professional. Only her darting eyes betrayed her nerves. "Sir, the tax forms you asked for," she said, hesitant.

"My desk, Irene."

She hurried forward, placed the folders neatly on the nearly empty desk, then retreated as quickly as she'd come.

He watched her go with dispassionate eyes, calculating before dismissing her entirely. Weak, that one. No spine, despite her impressive Ivy League résumé. He'd have to replace her soon. In his business, weakness cost lives as well as profit. There could be no tolerance for mistakes. Hadn't he had an object lesson in that principle?

He ground his teeth, turning to the cold New York laid out before him. The sky mirrored his eyes: flat gray, swirling with winter winds.

He'd met Will Mracek by chance. A rare errand he'd chosen to run himself, an antique novel of great value that needed repairing. Mracek's workshop and the man himself had the best reputation in the city. He'd been intrigued, too, by the reports of Will's mastery and how it had come at such a young age.

Walking into the shop, he'd felt an instant attraction to the young artisan. He was handsome, of course, with all the charms a young body and tousled dark hair could provide. Yet there had been something more—that sense of vulnerability about him, irresistibly combined with a carefully guarded passion.

Jean Claude had wanted him. It had been foolish—a whim of the kind he rarely indulged. But Will's innate charm won him over. Despite everything, he'd returned to the shop the next day and asked him to dinner.

During the first months of his affair, he convinced himself Will was a… passing interest. Will was sexually fulfilling, pliant to a point, but with enough willpower left to remain interesting. Jean Claude was drawn into his simple world, one away from the stresses of running a billion-dollar business that too often operated in the shadows. Will had never stained his hands with secrets, with dark thoughts. He'd never held a gun, never ordered blood drawn on foreign lands to keep the secrets-within-secrets needed to operate the most successful smuggling operation in the war-ravaged Middle East.

In his own way, Jean Claude had fallen in love.

Jean Claude tensed as he remembered the moment he realized what had happened. They'd been seeing each other for several months when Will had told him, with some excitement, of a trip he planned to take. A friend, distant for some time, whom he would visit in the summer.

Jealousy had speared him. He'd dissuaded Will, distracted him, asked him to move in with him the following week. In that moment he'd realized two things: that Will mattered to him, and that he must never be allowed to leave.

Nothing so precious could be allowed to stray from his grasp.

He slammed his fist onto the desk, one hard explosion of power. His face betrayed no expression. He prized control—demanded it of everyone, himself most of all, which made the "incident" so unforgivable.

Will was not meant to see the conversation Jean Claude had been forced to have with his associate in the home office he usually reserved for his legitimate business transactions. But the level of surveillance on his "official" locations had forced him to bring the unpleasant deed home, and… well. Things fell apart.

He'd believed that Will would come home after he fled the murder, that Will was *his* and would obey despite his fear. It was the only reason he'd allowed Will to leave the building in the first place. But Will, his Will, had been in possession of willpower Jean Claude hadn't anticipated, and he had escaped.

This was bad—both for him and his company.

How one antique book repairer had managed to vanish from the vast powers at Jean Claude's disposal was beyond him. His contacts in the NYPD and the FBI, usually so helpful, had been unable to tell him anything.

Thinking of it now, Jean Claude felt his carefully controlled temper rising. He wanted Will back. Needed him. It went beyond the dangers of Will talking. Jean Claude had enough clout to diffuse any claims Will might make of what he had seen that day, and there was always the option of a knife in the dark. No, this was entirely personal. A burning desire, made of lust and love and unbending iron will that would not brook any disobedience.

Will's absence could not be tolerated. Jean Claude felt his fists tighten, his muscles like whipcords, as he thought of Will and what he'd do to him. Will would never again forget who owned him. And Jean Claude would never again have to be without the man he'd come to need so very much.

There was another knock. Louder. Bolder.

"What?" Jean Claude snapped, not turning. He heard heavy steps, the confidence that could only come from Adelaide, his personal secretary. Her long brown hair was caught in a tight ponytail held high above a classically beautiful face.

"We may have found him." Adelaide's voice rumbled through the room. "A stray e-mail from our contact in the FBI. Some agent looking into our European connections. Date on the thing's about the time Will disappeared."

Jean Claude turned and felt his muscles loosen. He was a hunter. No prey could evade him forever. "Tell me everything."

CHAPTER 10

HADRIAN LEANED against the bar, staring into the hearth across the room, letting his eyes relax at the sight of the dancing flames. Vaclav sprawled in front of the fire, toasting his white fur in a posture of complete, lazy content. Hadrian envied the dog his simple joy.

What the hell had he gotten himself into?

"You are dreaming," said a heavy voice from his right. He looked up and caught a menu-laden Ivan frowning at him over his mustache. Hadrian was surprised. Normally no one could sneak up on him. "What is wrong?"

"Wrong? Nothing. I'm fine. Here," he said, dropping the rag to reach out and take the pile of menus. He carried them out from behind the bar and began setting them along the heavy wooden tables that filled the main room. He felt Ivan's eyes on his back as he did so but didn't say anything else.

What could he say?

That he'd spent Friday evening thwarting a mugging? That he'd ended up saving a man he'd met only once before, a man running scared from something Hadrian wanted no part in? That this man was one of his few friends' relatives, and someone to be wary of, and a mystery surrounded by a palpable danger?

Truth was, he couldn't get Max out of his head. Perhaps that was the crux of it.

Friday night, he'd waited with Max, unable to leave or rid himself of the protective instinct that had taken over his rational mind. When John had shown up, Hadrian had expected a handshake or some token of their friendship. Instead, John looked between them suspiciously, listened stiffly as Max explained what had happened, and then hustled Max away with the kind of nervous control Hadrian had only ever seen in high-risk military operations. John had thanked him, sure. But Hadrian would have rather had an explanation, perhaps starting with why both John and Karel had failed to mention they had family coming to stay with them.

The whole thing stank. Hadrian had spent most of Saturday in bed, tossing and turning and trying to convince himself to be done with Max and his damned mystery.

He could still step away. He knew it, insisted that was the case. All he had to do was mind his own business, keep to his own life. He only saw John rarely, and Max was a random run-in at best. After all, what did he even know about Max, who he'd spoken to for less than an hour? He was short and handsome and combative. He liked to find his way into places he didn't belong, and he was brave but terrified, and when he blushed, Hadrian felt his heart speeding up.

Yeah, it would be really easy to let this whole thing go. If only he could stop dreaming about Max.

Twice that weekend he'd had the cabin dream, with the rug and the hearth and the sense of *home* he hadn't felt in over a decade. But those times he could see the other's face, and it was Max: Max smiling at him from the rug, Max glancing up at him through his flimsy glasses, eyes playful, loving….

"Dammit!" Hadrian cursed as he knocked into a glass left on one of the tables, sending it to the floor, shattering it. He closed his eyes and counted to ten before going back behind the bar to fetch the broom and dustpan.

Vaclav looked over at him as he began to sweep, whined.

Hadrian glanced up to see the dog staring at him with the canine equivalent of worry. "I'm okay, you big baby."

Vaclav yipped, somehow managing to inject disbelief, annoyance, and exasperation in the one sound, before settling back at the fire.

Hadrian shook his head, swept up the rest of the glass, and deposited it in the trash behind the bar just as Ivan pushed through the big kitchen doors. He had a steaming bowl in one hand.

"All right. Time to sit and eat," Ivan said, setting it down at a table by the bar. The comforting, earth-meat smell of boar goulash wafted over Hadrian, setting his mouth watering. "And then you will tell me why you are breaking my pub."

Hadrian met Ivan's eye and saw the stubborn wall behind them. He held up his hands in surrender and sat where Ivan indicated, knowing there was no point in arguing. He picked up knife and fork and dove into the dark brown gravy and the hunks of rangy, tender boar, cutting the richness with the bread dumplings that sat like fat stones on the side of the bowl. As his stomach filled, he felt some of the tension easing away, replaced with the warm comfort of Ivan's signature dish.

It was difficult to feel anything but quiet when he ate something so drenched in the spices and smells of the earth.

While he ate, Ivan sat in front of him, gazing across the pub with the patient air of a man who knows exactly who and what he is.

Hadrian finished, pushing the plate away, and met Ivan's eyes.

"You can tell me, or I can guess," Ivan said, one shaggy eyebrow raising. "But I have an idea that there is a man involved."

"There is someone."

"Good. It is long time since someone bothered you. Who is he?"

"That's just it," Hadrian said, running a hand over his close-cropped scalp. "He's... I don't know who he is. Complicated. He's the perfect bloody picture of complicated."

"So?" Ivan asked, shrugging.

"The whole thing is messy. And maybe dangerous." Hadrian toyed with his spoon. "And the man's hurting, but I don't know how or why."

"Well. Who is not?"

"But this is different," Hadrian insisted.

"Different? More than the alcoholic I gave a job to years ago? More than the man who screamed every night he lived in my flat until the nightmares stopped coming?" Ivan asked pointedly.

Hadrian blushed and looked away. He didn't like to remember those darker times. They were in the past—and they'd stay that way. And he didn't need anyone now, not someone who could mess him up, could destroy the hard-earned peace he'd finally won for himself.

He would forget Max. That was it—just forget him. After all, he barely knew the man. How hard could it be?

Ivan watched him a long moment, then held up his hands in defeat. "It is your life. But sometimes you must take a chance, *ne*?"

"Maybe. Or maybe that chance'll come back and bite you in the arse," Hadrian grumbled.

"A bite in the ass is not so bad once in a while," Ivan said, startling a laugh from Hadrian. "But I am just your boss. What do I know?"

"What're your orders, then?" Hadrian asked, half smiling now. Ivan had said his piece and would let Hadrian make his own decisions. That was part of what he loved about the big man.

"Do not break my things" was all Ivan said, making Hadrian laugh again. He stood and slapped Hadrian on the back. "Come. It will be time to open very soon."

Ivan's prediction was right. It wasn't long before the restaurant filled with the Sunday-lunch crowd. Jitka had her hands full, carrying fragrant plates of Goulash and Svíčková to the truly hungry, salads and small platters of meat and cheese to those looking for lighter fare. Hadrian found himself pouring pint after pint, splitting the rest of his time between washing dirty steins and filling clean ones. The lunch crowd was always hungry for a glass of beer, and he was happy to provide.

It kept his mind busy. There was less time to think about Max and the chaos he represented. The crowd carried him a good few hours before they hit four, when there'd be a brief lull before dinner started.

"So many! Tonight will bad," Jitka said, coming up behind the bar. He grunted in agreement as she reached beneath the bar, pulled out a water bottle, and uncapped it to take a long drink. She set it back under the bar, leaned forward on her forearms, and moaned. "I need sit."

"Want a coffee?" Hadrian offered, indicating the electric kettle. When Jitka nodded gratefully, he bent over to set up the pot. The pub would probably be empty for a little while. Time to recharge.

As he had that thought, he heard the door open upstairs.

"*Kurva*," Jitka cursed.

Hadrian laughed as she shuffled away to greet whoever was coming down the stairs. He turned to take advantage of the small break to grab his wet rag and start wiping down the bar. He had plenty of beer on tap, but he'd need to bring up a few cases of the bottled stuff before the dinner rush began. And he should have another go at the inventory list, make sure their supplier hadn't made any mistakes....

Someone cleared their throat in front of him. Hadrian looked up—straight into Max's dark eyes. He froze, trying to hide the mixture of excitement and annoyance that hit him, settling for surprise. "What're you doing here?" he asked, a little gruffer than he'd intended.

Max winced. "I just came by to say thanks. For Friday." He studied Hadrian's face from behind his glasses, and Hadrian watched those dark eyes comb over him, seeing perhaps more than he liked. Max's cheeks were touched with red from the cold, his hands pale where they twisted together on the bar. Hadrian had to bite back an urge to cover them with his own.

"You're welcome," Hadrian grunted, turning back to wiping the wood, needing to occupy his fingers before they betrayed him. "You make a habit of getting into trouble?"

In response, Max blew out his cheeks. Hadrian glanced up to see a mix of exasperation and cynicism run over his face. He was so expressive, this one. How had he survived so long? "Seems like I do. I don't know if I have bad judgment or the world's worst luck," Max said, shrugging.

"Sounds like both."

A startled laugh broke from Max, and Hadrian couldn't help smiling in response.

"Do you want a drink?" he asked, nodding at the rows of beer behind him.

Max looked over, then shook his head. "No, thanks. I gotta get going. But I… well, it's stupid."

Hadrian tilted his head, read the embarrassment in Max's face. "I'll not dock you points, this time," he coaxed, softening his voice.

Max bit his lip and reached into the pocket of his felt coat. Out came a small package, wrapped in neatly folded brown paper and about the size of a thin hardcover book.

Hadrian took it and ran his callused fingers over the wrapping. It was charming—old-fashioned in his favorite way. "You don't need to give me a present for doing the right thing," Hadrian said, looking up to meet those dark eyes.

Max shrugged but didn't look away. There was something shifting behind his eyes. Something soft and afraid and beautiful. "I wanted to. And Karel told me this was your thing, so…." He trailed off, his awkwardness showing in every fidgeting line of his body.

Hadrian nodded and carefully slipped a finger beneath the brown paper, opening it with a quiet rip. He set it aside, revealing a cloth-bound copy of *R.U.R.*, Karel Čapek's great science-fiction classic and the novel that had created the word "robot." Hadrian ran his hands down the cover, feeling the moss-green linen and the gold lettering painted onto the front. It was of a style he'd not seen before. A beautiful book. "Where did you get this?" he asked, shocked.

"That bookstore—they had a copy. In the back," Max said. "John mentioned you liked science fiction, and…."

Hadrian looked up sharply. Max was hiding something.

"You're a terrible liar," Hadrian said, raising an eyebrow.

"I'm not—"

"Relax. Thank you," he said, splaying his big hands across the cover. There was something here. Hadrian felt it in the book, the cloth itself humming with something he couldn't yet identify. He met Max's eyes with his own and felt them pulling him in.

It wasn't too late. He could stop this now, before it got worse. Before he was unable to.

"Have dinner with me," he said instead, shocking both of them.

Max stepped back. "What?"

"Have dinner with me," Hadrian repeated. He held very still, sensing the danger there. Max eyed him like he was a wild animal, poised to flee, held back by… what?

Max met Hadrian's gaze and swallowed hard. "I'm not sure that's a good idea," he said, searching Hadrian's face, looking for something. "There's a lot you don't know about me."

Hadrian raised an eyebrow. Recklessness had seized him, and he'd lost all will to fight it. "Dinner's a good way to learn more about a person, isn't it?"

There was silence. Max bit his lip.

"It's just dinner," Hadrian went on, leaning forward now, just a little, his gaze locked on Max. He watched Max's Adam's apple rise and fall—fought the urge to lean forward and kiss it. When he saw Max notice his noticing, he felt something stir deeper in his belly.

"Two men, some food, a bit of conversation. Talking can't hurt you, lad."

A shadow passed over Max's face, and Hadrian again felt that prescience of danger. "You have no idea," Max said, stepping away, breaking the heat that had just begun to sizzle between them. "Words can take you all kinds of dangerous places."

"I've seen some skirmishes in my time," Hadrian said, meeting Max's eye. He let some of his own darkness shine through, following the instinct that had pushed him onto this ludicrous path in the first place. "Danger's afraid of me, not the other way around."

"Maybe," Max said. His voice was quiet. "But does that mean I should be afraid of you too?"

"No," Hadrian said instantly. He dropped the pretense, leaned forward, and held out his hand. Palm empty, inviting. "Never from me."

Max looked at him a moment longer, glanced at his hand, and took a deep breath. "Lunch. I've got tomorrow off," he finally said, meeting Hadrian's eyes with his own. *They are so warm,* Hadrian thought. *Like polished wood. A hint of summer forest.*

"Lunch, all right." Hadrian dropped his hand and smiled. "Meet me outside at noon tomorrow. It's a date."

"Tomorrow." Max nodded and hurried away.

Hadrian watched him clamber up the stairs, then heard the door open and hastily shut again.

"Who is he?" Jitka asked, returning with a frown.

"That," Hadrian said, a wry smile crooking the left side of his mouth, "was either the best or worst mistake I'm ever going to make."

CHAPTER 11

MAX WALKED blindly away from U Medvídků toward the crowds of Wenceslas Square. He needed to lose himself for a bit, get his thoughts together.

He had a date.

A *date*!

He blushed, thinking of Hadrian leaning against the counter, the way his shirt had ridden up. He'd been unable to stop himself from looking at his pale skin, stretched taut against those lean muscles....

He shuddered, and it had nothing to do with the February wind. Desire, left cold for so long, was waking up in him. It was hot and exciting, and part of him wanted it, wanted everything promised in those icy blue eyes.

But the rest of him was quaking in his boots. He wasn't ready for this. Not at all.

If he closed his eyes, he could still see the gun coming up, still see the man fall to the ground, his blood spreading into the carpet. That had been the consequence of him trusting someone. Death and betrayal and the sure knowledge that his life could end at any moment.

What the hell was he thinking?

"Oh! Sorry, sorry," Max muttered, quickly swerving to avoid walking into a Russian family taking photographs on the sidewalk. He shook his head, hurrying away without looking back, and felt his cheeks heating. He dodged out of the flow of tourist traffic, moving down a side street that led away from the chaos toward a small park he knew would be empty.

A few blocks later, he was slipping between the snowy trees, making his way to a bench someone had swept clear of snow earlier in the day. He sat, breathing deep, bracing himself with his forearms propped against his legs. Behind him, the trees wove together to make a wall packed with snow, muffling the noises of the city and leaving him in a pocket of wintry silence. He focused on his breathing, let his gaze relax and take in the sloping field of snow before him, the far row of white-capped evergreens, and the tops of buildings peeking over them.

Reason returned in the silence, as the wind whispered around him.

"I did nothing wrong," he said to himself and the waiting trees. "Nothing. This is not my fault." He took a deep breath, letting the frosted air fill his lungs. As he exhaled, he felt the peace of the little park fill his empty spaces.

He had a date with a man who intrigued him. A man he felt curiously safe around—safer than he'd felt in years, even before Jean Claude had turned his life upside down. A man who'd saved his life instead of threatening it.

"My knight in black leather," Max said, half smiling. "And now I'm talking to myself."

Max stood, feeling calmer than he'd been a moment before. He could always stand Hadrian up. Part of him knew that would be best. If he did this, it would be another man at risk because of him, another potential complication. And yet….

It was time to stop hiding, to stop using his fears as a crutch. There was danger, yes, but there'd always be danger, as Friday night had proved. One couldn't live like a zombie, always hiding, always in fear. It was time to begin living again.

Standing, Max took out his wallet and checked the contents. He had a few colorful notes, mostly 100s and 200s, and a handful of the heavy gold-and-brass coins that gave Czech money its old-world charm. It should be enough for his purposes.

With a steadying breath, he left the park and its silence behind.

THE NEXT day, Max woke up early. He'd dreamed again of Jean Claude, of the day he left. But this time the dream was different.

It hadn't been the death he dreamed of, but the morning before. In the dream he lay in Jean Claude's arms, his cock hard up against Max's ass. Jean Claude was speaking French in his ear, drawing little circles on Max's bicep while he pressed his cock harder against Max's skin— teasing. Promising more. Max had sighed with pleasure, feeling himself grow hard. He'd turned, flushed, to face Jean Claude, and instead found himself staring into piercing blue eyes above a hawkish nose.

He'd run his hand over the velvet scruff of Hadrian's buzzed hair and kissed him. Hadrian pulled him tighter, rubbing their cocks together, the friction growing hotter and wetter by the moment. Dream Max had moaned and reached down to grasp Hadrian, feeling him slick and pulsing hot beneath his touch. Letting Hadrian spread his legs, Max felt Hadrian's strong fingers circle his asshole as he rose over Max, kissing him wildly as his fingers slipped inside, each movement bringing a moan to his lips. Hadrian pulled his hand away, and Max could have wept at the loss—and then Max screamed with pleasure as Hadrian's cock replaced his fingers. Hadrian thrust gently at first, then harder, faster, as Max begged for more. He felt the pressure build in his cock—his hands grabbed at Hadrian's back, pulling him closer—a wicked grin pressed against his neck—

He woke as he climaxed, leaving a mess in the sheets as he sat up, panting.

Max looked down at himself, shivered at the memory of the dream. He quickly balled up his sheets, a vague guilt hanging over him as he did so. "I just had a wet dream, and now I've got a date. Jesus, am I fifteen?" he muttered, as he pushed the bundle to the foot of the bed.

Shaken, he rolled out of bed and checked the clock, sighing in relief when he saw the early hour. Plenty of time to get dressed, to prepare himself and knock away whatever strangeness had prompted his morning wake-up call. And then…?

"Get it together," he muttered. "It's a stupid lunch date!"

He grabbed a towel and wrapped it tightly around his waist before heading toward the shower in the hallway. Luckily it was empty. His shower was as rejuvenating as it was cleansing. Max scrubbed his skin, feeling almost like he was shedding an older person. Shedding the weight he'd been carrying around, revealing new skin, clean skin. A clean body for a newly freed person. He caught himself whistling as he rinsed shampoo and conditioner from his hair.

He realized, with a wry smile, that the song he was whistling was "I'm Gonna Wash That Man Right Outa My Hair."

He stepped out of the shower, steam billowing about him, feeling lighter than he had in months. Stopping in front of the mirror, he wiped away the steam to inspect his reflection. He turned this way and that, looking at himself, really looking, for the first time since he'd left the States. He'd gotten too skinny, wasn't eating enough of Karel's delicious food. Still, it wasn't a bad skinny. He was lean, some muscle still left to him. Max ran a hand through his hair, flipped it left, then right, before rolling his eyes at himself and tousling it back into the mess it usually was.

"You're in a good mood," John said to him as Max stepped into the kitchen.

Max wore the new jeans he'd bought the day before, a slim pair of dark denim that flattered his short frame and paired well with the light gray sweater Karel had lent him.

John's brow furrowed as he took in the neat clothes and the freshly washed hair. "And dressed up. You got an interview you didn't tell me about?"

"Not exactly," Max said, shrugging. He pulled off his glasses and began to polish them on the edge of his sweater. "I'm meeting someone for lunch."

"Someone," John said, flatly. "Please tell me it's not Hadrian."

"Aren't you two friends?" Max frowned and pushed his glasses back into place.

"Friends, yeah. But that doesn't mean he's the best guy in the world," John shot back. "He used to be an alcoholic. And he's not exactly the type of guy you want someone from your family dating."

"What does that mean?"

John let out a long sigh. "He, well, he used to date a lot. A *lot*. I've seen him with at least a dozen people since I've known him and none of them for long. He's slowed down some in the past year, but… I just don't want you to be the next throwaway."

"He seemed very nice to me," Max said, slowly. "And I'm hardly going to sleep with him. Anyway, it's not like that. It's just lunch, John. Deeply public. Broad daylight and everything."

John's frown grew deeper. "Sure. Okay. Just…."

"Be careful. You think I don't know that?" Max met his eyes and felt his weariness return, his fear, the weight of it all. He didn't need a reminder of the threats others held. He'd had plenty of lessons already.

John's face softened. "I'm just trying to look out for you. Not like I've done such a great job so far."

"You can get mugged in any city, and it worked out okay. Look, is this going to be a problem?"

"You're not my ward," John said after a long moment. "Your life is your own. You can't blame me for wanting to keep you safe, though, can you?"

Max shook his head and forced a smile. "I'll see you tonight, okay? Promise. And besides—he tries anything funny…." He patted his pocket with half a smile.

"Good," John said, nodding. "Don't hesitate. He's a tough guy—he can take a Tasering without too much nerve damage."

CHAPTER 12

HADRIAN WAS dying for a cigarette.

He stood in the street outside U Medvídků, his hands tucked into his leather jacket, a gray knit scarf wrapped around his long neck. He'd left his head uncovered, welcoming the cold breeze on his shorn scalp. It kept him alert, on his toes.

Today was going to be interesting to say the least.

Butterflies he hadn't experienced since he was in his twenties were doing the samba in his stomach. He knew they didn't show—he had more than enough experience masking his emotions in all kinds of situations—but it wasn't the most pleasant feeling.

He bit his lip, trying hard to focus on the sensory memory of a cigarette dangling from his lips, the slow inhale of smoke burning his lungs, the catharsis of the exhale. His long form relaxed as he imagined it, muscle memories kicking into place, loosening his posture from its military stiffness.

Where was Max?

Hadrian had dressed as carefully as he ever did, choosing jeans he knew to be flattering, a black button-down that hugged his toned arms and made his hands look enticingly large, and charcoal boots to give the look an edge. He liked having an edge. It reminded him of what he'd once been, before he "retired."

Now, if only his date would show….

"Sorry, sorry!" said a voice from down the street.

Hadrian turned to see Max jogging down the snowy cobblestones, face red and out of breath. He looked good—cute and sexy all at once, with a dash of intellect in those sharp brown eyes. How did he do that?

Max stopped in front of Hadrian, panting, his glasses fogging with every exhale.

"Slow down, lad. Yer only fifteen minutes late," Hadrian said, unable to stop the smile crooking the left side of his face. "Though I have been freezing my bollocks off."

"I got lost," Max said, taking a deep breath and letting it out. He straightened, and the color along his cheeks bloomed from exertion to embarrassment. "I'm still figuring my way around the city and there are not enough street signs."

"Landmarks are the way to go in Prague. Start memorizing buildings. You'll have better luck."

"Yeah," Max said, raising an eyebrow. "I've never seen someplace with so many different styles of architecture. Even in New York, most of the buildings tend to look the same, depending on your neighborhood. Not like here."

"So you're from New York, then?" Hadrian asked, filing it away. Another key to the puzzle.

Max paled and tried to shrug it off. "Something like that."

Right, Hadrian thought. *Tread carefully.* "Well, you hungry?" he asked, deliberately keeping his voice light, casual.

Max relaxed just a smidge as he let New York go. "I could eat."

"How do you feel about walking?"

Max furrowed his eyebrows in confusion, and Hadrian made a note to get Max to make that adorably confused face at every opportunity. "Walking is a good way to go from A to B," he said slowly, searching Hadrian's face.

"All right, then. Our lunch date wasn't going to work if you were a lazy type."

"Was that a backhanded compliment or a veiled insult?" Max asked, cocking an eyebrow.

"Take it as you will," Hadrian said, grinning, and began walking down the street. His smile widened as Max hurried to catch up.

The street grew narrower, the paving stones heavy with snow and slush, the buildings leaning over them. Soon it opened onto a bigger thoroughfare, this one paved and full of cars and beeping horns, fat cables hung in the air between lanes. A loud hiss warned of an approaching tram, the massive train-like car dwarfing the cars and people around it. Max's eyes widened as a few pedestrians ran across the road before the tram, seemingly unconcerned about the giant beast gliding their way. They made it across only seconds before it breezed past, sending slush into the air and splashing it along the road.

"How many people get creamed by those things every day?" Max asked, shaking his head.

"Mostly just tourists," Hadrian said. "Idiots think the tram'll stop. Nothing stops those beasts except the occasional ice storm."

"Ice storm. Jesus."

"Welcome to Bohemia." Hadrian smiled.

He turned them right, moving them down the street along the tram tracks. The buildings around them grew bigger, grander. Gold crowned the gray stone statues perched on top of the buildings or jutted out from façades.

"And here we've got our first stop, and a personal favorite," he said, giving Max a showman's wave that directed his view across the street.

A massive opera house rose up in ancient columns and worn brick that somehow blended seamlessly into the modern glass-and-metal building beside it. It was as good a metaphor for Prague as any—an ancient building, majestic as the day she was raised, beside the best of modern Nouveau architecture. Old and new, living in harmony. Gold statues of horses, winged angels, and monks praying to an invisible God lined the top of the opera house. A banner unfurled across the front showed a ballerina dressed as Cinderella. Beneath her spinning form, *Popelku* was written in gold, scrolling letters.

Max stopped, looking at the building with wide, appreciative eyes.

Hadrian smiled. "You an opera fan?"

"Never been, but I always wanted to," Max said, taking in the grand building. "My father liked to listen to it while he worked."

"That's Národní divadlo, the national opera house," Hadrian said. "I've been inside once. It's beautiful."

"It must be," Max said. He turned to him with a half smile. "Not much in this city is ugly, it seems."

"It has its moments." Hadrian smiled. "C'mon. I thought you said you were hungry?"

He led Max across the street. Beneath the buildings, where the gold stone met modern metal, was a large archway that led through a low passage into a wide, open courtyard. Brightly colored rows of food tents had been set up inside. Hippies in hemp skirts and with dreadlocked hair manned the stalls alongside more normally dressed folk in ski jackets and long wool coats. Hundreds of others milled between the stalls, filling the air with conversation and high, fluting laughter. As they came closer, Hadrian could smell cigarette smoke mixing with meat and beer.

"What is this?" Max asked, looking at the colors, the food, the people. Something flashed across his face—some discomfort.

"Winter food festival," Hadrian said, raising his voice to be heard over the crowd. He frowned at Max, worried he'd misstepped again. "You okay? Not a big fan of crowds?"

Max shook his head but pasted on a smile. He brushed his hand across his front pocket—a move designed to be subtle, but Hadrian remembered what he carried there. He was glad Max had listened and moved it closer to hand. "No, it's fine. I… It's fine. I like festivals. And food."

"You sure? We can go somewhere else. There's some great pubs near here."

Max shook his head again, firmer this time. "No," he said, in a determined voice. "No. This is fine. It'll be fun."

"All right, then," Hadrian said. He grinned, more to break the tension than anything else. "Are you a vegetarian, got any allergies, that kind of thing?"

"No, luckily," Max said with an answering smile. It was shaky but there. "I'll eat anything except chicken wings."

"That's very specific."

"You'd hate them too if they'd given you a week's worth of food poisoning."

Hadrian winced. "No chicken wings, then. Let's see what else they've got. On me."

Max looked at him and cocked an eyebrow. "You sure? It may not look like it, but I can eat."

"That sounds like a challenge."

Max grinned, his eyes lighting up, and Hadrian let a sigh of relief slip as they joined the line for the nearest stall.

They made their way through the festival with systematic precision. Hadrian watched Max calculate the stalls, the line lengths, seeing his enthusiasm grow as whatever had caused him to tense up faded away.

A slight furrow would form between his brows before he'd point in a new direction, with Hadrian happily following behind. As they walked, Hadrian kept the conversation on the safe subject of food. It turned out that Max was something of a foodie. He loved all Spanish food, thought crepes were overrated, but could eat street-style döner kebabs at any time of the day. Hadrian listened to his passionate defense of the hot dog with a bemused grin, nodding as he pointed out that, yes, street hot dogs could be filled with anything, but wasn't that part of the point?

"It's a totally unique experience every time," Max said, gesturing with the bratwurst that had inspired this train of thought. They had wandered a little way from the festival and sat on a cleared portion of the steps that led from the back of the opera house to the low street behind it. "And you'll never mimic the taste of a street dog with something you get in the grocery store. Part of the flavor's in the street around it, you know? It's an experience meal."

"I never knew someone could be so passionate about hot dogs," Hadrian said around a bite of sausage.

"I like food," Max said, shrugging. He bit the last of his brat.

"You cook at all?"

Max laughed and shook his head. "Nope. I'm good at burning things, though. I can just about microwave leftovers without setting the kitchen on fire."

"How can you love food and not be able to make it?"

"Do you write?" Max asked, cocking an eyebrow.

"Write?"

"Yeah, you know, novels, books, all that science fiction I hear you like to read…."

Hadrian laughed. "Point taken, lad." Still smiling, he took the last bite of his sausage and stood, brushing his hands along his jeans to clear them of crumbs. He didn't miss Max following the movement. "C'mon," he said, holding his hand out to Max, who looked at his hand, hesitating. "I'm not going to bite ya, Jesus," Hadrian said, wiggling his fingers.

"You might," Max shot back. Still, he put his hand in Hadrian's.

Hadrian clasped his fingers gently and drew Max up, bringing him close just for a moment. Max's cheeks flushed as their chests brushed before Hadrian let him go and stepped back.

"Thank you for lunch," Max said, coughing and looking away.

"S'not over yet, unless you want it to be," Hadrian said, rocking back on his heels. "Have you got more time, or do you need to be back?"

Max met his eyes, searching, the blush barely faded from his cheeks. "I might have some time. What were you thinking?"

"A little entertainment," Hadrian said.

Max let out a small huff. "You like mysteries, huh?"

"I asked you to lunch, didn't I?" Hadrian returned.

Max's cheeks flushed.

They began walking away from the opera house, following the tramlines deeper into the city. Here, crowded McDonald's sat across the street from antique bookstores filled with glittering Klimt illustrations and souvenirs. Above, the stone façades spoke of ages of lost grandeur and the dirty, blank stone of years of Communist rule. Beggars knelt on the street corners, hats in hand, hoping for crowns from the passersby, while tour groups wrapped in jewel-toned puffy jackets wandered open-mouthed through the streets. Meanwhile, the people who actually lived in Prague hurried on their way, heads down and scowling, weaving between the crowds with all the impatience of someone going somewhere very important, very quickly.

"It reminds me a little of New York," Max said, during a lull in their conversation. "The people, I mean. Always in a hurry, annoyed by all the tourists dragging their feet and clogging the sidewalks…."

"Not like my home at all," Hadrian mused, placing his hand on the small of Max's back to steer him around a burger someone had dropped in the street. He let his hand linger, just a moment, not wanting to break the contact.

Max shivered but didn't say anything as Hadrian took his hand away. "Where are you from? England?"

"That's me," Hadrian said. "North of England, up by Newcastle. Not too far from the Scots border."

"How did you end up here?"

"For that, you'll need to buy me dinner," Hadrian said, evading.

Max glanced at him from the corner of his eye. "Maybe I will," he said, then quickly looked away.

Hadrian hid his smile.

74

"Your name… it's unusual," Max went on, as they left the main street for a wide cobblestoned avenue, lined on either side by restaurants and outdoor heaters. Tourists lingered here, browsing elegant store windows and looking through the menus in front of the restaurants. A murmur of distant guitars and conversation bounced between the stones, weaving background music around them. More people streamed in and out of the Metro entrances at the end, marked only by an entry arch in the wall and a large green M in a gray square.

"Nothing unusual about it," Hadrian said gruffly. He frowned, hoping Max would drop it.

"No, there's definitely something," Max said.

Despite his annoyance, Hadrian watched Max's expressive face from the corner of his eye. There it was again, that enticing wrinkle between his eyes, the look of concentration behind his silver-rimmed glasses.

"Oh!" Max said, breaking into a smile.

Hadrian groaned, bracing himself for what came next.

"Hadrian's Wall. Isn't that the defensive wall made by the Romans when they were in Britain? Runs across the country? Were you named after a landmark?" Max was laughing now, eyes sparkling with mirth.

"Hadrian was an emperor first, I'll have you know," Hadrian said, rolling his eyes. "Not a bloody wall."

"But…. Hadrian Walls. You were named after the wall, not the emperor."

"I might have been. My mum's got an interesting sense of humor."

"That's great," Max said, laughing. "I mean, it's a very unique name," he added, trying to suppress a grin and totally failing.

"Unique is one way to put it," Hadrian said, shaking his head.

They came to the end of the street, where it opened up to a wide, noisy avenue that stretched up the hill. On either side, buildings covered in gilt lettering and romantic signs crowded together, while down the center were wide gardens edged in high-trimmed hedges, covered at the moment in snow and ice. Through all this strolled hundreds of vendors, buskers and artists painted like living statues, all competing for attention from the mass of tourists that streamed up and down the cobblestones in the cold air.

Crowning the top was a proud statue of a military man, bold and astride a horse three times the size of its real counterpart. Behind them, an old ornate building, turned black with age but covered in gilt-edged statues, stood like a stately king overlooking his kingdom. It looked like a palace, something a royal family would use for their summer home in the city.

"Wenceslas Square," Hadrian said, shoving his hands in his pockets. "And that's the National Museum of Prague lording over it all."

"I've been here," Max said. "Very nice. Lots of cobblestones. And people."

As he spoke, Hadrian became aware of a distant chanting coming closer. He looked up the square and saw a straggling column of saffron-robed Hare Krishnas beating an overly cheerful path through the people and snow alike. They must have been freezing, though one wouldn't know it from their slaphappy expressions. "Bloody cultists," Hadrian said, frowning. "Here all the time. Right nuisance."

"I always wonder, what do they do all day?" Max said, watching them come closer with a look not unlike an anthropologist observing a new species of bug. "When they're not out singing and all that. Do they have jobs? Does Jim the drumbeater work in IT?"

Hadrian guffawed as Max watched with a startled grin. "A saffron-robed computer nerd," Hadrian said, still chuckling. "Jesus. I never wondered that. But they've got to have work."

"Unless they all live in some kind of compound. They'd have to paint it yellow, of course. And there'd be noise complaints from the neighbors."

Hadrian snorted with laughter and grinned at Max. "You're wicked. Ah, they're coming this way. Let's move, shall we?"

"Sure," Max said.

They sidestepped the approaching column of singers, Hadrian still chuckling. When he could breathe again, he began pointing out the buildings, telling Max their rich histories through the Renaissance, two world wars, and the rise and fall of Communism. Max drank the history of the square with rapt attention, following what Hadrian said and asking questions.

They stopped next to a Starbucks that stood near the hotel where Vaclav Havel had given his famous speech in 1989. Hadrian watched Max study the building, eyes squinted as if reading the history from the stones themselves.

"You like all this history stuff," Hadrian said. "You've been here a few months, you say, but you haven't done any of these walking tours?"

A shadow fell across Max's face. "I was waiting, I guess."

"For what?"

"To feel like this was real," Max said, the words coming out in a rush. "To feel like I was...." He shook his head. "It doesn't matter. I'm here now, anyway." He turned and smiled faintly at Hadrian.

"That you are, lad. Ah—our entertainment has arrived," he said. He sat back against a protruding ledge that created a natural seat, and gently pulled Max down with him.

"Where?"

"Just watch."

On the corner in front of them, three middle-aged men were setting up some kind of performance. The shortest and fattest, with a magnificently drooping mustache, seemed to be in charge. He directed his taller, thinner comrades to set a wooden box on the sidewalk, with a box of CDs and an empty hat laid before it. He set himself down on the crate, spreading his legs wide before tossing the end of his scarf over his shoulder and nodding. The man on his right pulled an upright bass as tall as he was out of a black case and began plucking the strings, listening for the right notes, twisting a peg and adjusting a tuner as needed. The other reached behind the box and pulled out a shining brass trumpet.

"Buskers?" Max asked.

"Of a sort. These lads are the best in Prague. Just wait."

They watched as the little band set up, people flowing around them. Max shivered, once, and pulled his coat tighter. Hadrian had the urge to put his arm around him but resisted, knowing it was too soon.

The man sitting suddenly held up three fingers and smiled. The others nodded, holding their instruments at the ready. The man with the trumpet took a deep breath, and the bassist wriggled his fingers above his strings.

"*Jedna, dva, tři!*"

The band burst into action, sending bright trumpet music flowing above the murmuring crowd around them. People slowed, then stopped where they stood, turning to listen to the colorful sound. A moment later the bassist jumped in, his fingers dancing over his strings and sending low notes vibrating through the onlookers' bellies. Then the man on the box began drumming between his legs, the noise hollow and exciting, sending feet tapping. Within moments, listeners were coming forward and dropping coins into their hat, a few leaving large notes and taking a CD with them.

Hadrian looked over at Max and was glad to see a smile on his face.

"They *are* good," Max said, catching Hadrian watching him.

"They play pubs too. I've been to a few of their gigs. They do Louisiana blues like no one else."

They listened for a few songs, as the band went from vibrant marching music to a slow, soulful blues and back to a pulse-pounding samba before stopping to take a bow. Max clapped at Hadrian's side, then reached into his pocket and pulled out a handful of change. Hadrian watched as he pushed through the crowd to drop the coins in the band's hat before coming back to where Hadrian was sitting. "That was great," he said as he sat. His eyes were warm behind his silver glasses.

Something turned over in Hadrian's chest. He pushed it down, fast—too much. Too soon.

What was this man doing to him?

Looking at Max, flushed with the wind pushing through his hair, the strangest of feelings filled Hadrian. He wanted to take him to the mountains, to show him the beautiful green forests of Český ráj and the Czech countryside. At the same time, he saw them in restaurants, in Paris, in Rome. Anything to keep that look on his face, that wonder and happiness mingled with a bloom of new excitement.

Hadrian took a deep breath, then opened his mouth to ask—

A loud beeping interrupted them.

Hadrian cursed, reaching into his pocket to pull out his phone. It was three already, and his alarm was going off. He'd have to hurry if he was going to make it back to U Medvídků in time for his shift.

"Time's up?" Max said, with a small frown.

"Gotta go to work," Hadrian said.

"Of course. Um… I had fun today. Thank you. It was good to get out and see the city." Max bit his lip, wove his fingers together, and twisted them, withdrawing from the little space the two of them had been occupying.

That won't do, Hadrian thought. "Doesn't have to be the last time. You might not be able to cook, but I can. Let me make you dinner."

"Not at your house," Max burst out, and Hadrian hated the shadow of fear in his eyes, felt the urge to banish it, no matter what it took. "Sorry, I—"

"It's okay, lad. That's fine. Would a restaurant do?"

"Well…." Max took a deep breath while Hadrian held his. "I still haven't tried goulash," he said, carefully.

"That can be arranged," Hadrian said. He moved closer, going slowly, letting Max see every move he made.

Max shivered but didn't move, instead looking up at Hadrian through half-lidded eyes. His lips parted slightly, and Hadrian saw how full they were.

"Can I touch you, lad?" Hadrian asked, voice low.

"Yes," Max whispered.

Gently, carefully, Hadrian lifted a hand and laid it against Max's cheek. His skin was cold and soft.

Max leaned into his touch. "This is a bad idea, you know. I—"

"You're dangerous, you're trouble, you're complicated," Hadrian interrupted, rubbing his thumb along the ridge of Max's cheekbone. "I know. I don't care."

"I'm just trying to be honest," Max said, and Hadrian could hear that truth in his voice. "There are parts of me that are broken. I don't know if they can be fixed. I don't know what you're expecting, but I probably can't give it to you."

"I. Don't. Care," Hadrian repeated, voice gentle but firm. "All I want is the chance to know you better."

"Really?" Max asked, and the surprise—the genuine surprise, almost shock—pushed Hadrian the extra step he needed.

He leaned down, pressed his thin lips against the softness of Max's mouth, and felt Max trembling beneath him. Hadrian held himself very still, rubbing thumb over Max's cheek, trying to say with his body what his mouth could not: *You're safe. Let me know you.*

Slowly, Max yielded to him. His hands came up to grasp the line of Hadrian's waist, like birds alighting on his hips. Then with a sigh, Max melted into him, that small body folding into his chest, hands taking a surer purchase, pulling Hadrian to him. Angling his head for more, Max parted his lips, inviting, and Hadrian answered with a gentle flick of his tongue.

Max tasted like the winter wind.

After a moment, Hadrian pulled away, breathing harder than he'd been moments before. He watched Max carefully, as he opened his brown eyes, looking terrified and like he wanted more all at once.

"Okay," Max said, pulling back. Hadrian forced his hands to his side, giving Max space, letting him decide what happened next. Max licked his lips, eyes darting to the square, then back to him. "I… give me your phone," Max suddenly commanded, and Hadrian obeyed, handing his phone to Max. Quick fingers danced over the screen before hitting send. "Here." He thrust the phone back at Hadrian. The text messages were open, a plain *hi* sent to a new number. "That's me, if you want to… well. That's me, anyway."

"Thank you," Hadrian said, slipping the phone back in his pocket. He thought about reaching out again, stealing another taste of those soft lips, but read the vulnerability in Max's face and held himself back.

He'd have to be slow with this one. Careful.

"So. Goulash."

"Goulash." Max nodded, breathing deep.

"I'll look forward to it," Hadrian said. He stood and moved away, fighting the urge to kiss him again. Instead, he smiled. "See you later, Max."

"Yeah," Max said, licking his lips. "Later."

His smile stayed in Hadrian's mind as he turned and began the long walk back to U Medvídků.

There was potential there, and a mystery Hadrian knew he would have to solve. He'd have to go slow, that was clear. Unlike his past lovers, if he could even call them that, a smile and a flash of charm wouldn't win Max over. The wounds Max was sporting were deep and painful, and would require honesty, proof that Hadrian could be trusted.

It would be hard, but Hadrian felt something—some gut feeling—urging him on. It was becoming clear that Max was worth waiting for, despite all his hints of trouble.

Hadrian smiled. For the first time in a long time, he had something he was looking forward to.

CHAPTER 13

JOHN STOOD in his small kitchen, antsy. His arms were folded against his chest, breath fogging against the window he leaned beside. Worry creased his forehead. He was thinking of Max, out with Hadrian, and the thought set his blood boiling.

As he stood fidgeting, he heard a soft sound as Karel padded into the kitchen. It was followed by the gentle hiss and scrape of their coffeemaker, a clink of glass on ceramic, then the soothing noise of coffee being poured.

John had stopped home for lunch in between his classes, which had reminded him of where Max was. With Hadrian. And John couldn't let it go. He kept thinking of Hadrian's other flings, all of them short-term, barely long enough to be called a relationship. "Fuck buddies" was more appropriate.

Max deserved better.

"I don't like it," John said, looking out onto the snowy street below. People scurried like little black ants over the snow, in a view that should have been idyllic but was somehow unnerving. They moved too fast, their motions almost frenetic. He turned to face Karel.

"I have known Hadrian for half of a decade," Karel said. He was leaning on the counter, his long arms folded, a cup of coffee steaming by his elbow. "Ivan for longer. Do you doubt our judgment?"

"What? No, of course not," John said, scowling. "He's fine, I guess. But not for Max. Max needs someone—"

"Kinder? I know of no greater heart than Hadrian's." Karel picked up his coffee and took a long sip. "He is very quiet. He can be quite rude. But do not doubt his goodness."

"It doesn't matter how good he is," John said, shaking his head. "Max just got out of a relationship. One where his trust was broken. You've heard him crying in his sleep."

A shadow passed over Karel's eyes. "I have."

81

"So how can you support this? Hadrian's been through more partners than tissues in the past two years. He doesn't date—he sleeps around and then returns to that lair of an apartment of his. He's happy enough to be alone all the time. Why would you want that for Max?"

"Who says that's what Hadrian wants?"

"I think history speaks for itself."

Karel raised an eyebrow. "Oh? Well, that is for Max to decide. It is you who has made this a problem," he said, setting down his coffee. "You must let Max make his own choices. Concern is fine, yes. But you cannot meddle."

"Not if they're the wrong choices," John shot back.

"Especially if they are wrong choices. He is twenty-seven years old. He has lost everything he had. And now he runs from a man who lied to him in the worst way, who would kill him when he should have loved him."

"See, that was—"

"Would you stop him from taking back his life? From trusting himself?"

John fell silent.

Karel took a deep breath and shook his head. "You want to do kindness. That is good, and I love that you would help your family like this. But a man cannot be made to doubt himself. He must make his own choices. His own way. And now you would stop him controlling his own life, just when he took it back? I will not let you, John. Because I love you and him. I will not let you destroy yourselves." He came over to stand before John and ran his long fingers through John's sandy hair. "Please, think of what I have said. Max is a grown man. This is a chance for him to find himself. To heal. Do not interfere, *miláčku*."

John took a deep breath and let Karel's hands soothe him. "I just want to keep him safe," he said, eventually. "I cut out my family so much when I came here. When he called me, I thought I had a second chance."

"You have, my mouse," Karel said, and leaned down to kiss him. "Just do not be a… what is that term… dumbass." He stepped back. "It is not easy to know what is the best way. Sometimes it is more important to know when not to get in the way of someone else. No matter that you love them."

"I guess," John said. He sighed again and glanced at Karel's coffee. "What are the odds of you making me a cup?"

Karel's mouth lifted in the half smile John loved. "Perhaps I could. Perhaps certain favors would need to be given in exchange."

"What? I—oh," John said, and smiled. He placed his hands on Karel's waist and pulled him flush against him. "That could be arranged."

CHAPTER 14

CHARLES GIRARD took a deep breath and bit back the long string of French curses he wanted to spew at the heavy man in front of his desk. Instead, he pasted on his best customer service smile, reminding himself that these *imbeciles* would be far away from him and on a plane very, very soon. "I am sorry, monsieur, you must either pay the oversize baggage fee or remove some of the weight from your suitcase," he said, trying to sound apologetic, as though it were his fault the idiot hadn't bothered to weigh his bags before arriving.

The man sniffed, tugging up the belt that struggled to keep his pants where they ought to be. "I've never had this problem before. It's only a few pounds overweight. This is disgraceful."

Charles pursed his lips, nodded as if agreeing. "But it is policy. My hands are tied. Perhaps you'd make your decision over there? You may return to my window when you are finished. *Merci.*"

The man sniffed again but finally began dragging his bag away, grumbling beneath his breath.

Charles permitted himself a moment to collect himself before smoothing his thinning hair back and pressing the button that would send the next irate passenger to his check-in window. His eyes widened when he saw the statuesque beauty who approached, a small rat-faced man at her side. They seemed to be luggageless. The only thing they carried was a small leather duffel bag that the man had slung over his back. "*Bonjour, madame, monsieur.* Boarding passes?"

The woman laid two passes on the counter with a perfectly manicured hand. "We are on our honeymoon," she said, glancing at the ugly man at her side with an expression that said the opposite.

Charles looked down, noting his pinched face and that he only reached up to her shoulder—and that was being generous. "Oh?" he said, taking the passes with another smile. "Have you any luggage to check?"

The woman's mouth tightened. There was something cold about her face—a hint of the shark, not enough movement in her eyes.

"We travel light," piped up the man at her side. His voice was bland. Not at all what you'd expect from such an ugly figure. "Pride ourselves on economy in all things."

"Hmm," Charles said, looking them up and down before going to process their passes. "Ah, I see you are headed to Prague next? A beautiful city. Have you been before?"

"Our first visit," the man said with his utterly forgettable voice. "We hope it will be rewarding, indeed."

Charles nodded, looking down at their forms. Something about the couple put him off. He processed them as quickly as possible before handing them back their passports and boarding passes. "Have a pleasant flight," he said, though without some of his usual zip.

"We will, thank you," the rat-faced man replied.

Charles watched them walk away, dread left in their place. There had been something strange about them. Something very strange indeed.

CHAPTER 15

"I CAN'T believe we're finished," Maggie said, heaving a sigh of relief. She had collapsed onto a bar stool in a tiny pub behind Foxrod, her body slumped on the dirty wood, a pint losing its fizz at her elbow.

Max sat next to her, drained of energy, a cold soda in hand. "Just need to wait for the results now," he said, heaving a sigh. "I'm pretty sure I screwed myself on that grammar exam. It's not fair—I've been out of school for years. I'm no good at test-taking."

"You're not the one who failed out of college the first time," Maggie said morosely, then pulled her pint over and took a sip. She frowned. "I can't keep all these stupid rules in my head. Who cares about the difference between a modal and an auxiliary verb? Really?"

"Stop, please," Max said, holding up a hand as if to ward off any other mention of grammar.

They sat back, listening to the ambient rumblings of the bar at their backs. The past two weeks had been… intense was the word, Max thought. As they'd gotten closer to the end of their course, the assignments, which had been manageable up to that point, had gotten fatter and longer, till he found himself staying up late every night just trying to finish some of them. And when that had ended, there was today's grammar exam to study for—an exam created by Trinity University in the UK and proctored by an annoying man who sniffled through the entire two hours.

Max huffed out his cheeks. He'd felt like he was back in school, suddenly too small for his body, a boy again. And with all the work, he hadn't managed to keep his dinner date with Hadrian. He took a sip of his Coke, his mind wandering to Hadrian: how strong he'd felt beneath his jacket, the way he'd leaned down, kissed him with those gentle lips….

Max wanted more.

But the thing was, he *had* seen Hadrian—a few times for coffee, snatched between leaving Foxrod and studying till half past two in the morning. On the weekend they'd again met for a walking lunch, cut short by Max's need to return home and finish an essay.

Each time had been wonderful. Max had felt so comfortable, relaxed in a way he hadn't been in months, if not years. Like he could be entirely himself and anything he said was okay. More importantly, he had felt safe for the first time in a long time—something he hadn't had even with Jean Claude, when he was still pretending to be a good man. With him, Max had never been able to escape the feeling of being a little on edge. At the time he'd put it down to Jean Claude's powerful job. Now he knew better, of course.

A delicious, curling flame lit deep in his stomach when he thought about repeating that kiss he'd shared with Hadrian. Maybe taking it further…. He shivered, thinking of the dream he'd had before their first date. How much he wanted to see if the real Hadrian felt as good beneath his fingers. But Hadrian hadn't touched him once, except for the shoulder, his back… all very nice, but certainly not what he was craving. It was like he was being gentle with him. Taking care.

Max bit his lip. He made a resolution: next time they met, he would be the one to instigate the kissing. He was surprised to realize he was ready for it. More than that—he needed it. Needed *him*.

"Good God," said an English accent over his shoulder, breaking him from his reverie. "Come here, you lot. We need to commiserate."

Max turned to see Christopher and Donovan coming into the bar. They waved them over before grabbing a table, and Max and Maggie went to join them with their drinks.

Donovan saw what they were carrying and shook his head. "No, nope, that won't do. Today was a whiskey-level of needing to be drunk. You want anything?" he asked Christopher as he stood.

"I'll have a double," Christopher said glumly.

Donovan clapped him on the back before heading to the bar, his bulk parting the way with ease.

"Hey, it wasn't that bad, was it?" Maggie asked, seeing Christopher's long face.

He shook his head. "I don't want to talk about it," he said, and dropped his head onto the table. "I just want to be drunk. Very, gloriously drunk."

Maggie looked at Max, who shrugged. "When do we hear our results?" she asked after a moment.

"We should get them e-mailed in the next hour," Max said. "They've got a quick turnover, I guess. Either of you have a smartphone?"

"Yeah, of course." Maggie frowned at him. "You don't?"

Max shook his head, pulling out the tiny clunker he'd bought when he'd come to Prague. A used flip phone, made before they started putting GPS chips in. Remembering New York, he'd made sure to specify that it be GPS-free when Karel had taken him to the store. "I keep it simple."

There was a clunk as Donovan returned, setting two double whiskeys on the table with one hand and hugging a pair of pints to himself with the other. "These," he said, tapping the whiskey glasses, "are to take the edge off. Cheers, mate." He picked up his glass and held it to Christopher's.

Max watched as they downed their shots, chasing them with beer. Just then his phone buzzed. He snatched it off the table before anyone could see and opened the message waiting for him, his heart pounding.

It was from Hadrian, of course. No one else texted him. He couldn't help the small smile on his face as he read it.

Test go well? If yes, we can celebrate with dinner tomorrow. If no, we can commiserate over dinner tomorrow. Food and sparkling company either way.

Max bit his lip, then began typing before he could change his mind. *Yes. Went okay, maybe. Where/when?*

"Who's that?"

Max's head shot up. There was something strange in Christopher's tone. A sourness. He was frowning at Max's phone. "A friend," Max said, trying to keep his voice casual and not sure he succeeded. "Just wondering about the exam."

"I didn't know you knew anyone else here. You never go out."

Max frowned at his tone. It was almost accusatory.

"It's not like he has to check with us," Maggie said. There was a note of warning in her voice. "I'm sure you know plenty of people we don't."

"Poor bugger's jealous!" Donovan burst out, his face going red as he exploded with laughter. "Max ain't allowed to have other friends now, Christopher? Or maybe you wanted to be special friends?" He snorted, clearly pleased with his own joke, but Max didn't miss the way Christopher's cheeks flushed.

"Shut up," Christopher said, glaring at Donovan. "That's not what I meant. I was just curious."

"It's okay," Max said, but he put the phone back in his pocket. It wasn't okay, not really. Something in Christopher's tone was off, and Max was astute enough to know he was jealous—never mind that Max had been careful not to show him any special affection. He hid a sigh. He liked Christopher, and he didn't have enough friends to let one go lightly, over something so stupid as unreturned feelings.

"Oh! I passed! A-plus, baby!" Maggie's excited squeal broke the mounting tension. She was reading an e-mail on her smartphone, her smile wide and full of relief.

"That's great, Mags," Donovan said.

Suddenly everyone was pulling out their phones, racing to check their scores. Maggie let Max use hers. He held his breath as he waited for the e-mail to load, then let it out upon seeing he'd passed. And not only passed—he'd managed to scrape by with an A-.

"Shit," Christopher said, looking down at his phone. Without saying anything to the table, he suddenly stood, grabbed his jacket and stormed out of the bar.

"That's not good," Maggie said, staring after him.

"No, poor guy must have failed," Donovan said. "Christ. He'll have to take the course again next month."

Max said nothing, just watched Christopher leave. He had an odd feeling, almost a premonition. Something bad was brewing there.

"Well… not to be callous, but… we passed!" Maggie said, shrugging. "Let's celebrate a little, huh? Now we just need to find work and housing and—"

"Shh," Donovan said, closing his eyes and shaking his head. "Not yet. Today, we drink. Work can wait till the weekend, eh?"

"Yeah," Max said, shaking his head to clear it of any lingering unpleasantness. It was not the time to be dwelling on dark thoughts and unlikely possibilities. He had passed, after all, and it was damn time he had something to celebrate. He held up his soda. "Cheers, guys. To us. A new beginning."

They clinked their glasses, smiling. As they did so, Max felt his pocket vibrate and knew it was Hadrian.

Things were starting to look up—really up. Monday he'd start looking for work and then a place of his own. It was time to stop living with John and Karel—time to reclaim the next piece of his independence.

Just then, Debbie walked in wearing a wide grin. "Did you guys do okay? I passed! I can't believe it!"

Max smiled, letting himself fall into the rhythm of this strange groups of friends he'd found. Their chatter chased away the last kernels of dread, leaving him a little lighter.

This was a good place. A good time.

He took a sip of his soda. Here was to hoping it would last.

CHAPTER 16

NOT FOR the first time, Hadrian found himself scowling at the gray sky, wishing winter would hurry up and leave already. He'd woken up early once again on his supposedly lazy Saturday morning, found himself restless, and headed out for a walk. Without meaning to, his feet had taken him on the familiar path through small streets and tramlines to the square above the Jiřího z Poděbrad Metro in Vinohrady. Snow and slush covered the usually green square, with only the thin skeletons of trees popping out from amidst the white. At its center, a massive boxlike church jutted out like a gray tombstone. The plaster saints on its fronts, grim and white as the snow below, seemed particularly appropriate.

Today, the first of March, and there was still snow!

He sighed, looking with longing at the strip of concrete on the side of the square. In all other seasons, it would be filled with stalls selling vegetables and fruits, handmade pottery, and buckets of deliciously briny sauerkraut. Before Christmas, there was the Christmas market, and the vendors would perfume the air with hot Glüwein. There would be buckets of Christmas trout on every corner, and stalls full of wooden and straw ornaments….

But that was another season. Another season where snow was far more appropriate than now.

He glanced up at the large clock set in the face of the church and huffed. It was barely noon. There was another reason for his crank, and it was mostly impatience. He had a dinner date with Max tonight. A proper, sit-down, romantic affair in a real restaurant. And he was nervous.

He needed to do something to while away the time before that evening. He thought back to his house, the dismal state of his kitchen, and rubbed his nose. Grocery shopping it would have to be.

With a sigh, he tried to resign himself to at least another month of cold and supermarket shopping until the market opened again. He turned away from the desolate scene and walked along the sidewalk, the church looming on his left and the street with its tramline on his right. Cars whirled through the slush, filling the air with the swish-splash of dirty water flying onto the curbs. The buildings here were gorgeous, though even their sculpted fronts and colorful plaster failed to relieve the gloom.

He crossed an intersection, passing a shop that sold imported Mediterranean groceries and a closed comic book store amongst the restaurants and furniture stores. The big Albert's was on the right, a grim store with flat windows beneath an unusually ugly building for this part of Prague. A tired-looking hound dog sat patiently waiting by the entrance. Hadrian stopped to pat its head before stepping through the sliding doors.

Inside, America's Top 40 blared from the speakers. He grabbed a grocery basket and passed through the swinging gates into the produce section. It all looked a bit drab, a bit wilted. Again he thought of the farmer's market with longing.

"You're not such a snob as you can't eat a wilty apple, Hadrian Walls," he chided himself. He picked up the offending fruit with a slight smile. His mother had never been a good cook, and they hadn't had the money for the freshest fruit. Their groceries had often come from the bargain bin, and he'd never thought twice about a brown spot on an apple.

"Hadrian?"

He turned to see John standing there, a basket full of vegetables on his arm, a stubborn frown on his compact, honest face. "What are you doing here?"

"John, mate. This is a grocery store. What do you think?"

John's frown deepened. "Right." He shifted from his right to his left foot.

"Haven't seen you at U Medvídků lately," Hadrian said, noting the way John's hand tightened on his basket and the corner of his mouth pinched.

"I've been busy with work. Lots to do, you know."

"It's just I thought you'd want to talk about Max and me," Hadrian said, looking him in the eye. He hadn't been raised to beat around the bush, and this needed to be addressed. "Since we've been seeing each other."

Anger flashed across John's face. "He's a grown man. He can see whoever he wants."

Hadrian couldn't help the smile that quirked up the side of his face. "Karel talked to you, huh?"

"He might've."

"Look, John, yer my friend," Hadrian started slowly. He needed to be careful here. "I'm not doing anything untoward with him. It's just been coffee and lunch."

"Dinner tonight," John said, raising an eyebrow.

"Yeah. We've got a date for dinner. Does he have a curfew?"

"I'm not trying to be difficult." John took a deep breath and ran a hand over his face. "But you don't know what he's been through. I do. You couldn't blame me for being a little protective."

"I'm not blaming you, mate," Hadrian said. Now he was the one shifting back and forth on his feet. "This is a little unusual, the whole thing. I know he's gone through… something. No," he said, holding up his hand to forestall John. "Don't tell me. That's on Max. I want to hear it when he's ready. But I'm not going to hurt him."

"You forget that we're friends, Hadrian," John said, shaking his head. "I know what you went through when you came here. Karel mentioned it too. The drinking. Whatever you went through before you came here, it left a scar on you. Max has too many scars to carry yours as well."

Anger sent electricity zipping along his skin. He felt himself stiffen, felt his back go ramrod straight. Flashes of the man he'd been, the man he'd worked so hard to heal, ran through his mind. Yes, he'd had a problem with alcohol. It had been the only way to quiet the echoes of what he'd seen. But he'd never touched a soul. The only one he'd hurt during all that was himself. A phantom throb along his wrist reminded him of that forgotten pain. He closed his eyes and willed it away.

"I've not had a drop in five years, and you know it. And I never hurt anyone else."

"Okay. So you won't drink. Great. But how long should I expect this to last before you send him home with a broken heart?"

"Excuse me?" A vein began to throb in Hadrian's forehead.

"I know you don't really date, Hadrian. You sleep around. Forgive me if I don't want my cousin to be just another addition to your long list."

Hadrian stared at him, his mind racing with retorts. So what if he'd slept around some? What difference did that make? He'd never lied to anyone, never led them to believe they were getting more than he had to offer. He thought again of Max, thought of how careful they'd been, how patient. The idea of hurting him made Hadrian's stomach churn.

"I want to be angry with you right now," he finally said. "That's a lot of evil you're accusing me of, and I don't think it's entirely deserved."

John looked a little uncomfortable. A tinge regretful. Good.

"But I can't." Hadrian sighed after a long moment. "I understand. You love him. I'm starting to see how easy that is to do. But I promise I won't hurt him. I just want to see where this... thing... between us goes. I'm being careful, John. Careful as I can."

John grunted. "You can't promise you won't hurt him."

"For Christ's sake, can anyone promise not to hurt another? I promise not to do it on purpose. I promise to be careful. Will that do you?"

"I guess it will have to," John finally said. He took a deep breath and let it out, hard. "Karel was right. I should have kept my mouth shut."

"He's a smart one, that Karel," Hadrian said. "You know he was one of my first friends when I started working for Ivan?"

"I know," John said. "I got lucky." He looked up, catching a woman watching them, not hiding the look of fascination on her face.

"Maybe we could talk elsewhere," Hadrian said. He turned to the woman and gave her a cheeky wave. "Hear anything interesting, darling?"

The woman blushed and muttered something in Czech before turning away.

"I've got to get going, actually," John said, hefting his basket. "Karel took it into his head to roast a chicken for lunch. He'll be wanting these."

"Yeah, well...." Hadrian steeled himself. "Look. I don't want to sour things between us. You're my friend, John. As much as I have friends. Come by U Medvídků this week, have a pint."

"We'll see," John said, then bit his lip. For the first time, Hadrian saw how John and Max were related—there was something about the face, maybe the mouth, the shape of the nose. Then John sighed and it was gone. "I've got to go," John said.

Hadrian nodded. "I'll see you around."

John didn't reply.

Hadrian watched him walk away—though perhaps walk was too mild for the way he was hurrying. He sighed, set the spotted apple he hadn't let go of in his basket. There was hope for broken things. He had to believe that, no matter how guilty John had made him feel.

And he did feel guilty, which was ridiculous. They'd barely kissed, after all. Max was a grown man. No one knew what Hadrian dreamed about.

He caught the eye of the woman who'd been spying on them. She sniffed and said something in Czech. He caught enough to understand that it was a scolding. "Lovely day," he said in return, smiling through clenched teeth. He gripped his basket more tightly and hurried past her.

He finished shopping quickly, making sure to avoid John before he could flee the store. The whole encounter left him with a sour taste in his mouth. Why was everyone and their sodding mother trying to warn him off this man?

"If he's that much trouble, why'd you make him such a damned sexy mystery?" Hadrian growled at the sky as he left the shop. Only gray clouds looked back.

He took a deep breath and checked the time on his phone: 1:00 p.m. Another five hours to kill—about four and a half too many. Too much time to overthink things. To be forced to see how bad of an idea this might be.

"You've never turned your cheek at a challenge," Hadrian said to himself as he crossed a street and turned into a gray, snowy park. He thought of the apple in his grocery bag, of the brown spots on its skin. He knew it would taste just as sweet on the inside, for all its bruising. It only needed to be handled with care.

CHAPTER 17

THIS TIME, Max made sure he was early.

Probably too early, everything considered. He and Hadrian had made arrangements to meet at the restaurant, rather than U Medvídků or either of their apartments. Keeping things neutral. Max sat there now, a green tea cooling on the table before him, hand splayed against the wood. It was a dark, traditional pub, with low ceilings and big carved booths that hid diners from one another. He'd been seated in the corner next to a window, the glass edged in frost, creating an intimate space that seemed separate from the rest of the world. Through the window he could see the night sky growing dark. He watched, thoughtful, as the lamps began to wink alive down the street.

The day had started on a good note. He'd been asked to stay at Foxrod, this time as a teacher, with six classes scheduled through the week starting that Monday. The e-mail had come with a small sense of relief—he'd started to worry about finding work now that his course was finished. The classes at Foxrod were a good launching point, and it was quite the compliment from his teachers. Only he and Maggie had been asked to stay.

He'd spent the rest of the morning e-mailing résumés to language schools in the city. It had taken a few hours just to make his "base" résumé—full of made-up jobs and a fake college degree in English to match the one on his fake visa.

His mind wandered as he stared out the window. There was something comforting about all that old wood, polished by generations of busy hands, the low saffron lighting making the varnish glow. He felt anonymous here. Safe. Something womb-like in the wood. It made him think of nights spent at his drafting table, molding supple leather to the boards that made the cover, sewing pages together by hand, carefully smoothing marbled endpapers to hide the seams. At the end he'd hold the book in his hands and marvel at its weight, that he'd made this thing, brought it to life.

There was a magic to it that he'd found nowhere else in this world.

Movement beyond the window caught his eye. He focused, felt himself blush as he saw Hadrian making his way down the street. His head was down against the wind, and he hadn't noticed Max in the window.

"I am in trouble," Max whispered to himself as Hadrian drew near.

He studied the other with an artist's eye. Hadrian's movements held a touch of mercury, of the metal's strength, but fluid, loose. It was the same grace a panther carried as it lounged in the trees. Always languid, yet coiled in waiting. One couldn't be in his presence without feeling that power, that *potential*. For what, Max couldn't yet say. It was dangerous but not violent. Fierce, yet protective. Maybe the contrast was the reason Max couldn't turn away, despite the clamors of his common sense.

Just then Hadrian looked up. Max's heart skipped a proverbial beat. No, it wasn't his fierceness—it was those eyes. Like deep ice that should have been cold but instead warmed him. Eyes that had looked into the darkness and pulled themselves back.

He saw them in his dreams, every time he shut his own.

As Hadrian drew closer, Max turned away from the window, face flushed, and pretended to be studying the leather-bound menu in front of him. He heard the door at the front of the restaurant open, a murmured voice in Czech, followed by Hadrian's brash accent.

Here we go, Max thought, stomach jumping.

"Hey."

He looked up to see Hadrian standing beside the table, his hands tucked into his pockets. His leather jacket was missing—presumably taken by the waitress, who'd whisked Max's coat away when he walked in. Instead, Hadrian wore a cream knit fisherman's sweater over tight black jeans. The simple look flattered him, made his shoulders broader, served to highlight the strong features of his face.

"Hey," Max said, hoping he didn't look like a complete idiot. Reflexively he pushed his glasses back up his nose, started to get up, then sat again. "I'm not actually sure—is this a hugging moment?"

Hadrian snorted and shook his head, but he smiled at Max, a warm smile. "Your guess is as good as mine. Not been on a proper date-date in years."

Biting his lip, Max took a chance. He stood and pushed himself onto his toes, high enough to brush his lips across Hadrian's cheek. It was sharp with stubble. Max liked the feeling.

"Okay, that's not a bad start," Hadrian said with a small grin.

Max sat, his face red, and looked off to the side. "Well, when in Rome," he said, laughing nervously.

Hadrian joined him, his knees brushed Max's as he did so, sending shivers through him. "You're early," Hadrian said, braiding his fingers together on the table between them. "Nice change of pace, that."

"I seem to only have two settings," Max said ruefully. He met Hadrian's eyes, saw amusement in their icy blue depths. "Too late or way too early."

"So you've no sense of time or propriety of place," Hadrian said, half smiling. "Good thing you're smart and handsome. Nice work on your course, by the way. John says it's a bitch and a half to finish."

Max shrugged, uncomfortable with the praise. "Thanks. It was hard. I'm not going to lie. It's been… a long time since I did anything academic."

"What did you do in school, then? Or did you finish after high school?"

Max bit his lip. "I have an English degree," he said, stumbling over his words. It didn't feel good to lie.

"Oh?" Hadrian frowned. "I'll say it again, you don't seem the type. You've got artist's hands." He reached out and ran a rough finger over Max's curled fingers.

Surprised at the touch, Max didn't turn away. He let Hadrian tease his fingers out, running that rough working hand over his own skin.

"See?" Hadrian said, tracing an old callus on the base of Max's index finger. "Skin's smoothed over some, it's softer than it ought to be, but it's there."

Max looked up, meeting those blue eyes. They bored into him. He had the sense Hadrian knew him better than was possible. "I did art, as well," Max said, still skating at the edge of the truth. "Painting. And book… well, mostly painting. I prefer it, to be honest. It was essential to me. Like breathing. I wanted to make things."

"Book… what?" Hadrian pushed. Then a light went on behind his eyes. "As in bookbinding? Christ, lad, did you make that cover yourself?"

Max looked away, thinking of the book he'd given Hadrian as thanks for saving him from the mugger. By his standards it had been shoddy work. Just a few pieces of stiff cardboard and some cloth he'd found in a local arts and crafts shop. He'd told the truth inasmuch as he'd recovered the insides of the book from a paperback copy in Čapek's. "It was nothing," Max said, shaking his head.

"Nothing? Thing is gorgeous," Hadrian insisted. "If that's nothing, then you've got some real talent hidden in you. So why'd you stop?"

"It's complicated."

"Tell me," Hadrian coaxed. He fell quiet, keeping his finger swirling against Max's palm, comforting Max, sending signals to his brain that screamed *Safety! Secret!*

"I didn't want to," Max eventually said, voice low. He closed his eyes and heard the deceptively quiet click of Jean Claude's gun. "But I had to leave it behind. It wasn't…." *Safe*, he wanted to say. "Secure. Financially, I mean." He looked out the window. It was dark now. The snow lit in sodium-yellow shadows from the street lamps.

"It's never too late, lad," Hadrian said. He took his hand away and folded his arms against the tabletop. Max felt suddenly cold, like he'd stepped from sunlight to shade. "It's waiting for you. If you're that passionate, it won't be gone."

Max smiled, glancing up at Hadrian. "I hope so. Ah—the waitress is coming."

"Still want that goulash?" Hadrian asked.

Max smiled, nodded, and watched as Hadrian ordered in clunky Czech from their uninterested waitress. She nodded at whatever he said, then turned and hurried away without a hint of a smile. "She was friendly," Max said as they watched her retreat.

Hadrian shrugged. "Lots of waiters like that here. Still too close to communism for the American 'service with a smile' to have taken root. It's changing, but slowly." He looked after their waitress with something like fondness. "Truth be told, I'll be sad if it goes. There's something about that casual 'fuck you' attitude. No pretense, like. Shit job is a shit job, after all."

"I can see that. Better to be honest," Max said, thinking of Jean Claude, of his kindness, his double-crossing. The dead man at his feet. "I hate falseness."

"Seems like it," Hadrian said, nodding toward his hand.

Max glanced down, saw it was curled into a fist, and had to force himself to relax. When he looked up, Hadrian was still watching him.

"You're an interesting one," Hadrian said. In the dim light and the shadows, only his face seemed real. "You're not telling the truth, for one."

Panic clenched Max's chest. "What? I—"

"Let me finish," Hadrian said. "You aren't telling the truth, but I also don't think you're a liar. I can smell out liars. Always have. And you blush too much to be anything but honest, when you can."

"That... might be the case," Max said carefully. The clutch on his chest didn't let up. He took a cautious breath. "What else do you see?"

"Plain as the nose on my face that you're running from something, and it's got you scared. John's watching you like a hawk, Karel's mother-henning you, and every time I try to get a straight answer, I end up turned around." He shifted his head, changing the angle of the shadows streaking down his face. "Yet you don't seem like you did anything wrong. Not a criminal, surely. The blush, again. And—you're too kind."

"Can you smell that too?" Max bit out. He curled his hand into a fist again and felt a wave of anger surging through him. "Since I'm so easy to read."

"You're not," Hadrian said again. He barely moved, didn't seem to react to Max's anger. "You're a mystery. Through and through. Some kind of puppy that ended up on my doorstep, yet you've claws too. I can't get a hold of you, and that's my biggest skill set."

"Reading people?"

"It's kept me alive this long," Hadrian said, shrugging. "Saved my skin a few times."

"You know, you keep talking about me being a mystery," Max said. He could feel indignation bubbling inside him, riding that hot wave of anger tinged with something baser. "But I know next to nothing about you. What did you do before you came to Prague? Who were you? You

100

talk sometimes like you were some kind of, I don't know, criminal or tough guy. It's infuriating."

"I don't like talking about my past," Hadrian started, leaning back. He pulled his arms off the table and settled them in his lap.

"But mine's fine to speculate about," Max snapped. He felt that anger rising, his grip loosening. "You're not the only one who can smell bullshit."

Hadrian was silent a long moment. Max's words swung in the air, heavy, a garland of poison hanging between them.

"I was in the Royal Air Force for five years," Hadrian finally said, breaking the silence. He fixed his eyes on Max, catching him in his gaze, and Max froze, unable to move. "Joined up the day I turned eighteen. My mum didn't like it—still gives me an earful when we talk. But I had to go. Had to get away, and the Air Force was the fastest way of doing it. Besides—there was flying."

A smile, tinged with nostalgia, crossed Hadrian's face, then faded.

"It turns out I was pretty good at it too. Did my time in the Balkans, worked my way up to Wing Commander. Then the UN came calling. They sent my troop off to join the Peacekeepers. Was looking forward to that, like. Thought I'd make a difference. You'd think Kosovo would have shown me how naive that was."

He fell silent, his face in shadow. He wasn't looking at Max any longer. His eyes had drifted to the side, dropped into that quiet space where memories dominate. From the looks of things, it wasn't a happy one.

Max's anger evaporated as Hadrian spoke. Instead, shame rose within him, that he'd seen Hadrian as anything other than hurting. "Where did you end up?" Max prompted, choosing his words carefully when Hadrian didn't speak.

"MONUSCO. The UN permanent mission in the Congo," Hadrian said, meeting his eyes. "People do horrible things in war. Horrible things. And sometimes you can't stop them." For a second Hadrian's eyes were naked, vulnerable. Eyes in a hollow face that had seen terrible things. Then the shutters fell back, and he shrugged. "Gave it up after that. Couldn't crack it any longer, moved here instead. Took me a few years before I got my head back round the right way."

"I… I'm not sure what to say," Max said, slowly. "I can't imagine that was easy. Any of it."

"No. And—here's my full disclosure, now," Hadrian said, taking a deep breath. He squared his shoulders, his expression carefully guarded. "You should know that when I first got here I had some problems with alcohol. Guess you might have called me an alcoholic, but I don't like labeling myself. Slept around a lot. General self-destructive behavioral patterns. Quit the drinking about five years ago. As for the men, I was never dishonest. And as I never met anyone I wanted to see more than once or twice, I never did."

The unspoken *until now* hung in the air, sending crackling charges down Max's spine. Hadrian finally looked away, breaking some of the tension but not freeing them entirely.

Something warm was growing in Max's chest. A kind, almost tender feeling, replacing the annoyance of moments before. He was beginning to see that Hadrian, for all his brashness, his cocky way of speaking, was carrying his own wounds around.

Max waited till Hadrian met his eyes again. "It's nobody's business but your own what you did in the past," Max said. He realized he was speaking to himself as much as to Hadrian. "Only the now matters. That's all that can count."

Hadrian was looking at him strangely.

"What?" Max asked.

"You're unexpected, that's all," Hadrian said, still looking at him with that odd expression on his face.

Max frowned behind his silver glasses. *Unexpected? What does that mean?*

"There's one more thing," Hadrian said, taking a deep breath. "I haven't seen anyone but you since we met. You should know that."

"That's good," Max said, then winced. "I mean, me neither. You know."

"Good. That's good."

A warm awkwardness filled the space between them. Luckily the waitress chose that moment to serve their dinner. She dropped two plates of steaming, fragrant goulash onto the table, the gravy a rich mahogany that seeped into the bread and potato dumplings that lined the edge of the plate. Chunks of beef floated beside them, looking tender enough to melt in your mouth.

"All right," Hadrian said, smiling at Max as the waitress fished place settings out of her apron pockets and plopped them beside their food. "This is a treat, you'll see."

Max turned to his own food as Hadrian began to eat with gusto. It smelled heavenly, the rich forest-meat-spice smell redolent with garlic and onions. Picking up his fork, he speared a piece of meat and brought it to his mouth. "Holy shit." Later, he might admit that he'd moaned just a little. "Jesus Christ, this is good."

Hadrian smiled and licked the end of his fork. "Told you they were the best. Make their own dumplings, spices, the lot. Best goulash in the city. Don't tell Ivan."

"Or Karel," Max laughed, and took another bite.

The mood quickly returned to the light banter they'd begun with as they made their way through their food. Max savored every bite and was disappointed when he looked into his bowl and realized it was empty. It was one of the best meals he'd ever eaten. It reminded him of his father's beef stew, but thicker, with a wild taste. Max sighed and set down his fork.

"Don't be so glum," Hadrian laughed. "There'll be other nights. More goulash. Have you tried Svíčková yet?"

"No. But I'll do it tomorrow if it's half as good as this," Max said.

"Oh, aye. You should come by U Medvídků one night. Ivan's is legendary," Hadrian said. "Keep me company at the bar."

Max smiled. "Maybe. I'd like that."

They spoke awhile longer, still avoiding anything heavy. Mostly they talked about books. Their tastes differed—Max preferred English literature, while Hadrian was a die-hard science-fiction fan—but there was enough overlap to keep their conversation flowing. Max found himself more charmed than he'd been before, if possible. Hadrian was funny as well as intelligent, with a wry sense of humor that spoke to Max's inner snarky New Yorker.

During a lull in the conversation Max glanced outside. He was surprised to see how dark it had gotten. Nothing had existed for him outside their bubble in all the time they were speaking.

The waitress suddenly appeared by their table. She looked irritated, her arms crossed against her voluminous bosom, as she fired something off to Hadrian in rapid Czech. Max caught a few words, enough that he wasn't surprised when Hadrian turned to him and said the restaurant was closing.

"Seems we've chatted more than we thought," Hadrian said, smiling. "It's near ten."

"Jeez." Max half smiled. He was almost a little sad—regretful. He wasn't ready for their date to end.

"Normally I'd say we should go get a drink," Hadrian said, raising an eyebrow. "But neither of us drinks." He turned the full force of his charm on Max, who couldn't help but squirm. Something hot stirred in him at the sight of Hadrian's rakish grin. He couldn't look away from Hadrian's eyes, noticing how long his dark lashes were, how they brushed his cheek as he blinked.

"We could get a coffee?" Max suggested.

"Not a bad thought," Hadrian said. His voice dropped, turning low, intimate. "I'm not ready to say good night to you yet, lad." He reached across the table, took Max's hand in his, and smoothed his palm out, running those callused fingers across his skin.

Max shivered as he met his gaze. "Me neither." He gathered his things as Hadrian went to pay, picking up his black coat from the peg beside the front door and wrapping it tightly around himself. Outside, he could hear the wind roaring down the street.

"Ready?" Hadrian said, appearing at his side. He grabbed his leather jacket and pulled it on before winding his purple scarf around his neck.

Max found himself watching his throat as he covered it, the long smooth column disappearing beneath the wool. "Yeah," Max said, blushing and looking away. He pushed out into the cold. The wind wasn't as strong as it had sounded. It sent cold icing across his cheeks, but he was grateful for it. It cooled the heat of his skin, made him feel more in control.

"This way," Hadrian said, nodding up the street where it grew narrower and the buildings looked older.

They began walking. The night was quiet, despite it being Saturday. No one else wandered the snowy streets beneath the faux gaslights. Nor did Max and Hadrian speak. The silence was a comfortable one, broken only by their shoes on the cobblestones and the sound of their breath.

Max glanced up at Hadrian as they walked. His face, profiled against the night, reminded Max of a Roman soldier, at the same time proud and sensitive, every feature strong, all framing those blue eyes. His heart skipped a beat.

Now or never.

"I—" Max started to say, then bit his lip. He stopped and waited for Hadrian to pause in front of him. His heart was pounding in his chest as he steadied himself.

"Yes?" Hadrian's voice was low as he turned around to face him. He waited while Max gathered his thoughts, searched his face.

"I've had a really nice time tonight," Max finally said, voice dropping at the end. He watched Hadrian watch him. The air around them felt too still, too silent, like the world had stopped and turned its eyes to them. He looked up at Hadrian, willing him to understand.

"If you're wanting me to kiss you, lad, you'd best tell me," Hadrian rasped, his voice deep.

"Kiss me, then," Max said, raising his chin defiantly.

"Thank Christ," Hadrian said, the words almost a prayer. And then he reached forward and cupped Max's head in his big hand, his free arm sliding around his waist, pulling Max close. He gasped as Hadrian pulled him flush against his long, lean body and pressed their lips together. They slid over Max's mouth, his neck, like hot silk that burned in the most deliciously dangerous way. Heat uncoiled in Max's belly as he gripped the slick leather of Hadrian's jacket, molding himself to Hadrian's taut chest, feeling those hands roam across his back.

There was a thump, and his back knocked into brick—but that big hand cradled his head gently, kept him safe even as Hadrian conquered his mouth. Max moaned as Hadrian flicked his lips with his tongue, parting them, darting back before returning to taste him. He opened with willing hunger, moaned again as Hadrian explored his mouth. The hand at his back pressed in harder, grinding them together, the hot denim deliciously tight around Max's waist. Max grew hard as he slid his hand down to grab Hadrian's ass. He could feel Hadrian's cock straining through his jeans, could feel it rubbing against his own, and he wanted nothing more than to get on his knees and take it in his mouth.

Max moaned again, his knees going weak. As if in answer, the kiss slowed.

Hadrian pulled his head back, just enough that Max could see his face, but kept their bodies pressed together.

Max never wanted him to move.

"Is this… okay?" Hadrian asked.

Max watched through hooded eyes as Hadrian searched his face, a soft frown creasing his cheeks. He loosened his grip on Max's hip and dropped his hand from Max's face, giving him a little space, letting him know he meant it when he asked if he were okay. The action sent warm shivers down Max's back. He felt like Hadrian could see into every part of him, to the deepest wells of his hidden places. It was frightening but beautiful. No one had looked at him like that for a long time. Maybe ever.

"Yes," Max said, half whispering. He brought up his hand and traced a line along Hadrian's cheek while he ran the other lightly over his ass.

Hadrian's eyes darkened. The look he gave Max sent his cock jumping. "Are you sure?" Hadrian asked again. "I don't want to go too quickly. I just wanted to kiss you again."

"You can kiss me whenever you want, so long as you do it like that," Max said, blushing.

Hadrian broke into a smile. "I'll take you up on that, lad. Christ. I could kiss you the rest of my life."

They didn't talk much after that.

Nor did they make it to the coffee shop.

Later, Hadrian walked Max to the front of his building. Max flushed as he dug in his pocket for his keys, almost dropping them in the snow in his nervousness. He wrestled with himself as he did so. He really, really wanted to invite Hadrian up. At least, his heart and his cock did. His brain was a little unsure.

"Do you…." Max said, as he turned the keys over in his hand. "Uh… do you want to—?"

"Whatever you're going to say, wait," Hadrian said. He reached out and closed Max's hand over his keys.

Max felt his heart sink to his stomach. It must have shown on his face, as Hadrian immediately shook his head. He held Max's hand tightly.

"Don't get me wrong," Hadrian said, his voice dropping again to that low, sexy growl that went right to Max's stomach. "I want to. Badly." He pulled Max flush against him, showing him just how much he'd like to come up. "But it's too soon. I don't want this to be something you regret. When we do, and I think we will, I want you to be ready. And I don't think you are yet."

Max bit his lip, then sighed. "Maybe not. But—just for the record—I want to too."

Hadrian raised an eyebrow. "I can feel that. Can I kiss you again?"

Max nodded, smiling.

Hadrian ducked his head down and kissed him with just enough heat to set Max's toes curling. Then he pulled back and leaned his forehead against Max's. His nose brushed against Max's like a caress.

Max closed his eyes and inhaled deeply of Hadrian's spicy, woodsy smell. He tried to fix in his memory the warmth of Hadrian's arms as they cradled him, the perfect fit of their bodies pressed together.

"Good night, then," Hadrian said, pulling away as Max opened his eyes. The loss of heat was palpable. The air felt colder than before.

"Good night," Max said, then took a deep breath. "Just, there's one more thing."

Hadrian raised an eyebrow, and Max felt his stomach jump with nerves.

"You said you could cook, right?" Max asked, trying to keep his voice steady.

"Aye."

"Then you can make me dinner," Max blurted out, his heart beating hard enough to hurt. "Next Saturday—if that works for you?"

A warm smile spread over Hadrian's face. "Saturday." The way he said it made it sound like a promise.

Max turned, climbed the steps up to his building, and fit his key in the door. He glanced over his shoulder and saw Hadrian standing on the sidewalk, a grin spread across his face. For lack of anything better, Max sent Hadrian an awkward little wave, prompting him to laugh.

Then he was inside, and the night was over.

CHAPTER 18

HADRIAN SMILED to himself as he opened the window above his small kitchen sink. A cool breeze rolled in, bringing with it the first taunting hints of warm spring air. Outside, the icicles that hung off the eaves of his building had been melting all day, creating a pleasant background of dripping water.

He had plenty of reasons to be in a great mood. That morning Ivan had offered him a small promotion, as much as anyone could be promoted when they were one of a handful of employees. It meant a little higher salary and a bit more flexibility in choosing his days off.

And then there was Max.

Hadrian turned to the hearty loaf of dark bread waiting for him on his old wooden cutting board. He pulled the bread knife out of the chopping block and sliced the crusty bread into small circles. He was in the mood for something light, something springlike. Chlebíčky, the open-faced Czech sandwiches, would suit just fine. When the bread was sliced, he smeared each piece with mayonnaise and topped it with a thin slice of swiss cheese and ham. A tomato wedge, freshly cut, followed with a small piece of pickle.

When he was finished, he had a plate of four open-faced sandwiches ready for eating. He carried it over to his reading chair and sat but didn't pick up a book. Instead, he contented himself with looking outside at the beautiful view. Rows of orange-tiled houses stretched in front of him, interspersed with square apartment buildings and the sloping roofs of more ornate, older structures. The sky was a perfect blue, and in the far distance, he could see Petřín Hill rising over the city, the castle keeping sentry beside it.

He hadn't expected Max to come into his life, but he was happy that he had.

Their date had been almost perfect. Once again he found himself struck by Max's surprisingly sarcastic tongue and charming propensity to blush. He was handsome and able to keep his own in a conversation full of banter, which was just how Hadrian liked it.

It was almost a little frightening just how quickly he'd become enamored, and how much power Max seemed to have over him.

When Max had grown angry at Hadrian's poking, he'd surprised himself by opening up, sharing as he was asking Max to do. He hadn't spoken to anyone of his experiences in the UN for a long time, and years had passed since he'd so much as mentioned the Air Force's name. He preferred it that way. As for the rest....

He closed his eyes and felt the heat of the sun on his back, the sweat turning the inside of his helmet slick, the itch of his uniform sticking to his back. He hurried to hand boxes of canned food and bottled water to grasping hands, knowing it wasn't enough, half his attention spent calculating how many he could get to before the supplies ran out, the other straining for the sounds of helicopters in the distance, knowing a chopper from the wrong side now would mean hundreds dead.

There were flashes—homemade pipe bombs exploding like fireworks, but they were in the crowd, not the sky, and the colors came from blood and clothes sent spiraling into the air, and that roaring noise was screaming.

His eyes snapped open, and he shook his head, then forced himself to look outside, to breathe deep, to remember where he was.

No, Max didn't need to know the rest. He'd already said so much more than he'd thought himself capable of sharing.

He saw again the softness in Max's eyes as he listened to Hadrian's story, a softness tempered by respect. That, there, was a look he wanted to preserve in his memory for the rest of his life. Sympathy without pity. Empathy, and only that, for his pain.

That would have been enough to make Max important to him. But their physical chemistry was a whole new level of hot, deepening with every interaction they had. The way he'd kissed Max in the snow... the way Max had pulled him closer....

Heat surged in his belly, and his cock swelled just remembering the way Max had felt pressed up against that wall. There had been promise there. Confirmation that their bodies worked well together, hints of what lovemaking could be like. The look on Max's face when he'd pulled away had been almost more than Hadrian could take. It had taken all of his self-control not to accept Max's offer, to follow him upstairs and ravish every inch of his body.

But he'd known it was the right thing to do. Max's look of gratitude afterward had confirmed it—and reinforced the fact that any steps taken forward would not be casual. What they had was strange, and special. He didn't want to screw this up, and part of that was showing Max that Hadrian was interested in him for *him*.

He looked around his flat, taking in the old wood, the comfortable sparseness of his space, and thought to his last actual, bona fide relationship. "Christ," Hadrian muttered as he did the math in his head. Had it really been two years?

He'd dated Alexej for a year before Alexej returned to his native Slovakia. They'd had fun, but that had been it. Beyond a single weekend's moping, it hadn't torn Hadrian's heart to see him leave.

Since then he'd had his share of one-night stands, of course. He enjoyed sex, had been told he was good at it, but nothing had attracted his attention, his imagination, like Max. The man had beguiled him in a surprisingly short time.

Sighing, Hadrian picked up one of his sandwiches and took a bite. There was only one barrier in their way now, and it was whatever dark secret Max was hiding from the world. It would have to be on Max's terms, if that were to be broached. For now, Hadrian was content to wait.

CHAPTER 19

DESPITE IT being Monday, Max found himself grinning as he made his way through the snowy, crowded sidewalks to the cafe near Foxrod, where he was meeting Maggie for lunch. There were still a few hours before his class was due to start, but he'd felt the need to get out of the flat, discuss things with someone. Maggie had sprung instantly to mind.

His dinner date had been playing on a nonstop loop ever since he'd left Hadrian at the door. A pleasant distraction—one that warmed him to his toes—but it was a distraction nonetheless. There was a chance that discussing it would get the date out of his mind long enough for him to concentrate on his new job.

He was paused at an intersection, waiting for a tram to go slithering past, when he spotted a familiar face down the street. It was Christopher, scowling at the ground as he wound through the lunch crowd. Max hesitated a moment, remembering the awkwardness of Christopher storming out of the pub on Friday. But Christopher would see him in a moment, and despite Max's reservations, he was his friend. Somewhat resigned, he raised his hand and called out his name.

Hearing him, Christopher looked up and his scowl faded into a small smile. "Hey, Max," he said, coming over.

"How are you?"

"I'm okay. Where you headed?"

Max nodded over his shoulder to the crowded street across from them. "I'm meeting Maggie for lunch at that little French place. Want to join?"

"Not today," Christopher said. "But let me walk you there?"

"Sure."

They checked the road for trams. When the coast was clear, they stepped off the sidewalk and onto the cobblestones. Christopher kept his hands in his pockets and didn't speak, despite having asked to walk together. Max felt the awkwardness but wasn't sure how to dissipate it.

Luckily he spotted the cafe after only a few minutes. Its outdoor seating area was still closed for the winter, but the windows were lively and displayed spring flowers and a hand-painted bicycle that cast some cheer over the lingering snow.

"Sure you don't want to join us?" Max asked, as they stopped outside the cafe. "They're pretty cheap, and the food's great."

"I can't stay long, sorry," Christopher said, fidgeting. He took a deep breath and fixed his eyes on a point somewhere above Max's shoulder. "But before you go, I need to apologize. I was incredibly rude on Friday. Never even congratulated you."

"Don't worry about it," Max said. He gave what he hoped was a sympathetic smile. "Seriously, man. I'm sorry you didn't pass. That sucks."

"Yeah, well. What are you going to do?"

"What happened? I studied with you—you seemed to be on top of everything."

"It wasn't the test," Christopher said, sounding miserable. "I aced that. It was my assignments. Couldn't get them up to passing."

"What?" Max frowned. "Why didn't you say you were having trouble? I would have helped you out, or Maggie, or anyone."

"Too damn proud," Christopher said, breaking again into that handsome grin. "Besides, I didn't want the guy I'm crushing on to know I couldn't hack it."

Max winced, feeling heat climb into his traitorous cheeks. He'd suspected as much, but he'd really hoped that either his suspicions were wrong or that Christopher wouldn't bring it up. Unsure of what to say, he stalled for time. "You—I—" Max shook his head. "Sorry, what?"

"Come on, like you didn't know." Christopher's grin turned rueful. "Thought I was pretty obvious."

"Well…." Max bit his lip. He took the safe route and changed the subject, eager to avoid any other confessions. "So what are you going to do now?"

Christopher shrugged. "Not sure yet. I could take the course again, but that's bloody expensive. Might be able to find work here without the certificate, but it would be difficult. Not many options for me, workwise."

"I'm so sorry," Max said, and meant it.

"Yeah, well. Such is life, right?" Christopher smiled then, a bit of his usual charm shining through the gloom. "Speaking of nothing—any chance you'd have dinner with me? I promise I'm as charming on a date as I am in class." He stepped forward and reached out to cup Max's elbow.

At his touch Max flinched back.

Christopher froze, then dropped his hand back to his side with an offended frown. "That's a pretty clear 'no.'"

"I'm sorry, Christopher," Max said, shaking his head. Better to be blunt, and honest. "I'm just not interested—no offense."

Christopher studied Max a moment, his face unreadable, then shrugged with a strained smile. "It's okay, I get it. I didn't think you were one for dating much anyway. I mean, you never come out with us, you don't drink—it's cool. Can't blame a guy for trying, though."

Annoyance flashed through Max. *Not one for dating? What is that supposed to mean?* "Actually—"

"Don't tell me you're straight?" Christopher said, eyebrows raised in a kind of skeptical arrogance that set Max's blood boiling. "I'm usually good at telling who is and isn't, and you definitely—"

"I'm seeing someone." Max watched as Chris's face changed. First his eyebrows rose, surprised—and then surprise morphed to an odd frown.

"What?"

"I'm seeing someone," Max said again, with a little less heat. "That's why I don't want to go out with you."

"Maggie said you weren't into dating," Christopher said, eyebrows drawn together.

"I wasn't. I'm not. Just… this one particular guy. It's been kind of a surprise, actually," Max said, shrugging and looking at the wall past Christopher's head. "Sometimes these things just happen." He looked up at Christopher and felt a flare of discomfort. There was a stormy expression on Christopher's face that made Max wince even as it stirred an answering anger in him.

"Is that who you were texting on Friday? Your 'friend'?"

"Yeah," Max said, curt. He looked around, hoping Maggie would pop up and spare him this.

"You sure you're not just winding me up?" Christopher pressed on, cracking a tight smile. "You can just say no. I won't bother you again."

"His name is Hadrian, and he's a bartender at U Medvídků if you need to check for yourself," Max snapped, feeling his temper crest.

Immediately he bit his tongue, wishing he could take his words back. Who he was or was not with was his own business, no one else's.

The cringe was followed by a rolling edge of fear. He couldn't allow himself to be this out of control. What if the next secret he spilled was his own? Max took a deep breath, trying to calm himself. He needed to salvage this before he said something worse.

"Look, I don't want to lose you as a friend, Christopher," Max said, trying to soften his tone. "I like you a lot. Just not in that way."

"I get it," Christopher gritted through tight teeth. "Sorry. I guess I was a little pushy, mate."

"It's okay," Max said, though it wasn't.

Christopher pasted a grin on his face, but Max could tell it was false. It was too tight at the edges. He glanced at his watch, then back at Max. "Look, I've got to go. Got an interview. I'll see you around, okay?"

"Sure," Max said.

He'd barely finished the word before Christopher turned and hurried off, almost smacking into a woman loaded with shopping bags as he did so.

Max watched him go with a furrowed brow, felt the lingering edges of his anger fade to discomfort. That had been unexpected and strangely aggressive. He'd known Christopher liked him, but there had been something distasteful in the way he'd been speaking. Unbidden, he felt that bad feeling return to his chest.

In the midst of this thought, someone came up behind him and tapped him on the shoulder. He whirled to see an odd, small man with a pinched face and uncombed flaxen hair standing behind him. He was about the same height as Max, but thinner. The impression he gave was vaguely ratlike.

"Sorry?" Max said, out of habit.

"Yes, you speak English?" the stranger asked. His voice was neutral, forgettable.

Max swallowed his distaste and pasted a friendly smile on his face. "Yes, do you need help?"

"I looking for language school Foxrod," the man said, returning the smile. "You know this school?"

Max hesitated a moment, trying to glance subtly into the cafe to see if Maggie had arrived yet. It looked empty, and Foxrod was only about a block away. He could take this man over if he hurried. "Yes, I am a teacher at Foxrod. I can walk you to the school."

The man's smile widened. "Thank you very kindly."

He followed Max away from the cafe, down the busy sidewalk. They passed a fast food chain and a bank before coming to the nondescript building that held Foxrod. It was big and flatly gray, surprisingly ugly for this part of the city, with an open first floor that created a kind of plaza beneath the building. Now, during the day, the plaza was crowded with people streaming through it to get to the street behind or the restaurants inside.

He could see how the man had missed the door. The entrance to Foxrod, a small glass door with a simple orange and blue sign on the front, would have easily been swallowed up in the confusion were it not for the large sign they'd stuck in the middle of the plaza, pointing right at the door. Today, for some reason, the sign was missing.

"Here you go," Max said, showing him the door. "I'm sorry, I need to go...."

"No, thank you," the man said. He studied Max with his strangely beady eyes. "You are kind." He gave Max an odd little bow before stepping inside.

Max watched him go, wondering, before hearing his name called from behind him. He turned to see Maggie coming down the plaza, an odd frown on her face. She was looking past him, toward the door of Foxrod where the strange man had just disappeared.

"Maggie? Hey, sorry I'm late," Max said as she stopped near him.

"You okay?" she said, her voice intent. "That guy bothering you?"

Max raised an eyebrow. He ran the encounter back through his mind, not seeing anything out of the ordinary besides the man's strange bow. "That guy? He's just a student. Needed directions. Why—something strange about him I missed?"

Maggie looked at him then, something sad flashing across her face. Then she smiled and shrugged as if nothing had happened. "No, don't worry about it. I just get a little paranoid, that's all. It's a big bad city out there."

Max didn't roll his eyes, but it was a close thing. She thought Prague was dangerous? If only she knew what lived in New York. "Let's get some food," he said, changing the subject. "I just had the weirdest run-in with Christopher. Also I maybe have a boyfriend now."

"What!" Predictably distracted, Maggie began interrogating him on their way back to the restaurant. It was enjoyable, felt good—normal—to be gossiping with her. And in the tide of news he had to share, Max forgot all about the strange Foxrod student.

CHAPTER 20

KAREL WAS well aware of how he appeared on the outside.

Calm, relaxed, and essentially harmless, with his long hair and video game T-shirts that, admittedly, he never bothered to fold. He knew that standing next to John, who habitually frowned when he wasn't actively smiling, he looked even more laid-back.

He used it to his advantage, knowing the whole time that it was just a charade.

He hadn't become one of the top game designers in the Czech Republic by relaxing all the time. Certainly his childhood, in the last throes of a Communist regime that had sent his grandparents to prison and nearly worked his father to death, couldn't have led to anything but a certain steel at his core. Growing to manhood in a country undergoing revolution had brought him new ideas, new weapons of the mind. He'd learned English quickly, with relative ease, and found his way into the tech center when it became clear that was the route for success in this new world. He managed to do so in a way that married possibility with his personal interests.

That was not to say he was unkind. Indeed, Karel believed that one caught more flies with honey than vinegar. He also believed in second chances and the goodness that could live inside even the darkest of men.

But he was prepared, if necessary, to do that which was hard, which was difficult. That had served him well, first in his career and then in loving John, who could be stubborn at the best of times. When John told him of his cousin, Max, Karel knew he must welcome him into their home. He was family—and Karel did not like those who would abuse others. He'd thought of the danger, then dismissed it as unimportant in the face of saving a young man's life.

Max had quickly cemented his place in Karel's heart. Here was a man like him: soft on the outside, hard as nails where it counted. Having survived so much and escaped when others would have perished, Max thoroughly deserved the chance to begin his life again.

Which was why, on a Wednesday afternoon, Karel decided to take his lunch at an old friend's.

"Karel!"

He smiled at Ivan's enthusiastic greeting as he stepped down into U Medvídků. The big man threw his arms around Karel and squeezed him tight. Vaclav, Ivan's faithful dog, was not far behind, and Karel happily ruffled his fur before reaching down to scratch behind his ears.

"It has been nearly a month since you came to visit," Ivan chided in Czech, as he stepped back. "This is not good. Friends must see each other more often, yes?"

"You are right. Forgive me," Karel said, giving a small theatrical bow that sent his hair spilling over one shoulder. Straightening, he went on. "We had deadlines at work, and then things at home have been quite busy."

"Yes," Ivan said, raising an eyebrow. "I hear you have family staying with you."

Karel read the look in Ivan's face, the respectful quest for gossip, and grinned. "I think your bartender has been telling stories."

"Him?" Ivan snorted. "That man is like a vault. He bottles everything inside. It is not healthy. But you must respect another man's privacy."

"Yes." Karel nodded. "Of course, you must also take care of your family."

Ivan met his eyes. "You must."

Karel broke into a smile. "I am starving, Ivan, and I have only the hour to eat. What can you make me?"

"I have some potato soup in the kitchen, some bread. Will that do?"

"Thank you. That would be perfect."

"Good. You are too skinny, you know."

"Every time you tell me this," Karel said, shrugging, "I think you are jealous."

Ivan laughed, smacking him on the back before stepping away. "Have a seat, maybe at the bar," he said, eyebrow raised. "It is comfortable. Our bartender will be back in a few minutes. Ah—speak of the devil," he added, giving Karel a knowing look before turning to head to the kitchen.

There was the sound of the front door opening, then slamming shut and footsteps treading carelessly down the steps. Karel smiled, tucking his hands into his back pockets, as Hadrian came around the corner and into the pub. His eyes widened, and then he grinned upon seeing Karel.

"All right, mate?" Hadrian said, coming over to clap Karel on the back. It took Karel half a second to register the switch to English. "How are you? Haven't seen you in a while."

"Busy, you know how it is," Karel said, smiling back. "We are almost finished with our new game. I have a lot of deadlines."

"Ah, well. You're here now, eh? And—is John with you?" Hadrian asked, some of the cheer dropping from his voice.

Karel frowned. "No. Then he has spoken to you about Max, I see."

Hadrian winced. "Just a little friendly warning, is all. Nothing I wouldn't say in the same circumstances."

"You must not listen to him. He is overprotective. You know how he is."

Hadrian's smile returned, just a little. "I remember when that creep started hanging around your studio."

"Yes, well. Truthfully I came to have lunch and to see you. It has been too long, you are right."

Hadrian nodded, waved him over to a bar stool, and went around to take his place behind the gleaming wood. "Something to drink?"

"Staropramen," Karel said, naming one of the many Czech beers on tap. He waited, comfortable in the quiet while Hadrian cleaned him a glass and poured the drink. "Thank you," he said, accepting the beer.

"So how've you been?" Hadrian asked, leaning his hip against the bar.

Karel shrugged. "Like I said, it has been busy. The new game had some problems in our beta run. Nothing we can't fix, but still… it makes things complicated."

"That's too bad. What was the problem?"

"Well," Karel said, then launched into an explanation of the last-minute glitch they'd discovered that turned the final boss from a vampire zombie into a cow in drag that shot sticks of butter out of its udders.

Hadrian laughed. "I dunno, sounds more like a bonus than a glitch."

Karel rolled his eyes. "Yes. A million crown bonus."

"Ah, never mind, then," Hadrian said, wincing. "Christ, I can hear my bank account screaming for mercy."

"Then you can imagine our pain." Karel grimaced. Someone in programming was going to be fired over that one. "The situation, it is unpleasant. Though we may keep it as an Easter egg."

"Could do," Hadrian said, nodding.

"When are you going to enter 2015 and buy a game system, Hadrian?" Karel asked with a grin. It was an old fight of theirs. Hadrian was as Luddite as they came, and Karel couldn't help but tease him.

"When you build something with as good graphics as those I can imagine in my head," Hadrian shot back. "Give me a book any day. Much less complicated. Portable. Fits in your hand."

"So do 3DSs," Karel said, then shook his head with a laugh. He glanced at Hadrian, saw the smile on his face, his relaxed posture, and hid a small smile as he brought the conversation around to his target. "Ah, enough. Let us talk of something more pleasant. I found a new recipe this week and I need test pigs. You should come over for dinner on Saturday. Unless you have a plan already?"

Hadrian winced. "Actually, I'm busy that night."

"Ah, with Max," Karel said, nodding as though he'd just remembered. "Yes, he mentioned something… will you go out?"

Hadrian quirked an eyebrow as Karel smiled politely. "You know, I always pegged you as the subtle one in your relationship," Hadrian finally groaned. "John's the brash one."

"This is not subtle?" Karel asked, grinning over the top of his beer.

Hadrian rolled his eyes. "Look, I'm going to cook him dinner on Saturday—"

"You're a very good cook."

"Yeah, so they tell me. But I'll say the same thing I said to John. I'm not going to hurt him, Karel."

"Will you let yourself be hurt, though?" Karel asked. He set down his beer, all playfulness aside. This was the crux of what he wanted to talk about, not some nonsense about Hadrian's past escapades.

"I—what are you talking about?"

"I have known you a long time now. I believe us to be friends—is this so?"

"Of course," Hadrian said, looking away. "You've seen me through a lot of bad times, Karel. Back when… well, you stuck by me. That's friendship."

They both fell quiet, remembering their first meeting. The long months of recovery when Hadrian could barely make it to work. How Karel had befriended him after Hadrian served him in U Medvídků, talked to him while he worked, given him comfort in a time when he was not far off from really damaging himself.

"And you have supported me too, through so many hardships. And I watched you return to yourself, to make a life here. But I have never seen you surrender to another person."

"Alexej—"

Karel tsked. "Please, he cannot count. There was no love in your eyes when you talked of him. You are a very closed person, Hadrian. Very private. It has kept you very safe all these years, after the time you will not talk about, that hurt you so badly. But it has also made you cold."

Hadrian sighed, rubbing a hand across his eyes. "Look, what are you trying to say?"

"I am trying to say just what I said: Will you let him hurt you? Will he be given that chance?"

Karel watched Hadrian pull his hand away, watched those astonishingly blue eyes furrowed first in confusion and then clarity. He was pleased Hadrian didn't answer right away. He stayed silent, waiting for whatever answers Hadrian would give him.

"I… I don't know," Hadrian finally said. "He's close. Closer than anyone has been, and we're only a few dates in. Later?" He stopped, frowning, then breathed deep. "But I'm trying, Karel. I feel for him, like— no one has ever—" He cursed, drumming his fingers on the bar. "I don't have the fancy words to put it in. I just can't stop thinking about him."

Karel watched him for a moment, then nodded, satisfied. Picking up his drink, he took a long sip, letting the cool beer soothe his throat, giving him a moment to gather his thoughts. When he was done, he set the beer on the wood and grinned up at Hadrian. "Excellent."

Hadrian rolled his eyes. "You're right confusing today. Poor John."

Karel waved him off, grin unfazed, and turned at the sound of the kitchen door opening. "Aha—lunch! Ivan, you are a king."

Ivan set his soup before him, then settled in to talk with them. After a while, Karel lost track of the conversation and focused on his lunch, enjoying the salty-sweet creaminess of the broth and the perfectly soft tenderness of the potato chunks that swam within it. He watched Hadrian from the corner of his eye, pleased at what he had learned today, at the potential he sensed between these two men for whom he cared so deeply.

If Hadrian's reaction was anything to go by, it seemed Max wasn't the only one off balance. And that suited Karel nicely.

CHAPTER 21

CHRISTOPHER DRAINED the last of his beer before setting the glass down with a miserable clunk on the bar. Around him, neon lights pulsed and club music blasted despite the bar being almost empty. It felt a little pathetic. The kind of scene he should be embarrassed to be part of at four o'clock on a Wednesday afternoon.

It suits me, he thought. *A pathetic scene for an utterly useless human being.*

"*Pivo, prosím*," he called to the bartender in clumsy Czech.

The bartender glanced at him, at the cluster of glasses by his elbow, and shrugged. Pouring him another beer, he set it down with a raised eyebrow and walked away.

"Fuckin' waste," Christopher muttered to himself before draining half the glass. He set it back a little less steadily than he had before. Around him, things were beginning to blur at the edges. The room tilted slightly. Good. He wasn't in the mood to be sober.

Life of late had been undeniably awful. First his fuck-up with the course, which had cost him several thousand dollars' worth of wasted time. It was his fault, he knew, for not taking it seriously and assuming he'd skate by on his test results alone. Foolish of him. But he'd thought he might still be in reach of a consolation prize in Max. Who'd have thought he was taken? Quiet, shy Max, going on dates with someone he met outside the course?

Christopher was not used to failing. Two counts were enough to drive him to drink.

He sighed, staring moodily into his glass. He'd have to decide soon if he were going back to the UK or not. His money was running low. If he found work, maybe he could stick around—but then, why bother?

"Excuse me," said a low voice over his shoulder.

Christopher turned bleary eyes to find a short, rat-faced man with thin blond hair smiling at him. "Help you?" he asked, drunk enough that the stranger's speaking English didn't strike him as odd.

123

"You are the only person here, besides myself," the man said, with a slight shrug. "I find that I would like some company. Would you mind if I bought you a drink?"

Christopher frowned, shifting away. "Sorry, mate, not interested."

The man looked surprised and then laughed, flashing his left hand. A gold ring glittered on his ring finger. "I did not wish to give you the wrong impression," he said. "Nothing of that nature. I promise, I only want a bit of company. A chat, perhaps."

Christopher frowned, then shrugged and nodded to the stool next to him. "Have a seat, then. Not sure I'll be good company just now, though."

"Oh? Why not?" the man asked. He took a careful seat beside Christopher, then waved at the bartender, indicating Christopher's beer with a nod.

"Fucked up, basically," Christopher said, taking another swallow from his beer. "Supposed to have gotten my qualification to teach English, failed the course. Almost two thousand pounds down the drain."

The other man tsked, shaking his head. "Ah, a business venture gone wrong. I am familiar."

"All my fault, though," Christopher said, glaring into his drink. "Couldn't ask for help. I'm an idiot."

"We have all got our failings," the rat-faced man said. He smiled as the bartender placed a beer in front of him, but didn't touch it. "Cheer up—perhaps you could try again? Where is your course? Here in Prague?"

"Yeah, Foxrod. It's a language school near Mustek. You a teacher?"

"Me? No, I'm not a teacher," the man said, shaking his head. "Though I considered it once. Never pursued it—to tell you the truth, there was a woman involved, and when that didn't work out, well…." He shrugged.

"Well, that's another thing we've got in common, then," Christopher said glumly.

A smile flashed across the stranger's face, too quick for Christopher to be sure of what he'd seen. "Oh? Is that part of your tale of woe?" the man asked, his voice casual.

"Unfortunately. I'm unlucky all around. They were on the course with me. Bloke named—" Christopher cut himself off, fighting a sudden chill that ran down his spine.

"Go on," the man said, nodding encouragement.

"Doesn't matter his name, I guess," Christopher said slowly. The chill remained. He couldn't shake it. Some instinct warned him to silence.

"I won't tell." The man winked and shifted slightly in his seat, edging closer, bridging the space between them.

Christopher frowned. "Why are you so eager to know? Just a name. Bit embarrassing for me, you know."

"Ah, nothing to be embarrassed over. A tale goes better when the characters are named, I think. And perhaps I know him," the man said with a smile. He shrugged and drew a small circle in the condensation left by his beer mug. "'Tis a small world, after all."

Christopher eyed him up and down, thinking. It couldn't matter, could it? Prague was a small world, with most expats knowing one another. Besides, Max was a grown man. He could take care of himself.

He clearly wanted nothing to do with Christopher, anyway.

"His name is Max," Christopher said, draining the rest of his drink. "Real smart, cute as hell. Quiet type, but friendly. I had a bit of a thing for him. Turns out he's already got a boyfriend." Christopher snorted unhappily, losing himself again in his story, forgetting some of the caution that had stung him.

The stranger pushed his untouched pint into Christopher's hands, and Christopher nodded his thanks, hand tightening on the cold glass. "Go on. And is this lover someone you know as well? A rival, perhaps. Another educated man like yourself?" The man smiled sympathetically.

"No, that's the thing—he's a bloody bartender!" Christopher said as he took a swig of the fresh pint. The bubbles rushed to his head in a cool wave of foam. That was what he needed—a pint and a good moan. Would set him up right quick.

"Perhaps you should take me to the beginning. Tell me, when did you begin this TEFL course?"

The world swimming, Christopher began to talk. Soon pints turned to whiskey, and as the liquor flowed, so did Christopher's words. The rat-faced man was a good listener. Christopher told him everything, getting it all off his chest. Words running like water as his drinks got smaller and consequently stronger. By the end Christopher could feel his memory going, the first edges of a blackout tinting his vision dark.

Much later, Christopher found himself with an arm slung over the man's shoulders. They were singing as they left the bar and made their way into the streets of Prague. Christopher watched as the sky spun in circles above him. It was dark, tonight. The clouds hid the stars. Even the street lamps seemed to have dimmed.

"Bloody hell time's it?" he asked. He giggled and tilted to the side. Only the small man beneath his arm kept him from falling into the snow.

"Don't worry, not too late," the man said, and fell silent.

Christopher felt him tug his arm, looked ahead, and saw the street narrowing in front of them. "Where we goin', mate?" he slurred. He shivered. "I'm cold. Think I might be sick." That struck him as funny, and he started laughing again. Everything was funny, and for the life of him, he couldn't figure out what he'd been worried about. "You're a good friend, you... hey, wus your name 'gain?" Christopher laughed. "Can't bloody remember. Making a right tit of myself."

"You don't need to worry about that," the man said. He shifted, sending Christopher's world spinning.

There was a pressure in his stomach. The thought that he might piss his pants wound its way through Christopher's subconscious and made him laugh some more. He looked around and saw his new friend was pulling him toward an alley. Perfect spot for a pee. "Right," Christopher said, lurching off the man and bracing himself on the brick. "Right, I gotta take a leak. Gimme a second." He stumbled down into the dark, stopped, propped himself up against the wall, and began fumbling with his fly. "Christ, how much we drink, mate?" he called back over his shoulder. "Stream like a bloody garden hose over here!"

There was silence behind him. A crunch, as if feet on fresh snow.

"Mate?" Christopher called back. Cold wind blew across his neck. He finished and fumbled his pants closed. Suddenly he wanted to be home.

There was a click. The sound of an exhale.

Something stung him, hard, on the back of his neck. He was falling into the snow, the ice cutting his face as he smashed into the ground. The air smelled of urine and garbage. Christopher had a moment of confusion, a wondering what had happened. Had he fallen?

Then blackness.

A SHORT while later, the rat-faced man pulled open the door of an unremarkable sedan and sat. The tall woman, broad-shouldered and gorgeous, was sitting in the driver's seat, staring fixedly at the street ahead of them.

"He's taken care of," the man said with a shrug. "Quiet. They won't find him for some time."

"You got everything we need?" she asked, voice disinterested.

The rat-faced man nodded. "More than we expected," he said, raising an eyebrow. "The boy has taken a lover. A bartender from a local restaurant."

The woman frowned. "He'll want to know. Make the call—include everything."

He nodded again, pulled out his phone, and dialed quickly. It rang twice before a cultured voice on the other end spoke.

"We've got him, monsieur," the rat-faced man said. His voice changed, dropping the pretension of before, smoothing into a broad accent. He nodded at something the other said, then handed the phone to the woman.

"Bonsoir," she said, listened intently for a few moments, then nodded. "As you say. We will be discreet. *Oui, oui. Au revoir.*" She hung up, having received their orders.

The rat-faced man looked at her expectantly. "Well?"

"Put on your seatbelt," she said, turning the ignition with a bored expression. The car roared to life beneath them. "We have work to do."

CHAPTER 22

HADRIAN SURVEYED his small kitchen, arms akimbo, sure he'd forgotten something. He wore black jeans and a matching cotton button-down, the top left open. A white half apron, stained from cooking misadventures past, was wrapped around his waist.

"Well, then," he said, frowning at the small space before him.

He had the pasta water simmering on the stove, salted and ready to receive the fresh linguine he'd picked up that afternoon. Wild mushrooms—a riot of browns, oranges, and yellows—from one of Ivan's farmer friends were marinating in a delicious blend of thyme and garlic. And finishing in the oven, filling the air with comforting smell of home, was a freshly baked rosemary focaccia, just waiting to be pulled out and dipped into the herbed olive oil he had waiting on the table.

Everything was fine. Dinner was going to be delicious. So why was he so worried?

"You know why," he muttered. Karel's words had been haunting him all week, spoiling some of his excitement for tonight. Could he let himself get hurt? Was that really necessary? "Can't I just have a nice friggin' dinner?" he scowled.

Grumbling, he stepped away from the kitchen and went to the small table he'd pulled underneath the window opposite his bed. Not that he'd admit it, but he'd gone out and bought new pasta bowls and glasses for tonight. The bowls, a white ceramic, had an asymmetric shape that had struck him in the store. The glasses themselves were plain, but considering most of his cups were the free plastic kind usually found in bars, they were a major improvement. In between sat the yellow bowl he'd picked up in the market the previous spring, holding oil ready for dipping.

He'd chosen this window for its view, one that would only improve as the sun went down and the golden gaslights of Prague lit up the night.

If things went well, they'd eat and talk and… well, they'd see. Whatever happened would happen.

He frowned, hating the nerves that ransacked his stomach. He was never nervous for a date, certainly not to make dinner for a man. Hadrian liked to be in control of himself. He took great care to project it at all times.

Only Max could wind him up like this.

He pulled his phone out of his pocket and glanced at the time: 7:10 p.m.

Max was unsurprisingly late.

"Should've guessed," he said, half smiling.

Just then the buzzer broke through the quiet in his flat. He felt his heart jump, just a little, as the nerves in his belly fluttered harder. He walked over to the door, his socks turning his movements silent. Pressing the intercom, he said, "Hello?"

"Hadrian?" Max said, charmingly unsure.

"'Lo, Max. Hop in the elevator. I'm the only door on seven," Hadrian said, pressing the button to open the front door.

"Right, okay," Max muttered, followed by the sound of the door opening.

Hadrian stepped back, glancing again at the kitchen, the table, and his bed and reading area. He'd always been a clean man—came from years of military discipline—but today he'd gone the extra mile and scrubbed everything.

He heard the elevator doors ping open, took a deep breath, and forced his body to relax. When Max knocked, it was as hesitant as his voice. Hadrian went over and opened the door, revealing Max standing with a small potted plant in the crook of his arm. His hair was disheveled from the wind, his cheeks pink, and his eyes bright behind his silver-rimmed glasses.

"Only ten minutes late. See, I'm getting better," Max said, smiling.

Hadrian let out a breath, feeling suddenly calm. He smiled, a thinner version to match Max's. "Not bad at all," he said, raising an eyebrow. "Come on in."

Max ducked his head before stepping inside. Hadrian closed the door behind him and turned to see Max taking in the apartment.

"It's so neat," he said, then visibly cringed. "I mean, not to say that I thought you were sloppy, it's just...."

"Hmmm?" Hadrian asked, his smile growing.

"Ah... never mind," Max said, his blush reaching his ears. Quickly, he took the plant from his arm and thrust it at Hadrian. "Here, this is for you. I was thinking flowers, and then I remembered you like to cook, and...."

Hadrian, somewhat bemused, took the plant from him and sniffed the feathery leaves that stretched along its stalks. "Fresh thyme," he said, surprised. "Thank you. This is lovely."

Max shrugged as Hadrian turned and set the plant on the small table he kept by the door for keys.

"Your coat," Hadrian murmured, stepping forward. He reached out to help Max out of the heavy felt, trailing his hands along Max's shoulders as he did so. He was delighted to feel Max shiver beneath his hands. Under the jacket, Max wore a thin sweater in cranberry red over the same tight jeans he'd had on the other day. "You look nice," he said, giving Max a once-over with a small smile.

"Thanks," Max said. "You too. Very chef-like."

Hadrian laughed and carried Max's coat to his armchair and laid it over the back. When he turned around, he saw Max staring at his feet.

"Ah—should I take my shoes off?"

"Up to you," Hadrian said with a shrug. "I tend to go the Czech way, but it doesn't really matter."

Max nodded, then reached down to pull off his black boots before setting them by the door. "Damn," he muttered.

Hadrian glanced down and saw a lurid yellow sock paired with a plainer black, and laughed. "Forgot people take their shoes off here, huh?" he said, chuckling.

Max took a deep breath, let it out, then looked sheepishly up at Hadrian. "To be honest, it wouldn't have occurred to me to check my socks even if I'd known."

"I think it's charming," Hadrian said, smoothing out his voice. He was delighted to see Max's blush returned.

"Whatever you're cooking smells fantastic," Max said quickly, stepping away from his shoes, and the subject.

"Hope you like Italian," Hadrian said, letting the socks go, not wanting to go from teasing to making Max uncomfortable. "I was feeling Mediterranean. Maybe it's the coming spring."

"Love it." Sniffing the air, a look of surprise shot over his face. "Is that focaccia?"

"Made it myself." Hadrian glanced at Max, still standing awkwardly in the entranceway, and felt a rush of affection. "Mind keeping me company while I finish our food?" he asked, tilting his head.

Max nodded. "Sure. What else would I do?" he added, with a small laugh.

"Well, it would make dinner a bit awkward if you didn't actually want to spend time with me," Hadrian said. He waited till Max walked over to him, then led him to the stool at the end of his counter, where Max sat, his body still stiff. That would have to change.

"Get you a drink?"

"Water is fine," Max said, taking in the kitchen. "What are you— oh," he said, as Hadrian walked over, reached into the cabinet by his head, and pulled out one of his new glasses. In doing so, Hadrian's chest brushed against Max's shoulder. Even that small contact sent heat pooling in Hadrian's belly.

Hadrian smiled to himself as he stepped away, leaving Max flustered on the stool. He pulled out a pitcher of water flavored with lemon rounds from the fridge and set it on the counter. "Mind a bit of citrus?" he purred.

"Sure," Max said, his voice lifting at the end. He coughed into his hand, looked away. "You know, sometimes I don't get you," he blurted out, then closed his eyes with a pained expression. "Can we forget I said that? Blame it on my horrible foot-in-mouth disease?"

"Hmm. I think I'll need further information first," Hadrian said, hiding his smile as he poured water into Max's glass. It was clear Max was off balance, in the best of ways. He'd have to be careful. Make sure it stayed fun.

"Well, I just meant that, you know, you're strange," Max said again. "No, let me restart. Okay, you're a bartender, right? An expat? And most of the expat-bar types I've seen in Prague have been the grungy, drink-away-their-life types. But here's you, and you don't even drink." He lost the cringe as he warmed to his subject, holding out his hands as he ticked down his fingers. "You love classic sci-fi, and crappy sci-fi. You're the cleanest person I know. But you're not fussy about clothes. I mean, I've seen the same outfit a few times, and you don't have any flashy jewelry or anything like that. You're quiet, but you kicked the shit out of that guy attacking me in the alley. You went from RAF soldier to bartender in Prague. And now I'm sitting in the cleanest apartment I've ever been in while you cook me gourmet Italian food and serve me lemon water. What the hell?"

Grinning, Hadrian set the glass on the counter beside Max before cocking his hip to the side and crossing his arms. "Been thinking a lot about me, eh?"

"What? I—no—I mean, yes, but—argh!" Max said, flustered. He reached out and took a long drink of water.

Hadrian looked at his throat as he swallowed, felt that rush of heat deep in his belly, and wondered again at the strange combination of cuteness and sexiness and quiet passion that hid in such a small body. "Relax, lad. Take that as a compliment, actually," Hadrian said, his own voice a bit strangled. He hoped it wasn't too obvious just how much he was enjoying having Max there.

"Well, good," Max said, huffing out a breath.

"You're a bit odd yourself, you know. Big mystery, flouncing your way into my life like you've done. I ought to be calling you strange."

"I don't *flounce*," Max said, but his voice was quiet. His hands stiffened around his glass.

Hadrian felt his tension, took a deep breath, and pulled back again, knowing that was dangerous territory. He wanted to push, but he reined it in, breathing deep. No, Max needed to want to tell him, to be comfortable enough to share whatever it was he was hiding.

"Better get this pasta boiling," he said, turning to the stove. He cranked up the heat beneath the pasta water, watching it with a trained eye until it bubbled before adding in the pasta. Next came the small pan on his stove's only other burner. He set the heat to low, then added the garlic-infused mushrooms and the oil they'd been marinating in. A pleasant smell of garlic and thyme sizzled out to join the warm focaccia scents from the oven.

"How did you get into cooking?" Max asked.

Hadrian turned to see Max watching intently as he worked at the stove. He was relaxing again, his hands loosening, as Hadrian sautéed the wild mushrooms. "My mum was a terrible cook," Hadrian said, smiling at the memory. "She used to swap ketchup for tomato sauce, to give you an idea."

"Ouch," Max winced. "That must have been... interesting."

"Disgusting is the word you're looking for. I got into cooking first as a way of preserving my stomach lining," Hadrian said, startling a laugh out of Max. "Then, in the Air Force, some of the blokes in my troop were into it. Odd hobby for a bunch of pilots, but it was fun. Interesting, like. After that I guess it just stuck with me. Always did like doing things myself."

"Smells like you've practiced a lot," Max said. "I always wished I could cook. But every time I try, I end up setting something on fire."

"Your folks any good at it? Or do you come from a line of kitchen disasters?"

Max shrugged, a faraway look coming into his eyes. "I never really knew my mother."

Hadrian winced, sure he'd stumbled upon yet another source of pain for Max. Yet he spoke with enough real indifference to put Hadrian's mind at ease.

"She took off when I was little—maybe two or three. I can't remember, obviously."

"And your father?"

Here a smile came over Max's face, and Hadrian wondered what memory had prompted that happy look. "He was a good, but limited, cook. He could make any soup you wanted. Best thing he did was a beef stew—used real wine, y'know? But anything drier and you'd have a burned pile of nothing on your plate." Max came back to the real world, refocused on Hadrian with a smile. "I guess I get my culinary skills from him, but without the redeeming qualities."

Hadrian shook his head. "How about I do the cooking, and you just focus on eating, then."

"That, I can do." He took a drink of his water as Hadrian flipped the mushrooms in the frying pan with a practiced flick of his wrist. "You've got a lot of books. Looked like some really nice editions. I didn't realize you collected, as well as read?"

"Yeah," Hadrian said. "Suppose that's my other hobby, really." He dipped a spoon into the pasta and pulled out a long string of linguine. "You can have a look if you like. This'll take a few more minutes."

Max nodded and wandered over to Hadrian's bookshelf.

As he cooked, Hadrian followed Max from the corner of his eye. He didn't miss the gleam of interest as Max ran his fingers over his first editions, trailing them along the frayed fabric of their covers. He picked up a few, ran his hands carefully along their edges, and inspected their bindings. He paused when he came across the present he'd given Hadrian.

Hadrian cursed to himself as Max frowned at it. He'd meant to move it before Max came over, make it a little less conspicuous. He wasn't sure if displaying it like that was normal. Max had seemed to want to downplay it.

Max moved away, and Hadrian breathed a sigh of relief. He turned off the stove and drained the pasta before adding it to the pan with the oil and mushroom sauce. He tossed it, coating it well before moving it to a large serving bowl. Pulling the focaccia out of the oven, he breathed deep of the rosemary before transferring it to a wooden cutting board.

"Ready to eat?" he asked, carrying the dishes to the little table by the window.

Max walked cautiously over. *Relax*, Hadrian wanted to say. *I'm not going to bite.*

"It looks great," Max said, taking in the food. "I love focaccia. And where did you get these mushrooms?"

"Ivan knows a guy who sells them," Hadrian said. "Big old bloke, wife's twice his size—they go mushroom-gathering all year round."

"Gathering? As in, from the woods?" he asked, eyeing the pasta as if a snake might be hiding inside.

"The Czechs have been harvesting forest mushrooms since there were mushrooms in the forest," Hadrian said, rolling his eyes. "My guy knows what he's doing."

"Hmm," Max said, sounding unconvinced.

They sat and Hadrian scooped the mushroom linguine onto their plates. Max picked up his fork, speared an orange mushroom, and stared at it carefully before steeling himself and taking a bite. His eyes went wide as a small moan escaped his lips that had Hadrian shifting uncomfortably on his chair.

"How come you're bartending at U Medvídků instead of cooking?"

Hadrian grinned and tore off a piece of the still-hot focaccia. "Ivan's the real chef, trust me. This might be good, but you haven't tasted heaven till you've had his food."

"It must be really special, then." Max looked up at Hadrian, smiling.

Hadrian returned the smile and dug into his own food. Gently he turned the conversation to work, asking Max about his new job at Foxrod, his students, living with his cousin.

"John? He and Karel are great. To tell you the truth, it's been nice living with them. I haven't had too much family around, and getting to know John better...."

"I understand," Hadrian said.

Max looked over with a raised eyebrow.

"My father died when I was thirteen. It was just me and my mum after that, and ever since I moved here, I've been much on my own."

"It's hard," Max said, meeting his eyes. "Not most days. Not when you're busy. But when you come home and you're tired and there's no one there."

"Aye." Hadrian nodded, reading his own quiet sadness reflected in Max's expression. "You learn to live without it."

"What about your mother?" Max asked, carefully. "Do you visit her often?"

"When I can," Hadrian said, and smiled, thinking of his crazy, colorful mother. "Tried to convince her to move out here. Got a walloping for that. Woman prizes her independence."

"She sounds fun," Max said, smiling.

"And you, lad?" Hadrian returned, carefully. "You said your mother left you, but your father...?"

Max looked away, his smile fading. "He passed away when I was eighteen. Car accident."

"That's too young," Hadrian said.

"What are you going to do? That's life. Sometimes it goes that way." Max shrugged and shook his head. Again that darkness passed over his face, that sadness tinged with fear. He looked out the window, something hard passing behind his eyes. "You say your mother prizes her independence? That's something I've learned to appreciate too."

Hadrian felt a chill run up his spine. They were getting closer to whatever it was Max was hiding. "Had to rely on yourself, I take it?"

"Yeah," Max said, voice growing bitter. His hand tightened into a fist on the edge of the table, his forearms tensing beneath the fabric of his sweater. "Didn't always do the best job."

"Hey—" Hadrian reached out and placed his hand over Max's. Max flinched, and Hadrian almost pulled away. Instead, he followed the instinct screaming at him and froze, waiting for Max to relax before touching him again. Carefully he covered Max's fingers with his own, felt them trembling, but Max didn't pull away.

Hadrian was close now. Maybe too close. Fear and self-loathing were pouring off Max in a way Hadrian didn't understand. He knew he should change the subject, knew he should back away, but couldn't help himself.

"You've found it now," Hadrian said, waiting for Max to meet his eyes. There it was again—such anger in those brown pools, self-loathing, and a mix of darkness that Hadrian felt echoed in himself, in older, more desperate times. "You've come to a foreign country, found a career for yourself, a new job, new life. Whatever it is that you're running from, you can't let it swallow you. Got to live in the present, lad. Here. Where people love you and care for you and your life is full of opportunity."

"You don't know what I'm running from," Max spat, surprising Hadrian. "It's not some small thing. I can never go back to the States, never see my apartment again, or my life, never speak my real name because he might come *and find me*—"

He threw a hand over his mouth, his eyes round with terror. His face paled, and it took Hadrian a second to realize why Max suddenly looked like some of the men he'd been with on the battlefield. He looked like he was going into shock.

"No, no, no, no," he whispered, as Hadrian watched him, unmoving. *His real name? He?*

Suddenly, Max was standing, running toward the door where he'd left his shoes, and pulling them on with trembling fingers.

Hadrian watched a moment before shaking himself out of shock and jumping to his feet. He hurried over to Max, his military calm-in-crisis training taking over where he wanted to panic. With gentle fingers he stopped Max's hand, carefully took the shoe from him, and set it aside.

"No, I've got to go, I've got to—" Max babbled, pushing his hair back from his face in flustered panic.

"Calm down." Hadrian put one hand on Max's shoulder and let the other find its way to his cheek, soothing, imparting some of his own calm into the other man. "You're not going out, not when you're like this. Come here."

"You don't understand," Max insisted, pulling back. He looked so lost behind his glasses, so lost and alone, like a soldier who'd been fighting for far too long. Hadrian's heart ached to see him like that. "I've said too much. You have to let me go, forget about me. I'll move to another city. Another country. I can't keep doing this—this *pretending*—all the while putting everyone I love in danger again. I'm so selfish, such a fucking coward."

Ice ran through Hadrian as Max talked about running away. He hadn't realized until that very moment how much Max had come to mean to him.

"You're no coward," Hadrian snapped. "And the only selfish one here is me."

Operating entirely on instinct, lost in the moment, in his own fear, Hadrian pulled Max to him and kissed him hard. There was nothing gentle about it—it was a bruising wake-up call, a desperate pleading to stay, a screaming of *need*.

Max stiffened in his arms.

"Stay," Hadrian said, breath ragged, as he pulled back to study Max's face. Max, lips swollen, breath coming fast, looked up and met his gaze. "Please," Hadrian added, knowing he was begging, but not caring.

And then Max was pushing him back, and they were falling into each other, all lips and teeth and rushing hands, two men needing each other in ways inexpressible except by touch, and the world was burning around them, and Hadrian couldn't have cared less if he survived the inferno.

CHAPTER 23

MAX HAD never felt this before.

His skin was aflame where Hadrian cradled his head, his neck, ran his hand down his arm. Burning—the most exquisite fire. He moaned as Hadrian's greedy hands pulled at his sweater, tugging it hard over Max's head in the scramble to touch. He gasped as Hadrian's fingers splayed against his bare back, tugging him closer. Their chests pressed, the sensitive skin around Max's nipples buzzing at the feel of Hadrian's cotton shirt and his hard muscles beneath it.

Max wound his arms around Hadrian's neck, holding tight, a drowning man clutching a plank to keep afloat. Max moaned as Hadrian's tongue caressed his lips, then opened his mouth to the beautiful invasion. It wasn't gentle, their lips bruising, chins banging together in their eagerness, but that was just how Max wanted it. His tongue danced beneath Hadrian's as he explored his mouth. He felt possessed—clinging to Hadrian, his strength the only thing keeping Max standing. Then he gasped when Hadrian's hands found their way to his ass, squeezing with just enough power to bring him to the edge of pain. Max's cock, already aching, throbbed. He could feel it straining against his jeans, dying for release, for those clever hands to set him free, to rub and squeeze and pull—

"Bed," Max groaned, grinding himself into Hadrian.

Together, they stumbled backward. Hadrian pushed Max down onto the bed, and Max let him, delighting in Hadrian's weight on top of him, in the bulge in his jeans that pressed against his own with such delicious anguish. Hadrian began thrusting against him, and Max lifted his hips to meet him as he explored the firm swell of Hadrian's ass with grasping, greedy fingers.

In a move too quick to follow, Hadrian propped himself up on one arm. Still plundering Max's mouth, his other hand found his nipple, pinched it until Max gasped, then wandered down the smooth skin of his belly to cup the swell of Max's cock through his jeans.

"Yes," Max cried, arching himself into Hadrian's hand. His skin, every nerve alight, was dying to be free of his clothes. He pressed his hips up again, hard, grinned at the hiss of pleasure that escaped Hadrian. He moved from Hadrian's ass to his chest, pulling his shirt open, and reached for the bare flesh he so desperately craved.

Suddenly Hadrian stopped. He took his hands away from Max, framing Max's face with his forearms.

Max made an embarrassing mew of disappointment at the loss.

"Wait, lad," Hadrian said, panting. He rested his forehead against Max and held himself perfectly still above him.

Max wriggled his hips, his body demanding friction, but Hadrian didn't move. "What?" he asked. He ground his hips up again, gritting his teeth. His cock was so hard it hurt. He didn't know how much longer he could take it.

"Are you sure?" Hadrian asked, meeting his eyes. He sounded hesitant for perhaps the first time since Max had met him. "You're upset. I don't want to do anything you're not ready for. I…. Jesus," Hadrian said, shuddering.

It took a moment for Hadrian's words to penetrate through Max's sex-starved brain. And then a warmth that had nothing to do with the lustful fire raging along his skin blossomed in Max's chest. Hadrian was giving him a choice, a chance to change his mind, to say no. Even here, in this most base of moments, Hadrian was trying to protect him.

That warmth exploded through him. A feeling—too new to put into words, and perhaps it wasn't *new*, but a *realization*—filled his chest.

In that moment, Max thought Hadrian beautiful. And he knew he was perilously close to falling in love with him.

"Fuck me, please," Max said in a quiet voice. He kept his eyes trained on Hadrian's blue infinities, losing himself in them. He'd never felt so safe in his life. So much *trust*. "I'm so sick of worrying and being careful and hiding what I want. I'm in control of my life for once. I want you to fuck me, and I know exactly what I'm doing."

Hadrian looked into his eyes, his brow furrowed.

Max gave him a small smile and reached up to stroke Hadrian's cheek. *Thank you*, he wanted to say. And, *trust me too*.

Finally, Hadrian grinned down at him. "You are wonderful," he said and pressed his lips back down onto Max's.

Max let out a cry of pleasure as that tongue took him once again. He thrust his hips up, demanding—and cried out again, this time in frustration as Hadrian pulled himself out of reach.

"No, wait." He lowered himself back onto Max, resting his weight there, letting the solid line of their bodies connect.

"Wait? For what? I'm okay, really," Max said, angling his hips so Hadrian couldn't miss just how okay he was.

"I've been thinking about this for more than a month now. I want to take it slow. Make it count." Hadrian grinned again, a rakish flash of white teeth that was not exactly tame.

Max felt the color rise to his cheeks as Hadrian kissed him once more, then slid down the bed. He left a trail of kisses along the thin skin beneath Max's chin, the hollow at the base of his throat, his nipple—and a lick there, a teasing flick of the tongue. Then Hadrian was off the bed, kneeling between Max's dangling legs and yanking his pants off in one smooth motion. Max sprang free, the air almost painfully cool against his fevered skin. He saw Hadrian grin as he gripped his thighs in powerful hands and took in Max's cock with greedy eyes. There was a second, as anticipation built, and then Max threw his head back as Hadrian's lips closed around the head of his cock.

It was almost too much—too much pleasure, too much feeling, too right there. He gasped again as Hadrian's tongue flicked out across his head, a quick burst that left his dick throbbing almost painfully. "T-Tease," Max stuttered and received a low chuckle from Hadrian in return.

"Mmm. But you look so lovely when you're squirming," Hadrian said. "Now—watch me."

Max raised his head, his eyes heavy-lidded. Hadrian met his gaze, those ice-blue eyes sparkling. Keeping his gaze, he tightened his hands on Max's thighs and lowered his mouth onto Max—and kept going. Max bit his lip to keep from screaming as Hadrian took him all the way in. He did scream, his hips bucking involuntarily, when his cock hit the back of Hadrian's throat. Hadrian drew back, dragging his lips along Max's cock, sucking hard—and then plunged back down.

Max grabbed the sheets in shaking hands, his hips moving in time with Hadrian's bobbing head, losing himself in the tongue and teeth that teased and sucked along the base. Hadrian's right hand moved from his thigh—Max only vaguely noticed, his mind on the electric sensations of those lips on his throbbing cock—and then he felt Hadrian's fingers on his taint, teasing the space with gentle touches that kneaded the tender flesh there, sending shivers through Max and making him tighten with desire.

He hadn't been fucked in so long. Not like this. And with that thought, he wanted Hadrian all the way—wanted to feel his cock inside him, wanted the pleasure, the deep *intimacy* that would come with the sheer joy of giving his ass to Hadrian.

He spread his legs a little wider, inviting that hand to go farther. His asshole ached with the need to be touched. "Please," Max said, panting, as Hadrian paused. "Please, will you... will you fuck me?" He opened his eyes to see Hadrian's gaze darken.

Hadrian lifted his head from his cock with a soft sucking sound, making Max cry out. "What are you asking me, lad?" The low timber of his voice sent shivers through Max.

"I want you to fuck me in the ass," Max said. He locked eyes with Hadrian, let him see his need. "Stick your cock in me and fuck me till I scream."

Hadrian's eyes flashed as he stood, and Max took in the glorious picture he made, shirt thrown open, pants tight, a fevered intensity to his eyes. He was like a dark god, with Max bared before him, and all Max could think was that he wanted that god inside him *right now*.

"P-Pants," Max panted, and Hadrian grinned. A moment later his shirt was on the ground. A zip, and Hadrian's pants joined the shirt, and Max got a view of his cock for the first time. It was larger than he'd thought, and thick, the head purple with desire. Seeing it, the cum already beading at its tip, bouncing slightly in the cool air, Max could have screamed. Instead, he squirmed against the sheets.

Hadrian's eyes darkened further. "You will be the end of me," he growled. He grabbed Max's waist with his strong hands, pushed him higher up the bed, crawled up between his legs, and nestled his cock between Max's cheeks, thrusting and grinding himself against Max.

Max groaned as Hadrian's cock brushed his tight pucker. Their lips met, teeth crashing and tongues tangling in uncontrolled passion as Hadrian took his body. Then Hadrian pulled back and rose to his knees between Max's legs. He leaned over, giving Max a good view of his long back, his smooth torso. Max panted, wanting that weight on him.

Hadrian reached into the bedside table and removed a small white bottle of lube. "You've done this before?" He opened the bottle and smeared a drop on his index finger.

"Yeah," Max said, voice throaty, gasping. "Only a few times, but… yeah. I like being on the bottom."

At his words Hadrian reached down and squeezed his own cock, moaning. Then he brought his hand to Max's ass and slid his finger over that hot little circle, massaging the edges, teasing but not entering.

Max felt his ass loosen, the muscles quiver, waiting for that moment when Hadrian would….

"Ahh!"

Hadrian slid a slim finger into Max, circling it once before removing it with a slick, wet sound. He grinned above Max and brought his mouth down to bite and suck at Max's neck before easing that finger in again, and again. As Max moaned, he felt himself widen, felt one finger become two. This time they stayed in him, circling, each movement sending a pulse through Max's cock.

"More," Max moaned, shifting his legs to spread wider. He felt Hadrian grin against the base of his neck.

There was a ripping of paper, the dry crinkling of latex rolling over skin, the click of the lube opening, and Hadrian's moan above him as he slicked himself. Max gasped as he felt the head of Hadrian's cock teasing his opening, felt him thrust once, gentle, not entering but testing. Stretching. Max opened for him, a hint of what was about to come.

"Scream for me," Hadrian growled, hands braced on either side of Max's head, and slid inside.

Max saw white—a cry of pure pleasure burst from his throat—

Together, they plunged into oblivion.

CHAPTER 24

AFTERWARD, WHEN Hadrian had rolled off Max and the world had stopped spinning, they lay panting beside each other. Hadrian was utterly spent. His body felt hot and cool and limp, like he'd had a fever or run a marathon. The only sound in the apartment was Max's gradually slowing breathing and the heavy thumping of his own heart.

When even that slowed, he heard Max shift beside him. A moment later, Max sat up, leaned back on one arm, and looked at Hadrian with a half-embarrassed smile.

Hadrian returned it. "Bit awkward now," he said, crooking his mouth to the side. "Always is after the first time."

"I enjoyed it," Max said, blushing.

Hadrian grinned and rolled onto his side, his hand coming out to play with the soft skin on the inside of Max's exposed thigh. "Aye," Hadrian said, feeling the echo of desire deep in his belly. "You were wonderful, lad."

"And you," Max said, his blush deepening. "It's been a while. And that was… intense, I think is the word."

Hadrian splayed his hand on Max's skin, felt the contrast of smooth flesh and the dark hairs that whorled against it.

"I'm just going to…," Max said, smiling sheepishly and gesturing down at himself.

"Sure," Hadrian said, pulling his hand away. "Bathroom's just beyond the kitchen."

"Okay," Max said.

Hadrian watched him hop off the bed and head to the bathroom, admiring the tightness of his ass, the little cleft between it and the rest of his slim back. When the bathroom door closed, Hadrian fell back on the bed and stared up at the ceiling. A moment later he heard the click and hiss of the shower running.

Jesus H. Christ.

143

He was exhausted, wrung out in the best way possible. That had been everything he'd imagined, and more. His brain came back to life slowly, the postcoital fog still clouding his eyes. He took in the musky smell of sex that mixed with his cotton sheets, the lingering rosemary in the air from their dinner, and the faint tinge of sweat binding them all together.

As he came back to life, he felt apprehension drift into his calm fog.

He hadn't forgotten what had precipitated their lovemaking. They would have to discuss it, as soon as Max came back. It couldn't wait any longer.

He'd known Max was hiding something big. Something dangerous. But now he had a better sense of the scale of the thing. If he was using a false name, it was something bad, and almost definitely dangerous. And it brought up a deeply uncomfortable question: If Max had lied to him about that, even for the best of reasons, what else had he been lying about?

How well did he know this man after all?

Frowning, Hadrian ran a hand down his chest, seeking a comforting touch. He knew Max's body now, and there, at least, he sensed there were no lies between them. Whatever this thing was that burned in both their skins was real—he'd felt it calling back to him, felt Max reaching out for him as he thrust inside him.

But what else could he count on?

He thought of what Max had said, having studied English, his abandoned passion for art—surely that was mixed up in this too. But how? Why?

A growing determination chased the last of the fog away. He'd find out what Max was hiding. If not, they were done. He ached at the very thought of ending things, but knew it was the only way he could go forward.

Karel had asked Hadrian if he would allow himself to be hurt. Yes, he realized in that moment. He'd let Max carve him up any which way he pleased—as long as he did it with the truth.

The shower turned off. A few moments later, the bathroom door opened and Max stepped out in a cloud of steam, Hadrian's raggedy brown towel wrapped around his waist. Some of Hadrian's resolve fled him at the sight of Max, water dripping down his chest, gorgeous brown hair plastered against his head. In the dim light from above, he looked like a character in a play, half lit by gold and shadows.

"So," Max said, his soft voice barely carrying across the room. "I guess we should talk."

"Come here," Hadrian said, sitting up on the bed.

Max shook his head. "No, this is going to be hard. I can't do it lying there with you. I…." He sighed. "Let me find my pants."

"All right," Hadrian said. "Then, in the true British spirit, I'm going to make us a cup of tea. That okay?"

Max, still in the shadows, nodded.

Hadrian stood and pulled on his own discarded pants before walking into the kitchen. He filled his kettle, an old-fashioned metal clunker that had seen a lot of use, and set it on the stove. He followed the ritual like clockwork: light the gas, wait for it to click before releasing the handle, pull the heavy ceramic mugs from the cabinet. Teabags—a black, milk-and-sugar builder's tea was called for tonight. He waited for the singsong whistle of the kettle. When it came, he poured the water carefully into the mugs, letting the sound of falling water fill the quiet apartment.

He doctored their tea with milk and sugar, then took a sip to ensure it was as strong as he liked it. It was just sweet enough to be bracing, without overpowering. Good. He had the feeling they were both going to need it.

Max was sitting in Hadrian's plush reading chair, chin propped on his fist, a faraway look in his eyes. He'd pulled his jeans back on, but nothing else. In the dim light, his mussed hair sent dark shadows over his face.

"Here," Hadrian said, handing a mug to him while setting the other on the reading table.

Max took it with a nod of thanks and watched as Hadrian pulled over a dining room chair to sit across from Max. He kept the small table between them. Max cradled his tea between his hands, warming them, but didn't drink.

"Last chance," he said, not looking at Hadrian. "I can leave before I drag you any deeper into my mess."

Hadrian waited a long minute, till Max looked up, and met his eyes. Terror, and an exhausted acceptance, shone through. Hadrian shook his head. "Tell me, Max. Whatever it is… just tell me."

Max took a deep breath, his hands tightening around his mug, and nodded. "Have you ever heard of the Nippur Tablet?"

"No."

"It's one of the oldest documents in the world," Max explained. "Beyond value. A clay tablet made in 1300 BC, about this size." He held out his hands to show a square about half a foot in width and height. "Records detail of a terrible famine in Nippur—that's in Iraq."

"Okay," Hadrian said, frowning. "What's that got to do with anything?"

Max bit his lip. "It was held in the city of Nippur, along with a large collection of Mesopotamian artifacts. Priceless pieces of history, some of the oldest writing we have left. After the Iraq war started winding down, the collection was meant to be under the protection of Iraqi troops trained by the US military. Should've been safe. But the tablet, along with about a million dollars' worth of other artifacts, was stolen last year."

Hadrian nodded. A vague memory came back to him, some article in a newspaper, or the Internet, he couldn't remember.

"The Iraqi troops guarding the site were all found shot in the back," Max went on. "Press had a field day with it. Looked like insurgents, you know? But then reports leaked that someone had seen private security contractors on site the night of the robbery, from a firm called Graywater that the US had subcontracted to secure a site in a neighboring city."

Hadrian felt dread pooling in his belly as Max paused to take a sip of tea. It was like listening to the plot of a thriller, in the worst way. What was Max mixed up in?

"Dead soldiers, stolen artifacts," Hadrian said, trying to keep his voice low but struggling to contain his impatience. "But that's all in the Middle East, and you're from New York City. What does this historical stuff have to do with anything? And the security firm?"

"It has less to do with Graywater and more to do with the owner," Max said and looked away. "A very dangerous man by the name of Jean Claude."

Hot jealousy spiked through Hadrian, startling him.

"He walked into my shop one day—"

"Your shop?"

"Yes—sorry—Jesus. There's so much to tell." Max took a deep breath and ran his hand through his hair. "I didn't major in English. I am... was... an artist. A book-restorer. Had my own shop too, was doing very well until… well, until all this." He looked up and met Hadrian's eyes. "I'm sorry I've lied to you. But you'll understand soon why I had to."

Hadrian frowned, letting his words sink in. Okay, he'd been prepared for this. Had known, on some level, that Max was only telling him half-truths. The hurt came, then ebbed slightly at the look of pain on Max's face. It was hard to be angry at a face like that.

"I guess that explains a lot," Hadrian said after a beat. They both glanced at the bookshelf, where Max's *Robot* was displayed to the room. "Sorry, lad. Continue. That man walked into your shop…."

"Jean Claude." Max nodded and winced in a way that sent hot needles down Hadrian's spine. "He was handsome, and charming, and he asked me out. It had been a while since I'd gone on a date, and I thought, 'Why not? It's my lucky day.'" He laughed, a dry, bitter sound. "Turned out to be the opposite. We dated for, what, three months? Just long enough that I was convinced I was in love with him. I didn't know much about what he did, and I didn't really care. He was well-off—I didn't know by how much until later—and he had the kind of job where you wear a thousand-dollar suit every day. I was infatuated. And then, when he asked me to move in with him, I said yes."

Max slumped, his back curved, hands hanging between his legs. He looked down into his tea like it was the only thing keeping him anchored to this world. "I'd been to his apartment before, of course, but this was different." His voice dropped lower. "It was going to be my home. It was huge—the bedroom alone was as big as my store. And he was so attentive; he made everything gentle, everything easy. The only place I wasn't given free rein was his office. Even then, it wasn't far. Just had to go down a floor from our living space. So the day after I moved in, I thought, 'Hey, let's surprise Jean Claude. I'll go grab him, we can get some lunch.' It was a Friday. I didn't think he'd be busy."

A haunted look came into Max's eyes. He looked up past Hadrian to the window, his eyes unfocused, lost in some memory. Hadrian didn't like the way his face paled.

"The door to his office was open a little. I was going to go in, but there was a man inside already. They were speaking. Jean Claude sounded angry. Said the man had been seen doing something they couldn't cover up." Max flinched and fell silent, his eyes closing like he'd heard a loud noise.

Hadrian had to fight hard with himself to remain seated. He was torn between wanting to comfort Max and to go outside, anywhere, and start a fight. Punch a wall. Do something to relieve the god-awful tension building inside him. "What happened?" Hadrian prompted, his voice flat.

"Jean Claude shot him," Max whispered.

Hadrian felt the breath leave him in one long, steady pull. So—it was violence, then. The old calm of battle stole over him, kept his body tense, ready.

"Shot him like it was nothing. In the middle of his office on a Friday afternoon," Max went on, not seeming to notice the eerie calm that had descended over Hadrian. "Then he saw me...."

"Did he hurt you?" Hadrian asked, voice low.

Max shook his head. "No. I left before they could stop me. Got outside, just started running. Didn't know where to go or what to do, but I was so scared. And I think, maybe, a little bit in shock. I don't know how long I ran for, but eventually I found an alleyway and hid inside. Jean Claude called me—ordered me to come home, told me he could explain. How do you explain a man bleeding all over the carpet?"

Max's eyes flashed with anger. "I smashed my phone. Totally panicked. I couldn't go to the police—Jean Claude made that clear. Then I remembered my cousin John. So I went into a supermarket and bought one of those disposable phones, and I called him. He told me to leave, right then, to go somewhere I'd never mentioned to Jean Claude.

"I found a homeless shelter in the Bronx. Stayed there a few days, while John was arranging for someone to find me." He bit his lip and looked away. "It wasn't a nice place, you know? I was scared. And I started to think, maybe there was an explanation. Maybe Jean Claude wasn't some kind of villain. Had I really seen what I thought I'd seen?" He ran his hands through his hair, his face frantic. "And... I missed him. For whatever it was worth, I loved him. You don't let go of that easily."

Hadrian stood, not able to sit any longer. He turned from Max, walked over to the window, and looked out at the nightscape below them, the golden lights of Prague winking innocently back. He gripped the sill, letting the wood leech some of the anger from him, some of the jealousy he didn't want to admit to. He knew, in that moment, he hated this man, this Jean Claude. Knew it as much as he knew that Max was telling the truth.

"I thought about going back," Max whispered behind him. "I think I might have, and that's something I'll have to live with for the rest of my life."

Hadrian watched Max's reflection in the glass. He hadn't moved, hadn't even seemed to notice Hadrian's standing. "What stopped you?" Hadrian kept his voice low, eyes on Max's blurred shape in the window.

"They had the news on at the shelter," Max said. His was voice dead, his body still as a statue. "There was a fire downtown. A bad one. I was watching and I recognized the street, and then I saw the awning from my shop, or what remained of it. He'd torched it. Everything I had, everything I'd loved before him. And there it was—just gone, like so much trash. That, I couldn't forgive."

Hadrian took a deep breath and turned when he was sure he could control himself. "How did you get here?"

"Susan—John's friend from the Marines—got me a week later. She saved my life. Kept me hidden, gave me a new ID, a visa, everything, and then got me on a plane out of Boston. And here I am." Max collapsed back in the chair.

"Jean Claude doesn't know you're here," Hadrian said, slowly. He was met with a bitter laugh.

"You think if he did I'd still be alive? I got the picture after he torched my store."

They were silent a long time. A million things ran through Hadrian's mind: anger, furious impotence, a surge of protectiveness that frightened him with its intensity. Mixed with them was a surge of relief.

At last he had Max's truth.

After minutes that seemed like hours, Max shifted in his chair, bringing Hadrian back out of himself.

"But you know the worst part?" Max whispered as though he were in a confessional. "The worst part was that it was my fault. All of it. My stupid naivety that did this."

Hadrian looked down at him, at his curved back, his bowed head, saw him shaking with... what? Guilt? Anger? It wouldn't do, whatever it was. He knew what it was to blame yourself for disasters not of your own making.

Hadrian glanced at Max's mug. "You've hardly touched your tea. That won't do."

"Is that all you can say?" Max looked at him with startled eyes. "After all that, you're worried about tea?"

"One thing you'll learn about the English—tea trumps almost anything," Hadrian said. In truth, the tea was a ruse, a task designed to give them both time to pull themselves together.

The sounds that filled the flat as he boiled more water and washed their mugs were comforting. Familiar. It was a kindness they both needed.

Hadrian pulled out two tea bags and dropped them into the mugs, before speaking again. "I've known such men before," he said, into the quiet flat. He poured boiling water into their mugs, watching the water stain dark where it touched the little bags of tea. "Such monsters as your Jean Claude. They hide themselves well. You can't blame yourself for falling into his trap."

Behind him, Max let out a bitter laugh. "I think I can. It was my fault, my—"

"No," Hadrian said, quietly but with conviction. Behind him, Max fell silent. "You were looking for love, as we all do. And that bastard twisted it round you. You can't blame anyone but him." He turned to see Max staring at him, those dark eyes veiled.

"So what now?" Max asked. He held himself perfectly still in the chair, as Hadrian paused beside the counter. "You wanted to hear my story. My real story."

"You weren't lying about the danger," Hadrian said carefully.

Max nodded and stood. "I understand, and I'm sorry for having brought you into this. Don't worry—I won't put you in danger any longer." He turned, made his way for the door.

"Wait." Hadrian strode across the room and stood behind Max, but didn't touch him. "I didn't say I wanted you to leave, now did I?"

Max shook but didn't turn. "How could I stay?" he whispered, still frozen, facing away from Hadrian. "I never should have gone out with you in the first place. Jean Claude will be looking for me.

Probably for the rest of my life, or his. And if he finds you with me, you'll pay too."

Hadrian took a deep breath. Slowly, gently, he stepped forward. He'd made his decision, he realized, when he'd stopped Max in the first place. Known already that whatever was chasing this man, Hadrian would protect him from it or die trying.

He needed Max. Simple, pure, as that.

"I can look after myself," Hadrian said. Gently, carefully, he put his hand on Max's shoulder, pulled him unresisting till he faced him, and saw the tears that streaked down his face. With his free hand, he reached out and wiped a thumb across Max's cheek, pushing away those tears. "I can look after you too, in a pinch," Hadrian said, half smiling. "I'll remind you of the mugging I've already spared you."

"This is different," Max whispered, his voice raw. "Graywater is a huge security firm. Jean Claude has ties to the police, the FBI…. He could find me here. And he's got a much better arsenal than a crazy mugger."

"If he does, he'll find himself going through your ex-Marine cousin. And if he makes it past John, he'll have me to contend with." Shouts and hoarse voices, screams and the bloody crunch of breaking bones ghosted through Hadrian's memory as he spoke. He felt his face harden. "I'm no stranger to evil, lad. I can dispatch it if I must."

"If anything happened to you, I'd never forgive myself," Max said. "I… feel very strongly for you."

Hadrian had the feeling he'd almost said something else. Felt it himself, but knew it wasn't time, not yet.

"And I you, lad," he said instead. "If you want to go, I'll not stop you. You're your own man. You choose your life as best you can." His voice dropped. He couldn't stop the look of gentleness that softened his face. "But I'd miss you every day of the rest of my life if you did."

Max bit his lip, studying Hadrian's eyes. For his part, Hadrian held still, let Max read the truth in his face, in the way he watched him. Then Max nodded, and Hadrian reached for him and pulled him tight.

"There's one more thing," Hadrian said, leaning back slightly, his eyes fixed on Max.

"What?"

Hadrian smiled. "What's your real name, lad?"

The tension drained from Max. "Will," he said, and the word was like a sigh. "Will Mracek. But… I'm starting to think that I like being Max better."

"Suits you," Hadrian whispered, and found his lips with his own.

Exhausted, words spent, they let their bodies speak where they could not.

CHAPTER 25

JOHN SAT frowning at the kitchen table, his students' practice TOEFL tests spread out in front of him. By his right hand was a cold cup of coffee, untouched since he'd first made it over an hour ago. He ran a hand through his sandy blond hair, tousling it further. Every few minutes he pulled out his phone, checking to see if there were any messages. Nothing.

"We have to stop meeting like this." Karel's voice, soft, came from the kitchen door.

Sighing, John turned to see him leaning against the doorjamb, looking deliciously rumpled in the thread-worn pajama pants he'd had since before they had started dating. He wore no top, letting the light play over his lean torso, highlighting the long chestnut hair that was coming free from its tie.

John took all this in and felt the compact muscles at his stomach jump. But then, thinking of Karel made him remember their first date, which reminded him that Max was on a date right now, which reminded him of just how worried he was. "Dammit," John muttered, slumping forward. "I can't stop running through things in my mind. What if he tells Hadrian?"

"Do you think he will?" Karel asked softly.

John bit his lip. He thought of the look on Max's face in the last few weeks, how he'd brightened when the weekend came up, how some of the independence, the fire he remembered from their childhood had returned to his expression. "I don't know."

Karel pursed his lips and padded into the kitchen. John watched him come as a small, happy voice in his head whispered, *He loves me.* Karel had always moved like a big cat. Now, in the evening light, as he looked at John with that smile and walked so gracefully, John couldn't help but feel his heart swell.

Sighing, he leaned his head back as Karel came to stand behind him, resting one long arm across John's chest as Karel teased his hair back into place.

"I think he should tell him," Karel mused, quietly.

"What!" John's head snapped up.

"Relax."

John let Karel push him back into his chair and bit back a retort as Karel's fingers danced across his scalp. "Why would you say that?" John asked a moment later. "His life depends on his being here being a secret. You and I are the only ones that know, and that's what's kept him safe so far. How can we trust Hadrian? Max barely knows him!"

"I think, perhaps, that Max knows him better than you think. He is in love with him."

"What!" This time John did sit up, turning with incredulity to Karel. "He's known him a month. Dated him for less. What are you talking about?"

"Sometimes it happens quickly," Karel said, with a small smile. "I knew that first night, after I saved your wallet."

"You did?" John asked, surprised. He hadn't told Karel he loved him till they'd been dating a few months, and Karel certainly hadn't said anything about it before that.

Still with that small smile, Karel nodded. "I did not want to frighten you. You were still so hurt. But I knew. When I kissed you, in the snow, I knew."

"Karel," John said, his voice dropping. That swelling in his heart grew. He stood, gathering Karel in his broad arms. "I don't deserve you."

"Yes, you do. You are a good man, my mouse. A brave one. Strong. Protective." He squeezed John's arm, sending shivers through him. "But today you must step back and trust Max."

John frowned. "It's not that I don't trust him."

"Then you do not trust me, who believes in his character?" Karel asked, voice growing sharp. "You do not trust Ivan, who hired Hadrian, to have good judgment?"

John sighed. "It's not that. Not really. When Will—Max—called me, I hadn't heard his voice for so long. He sounded so lost, so scared…. I'd do anything to keep him safe. But what he's running from might be bigger than what I can protect against. And every person who knows—yes, okay, even Hadrian—is another person I might fail to protect."

Unbidden, the memory of a hot wind rolled across his face. He closed his eyes, felt again the straps of his heavy pack digging into his shoulders, the oppressive heat of the sun and sand pushing him. Saw the soldiers he'd led, the dead faces of those he'd failed to bring home, staring at him, holding him accountable.

Lean arms pressed around him, breaking through the sand. He opened his eyes and looked up into Karel's brown gaze.

"You are thinking of the desert."

John nodded. "How can I not?"

Expression gentle, Karel leaned down and kissed him. "I do love you, my mouse."

John's heart jumped. Caught in the echoes of those lost moments, he felt, with a pang, just how lucky he'd been to find someone he could call home. "Let me take you to bed," John said, running his hand over the smooth ridge of Karel's spine. Karel shivered in his arms. "Remind me of what's real."

"I—"

A knock reverberated through the quiet apartment, making John jump. It was a strange knock—a pulse of three short bursts, followed by one hard one.

"Who is that?" John frowned, glancing at the clock above the stove. "It's past ten."

Karel stepped away, annoyance written on his face. "I cannot think of anyone who would knock like that." He moved toward the kitchen door.

John frowned. A feeling of dread came over him.

"Wait," he hissed, reaching out to grab Karel by the elbow. Karel stopped, his brows creased. In response, John met his eyes and shook his head. He held a finger up to his lips, then mimed for Karel to stay there. He didn't move until Karel nodded agreement.

Walking with quiet steps, John moved through the kitchen, not stopping as he reached out and pulled one of Karel's sharp Japanese cooking knives from the block by the sink. He held it by his side, keeping his body loose, ready to react, as he padded to the front hall. He thought of the gun in their bedroom, then dismissed it with an internal curse and a promise to keep it closer to the door.

Despite his stocky frame, he moved as quietly as Karel. Easier, he thought in a flash, to sneak without the weight of body armor. And more dangerous too.

Checking that the chain was in place above their door, he leaned forward, looking out the peephole. His brow crinkled when he took in the small smiling man who stood there. He had a slightly pointed chin, graying black hair, and beady eyes. Quickly John scanned his memory, trying to place the face. It wasn't anyone he knew and not one of the Graywater employees whose photographs he'd memorized when Max first arrived. Still, it could be someone new, or someone entirely unrelated....

That wave of dread returned, heightening his senses. His body buzzed with a battle awareness he'd never needed in the pleasant apartment he shared with Karel. He hoped he was being paranoid. Knew, logically, that in just a few minutes, he'd be back in bed with Karel. But he had to be sure.

As he debated, the man knocked again. More insistently.

"Hullo?" The stranger's voice, muffled, came through the door. He sounded English and spoke with a nervous quiver. "Hullo, I'm sorry, but I'm staying next door and I've forgotten my key. Hullo? Is anyone home?"

John bit his lip, hand moving toward the doorknob as he debated between logic and the gut feeling that had him holding a knife. But logic hadn't kept him alive in Iraq. The credit went to instinct—and discipline.

Letting out a breath, John stepped away from the door, ears straining for any sounds. He didn't relax until he heard feet moving down the hall. A moment later, he heard Karel at the entrance to the kitchen.

"Gone," John said simply.

The worry line between Karel's eyebrows relaxed. "Good. Who was it?"

"Someone staying next door. Locked out of the flat, he said." He took a deep breath and tried to relax the grip he had on the knife in his hand. It was then that he noticed his fingers were trembling, which was unusual. Violence typically served to steady him.

"Maybe we should have helped him," Karel said, then shook his head. "No. You were right. Better to be safe."

John looked at him, adrenaline still pumping through him. His eyes darkened at the flush that rose on Karel's cheeks under his gaze. "Let's go to bed," John said, eyeing Karel up and down. Karel tilted sideways, just a little, and John shook his head. The beginnings of a headache were warring with his other impulses and fogging his mind.

He took a deep breath, or tried to. Instead, he could barely fill his lungs.

Karel smiled. "Mm. Yes. And bring the… the…." He suddenly stumbled into John, who instinctively went to catch him—and found his arms unresponsive. The knife fell from his fingers as they dropped to the ground together, in a tumbled heap that John felt only from a distance. Like moving in syrup, he struggled to lift his head, to see Karel passing out across his chest.

He sniffed and caught the faint whiff of felt-tipped markers. Turning his head with painful slowness, he saw a haze of smoke emerging from beneath the front door.

He tried to grasp the kitchen knife, but his fingers wouldn't move. Numb, fading, he watched as the world twisted down into a black tunnel—and then everything went blank.

CHAPTER 26

MAX WOKE in Hadrian's arms, a beam of sunlight shining in his eyes. He froze for a moment, taking in the unfamiliar surroundings, the white sheets beneath him. There was something warm and long pressed up against his naked back, a heavy weight around his waist.

It took him a second to identify the weight as Hadrian's arm. Hadrian was spooning him from behind, his head pressed into the nape of Max's neck. As Max breathed deep, Hadrian murmured something in his sleep and pulled him closer. Slowly, Max relaxed back into him, letting his weight soothe him.

It was a nice feeling. A safe, warm feeling.

I could get used to this, Max thought. He laid a hand over Hadrian's where it pressed against his belly, lacing their fingers. In response Hadrian made a contented noise and nuzzled his neck.

Closing his eyes, Max tried to impress the moment on his memory, to savor it as much as possible. He'd never woken up like this before. Sure, he'd had his share of lovers, but none of them had been the cuddling type. Jean Claude especially had seemed to demand space even in his sleep, leaving Max at the far edge of the bed. But this…. Max decided he liked it very much. He smiled. He wouldn't have pegged the tough bartending Hadrian to be a snuggler. Just went to show how surprising life was.

Unfortunately that warm floating feeling didn't last long. As Max's mind cleared, the events of the previous night began to break through the sleepy fog that had protected him as he woke. He stiffened as his mind started racing.

He couldn't believe he'd told Hadrian all that. His shame, his danger—he'd revealed it all. What had he been thinking?

Foolish, that's what he was. And stupid. It wasn't that he didn't trust Hadrian—Max was finding that he did, unshakably. That was part of what scared him.

The last man he'd trusted had so viciously abused that trust. So what was Max doing now, handing it out like candy to the next man he'd slept with? When it came down to it, he'd really only known Hadrian for a little over a month. Barely that. And despite his preexisting friendship with Karel and John, there was really no proof that Hadrian was worthy of his trust.

Except that he'd made him stay when he wanted to run. He'd listened. And when it was done, and he knew fully the danger, he'd pulled Max into his arms and kissed him until Max forgot his fears.

Max bit his lip. He could trust Hadrian, he decided. But that didn't change the fact that he had a price on his head, and that by telling Hadrian, he'd brought him into danger as well.

He would have to stop seeing Hadrian. It was bad enough with John, but he had the feeling his cousin simply wouldn't let him disappear. Nor could he do it without John's help. But Hadrian, at least, could be protected.

The thought made him sick to his stomach. A wail rose, from somewhere deep inside him—a howl, like a wounded animal. He wanted to turn, to press his face to Hadrian's chest, wrap his arms around him, and never leave the bed.

But that was the dream of a child, and he was a man. No. Resolve hardened him, and he blinked away the tears that threatened to fall, choked back the lump in his throat. He'd made a mistake last night, and he'd have to own up to it.

Frowning, he reached over to the small bedside table and pulled on his glasses. The room snapped into sharp focus, chasing the last vestiges of sleep away.

"It's too... 'rly" came a grumbling, muffled voice from behind Max's head.

"What?" Max asked, as the arm tightened around his waist. He felt Hadrian's head lift and turned slightly to see him glaring blearily at him through half-closed eyes.

"Said, it's too early for whatever's got you worried. Go sleep." He fell back onto the pillow, pulling Max tighter with him, cuddling him with such grumpy affection that Max couldn't help but smile.

Glancing at the clock, Max saw it was eight. A perfectly respectable hour.

"Some people like to get up in the mornings." He turned around, watching Hadrian's face. It was creased on one side, where the pillows had left lines across his cheek. A faint shadow of morning stubble crossed his chin. Pain—a deep, throbbing ache—hit him in the chest. "You know. See the sun, seize the day, all that good stuff."

"Don' care," Hadrian growled. "Sun's overrated."

Max rolled his eyes. Impulsively, he leaned forward and pressed a kiss to that stubbled chin.

In response, Hadrian opened one eye. "Ah, well," he said, and sighed dramatically. "S'pose that's not the worst thing to wake up to."

Max smiled wider, then sobered. "Listen," he said, and pulled back slightly. "About last night. I—"

"If you're about to tell me that you're leaving and never coming back, for my own safety, or some such bollocks," Hadrian said, opening his eyes to glare at Max, "then you'd best rethink."

"Your life is in danger," Max protested. His heart thudded in his chest. He'd forgotten how perceptive Hadrian was.

"Less so than yours," Hadrian shot back. His eyes were wide open now, brow furrowed in annoyance. "Never pegged you as the selfish type."

Anger flared through Max. He shifted, propping himself up on his elbow. "Selfish? For wanting to keep you safe?"

"For disrespecting my feelings," Hadrian growled. "And disrespecting me. I make my own damned choices, and now you've warned me of any danger. I choose to stay with you. It's on my own head what happens. So get that through your thick skull. You ain't leaving a safe place for the sake of protecting me."

Max was silent. He met Hadrian's gaze stare for stare, felt Hadrian's will press against his, and knew, in his heart, that it wouldn't change his mind. For a brief moment, as Hadrian spoke, he'd let himself think, *What if?* But the road that led down had too many branches that ended in death—Hadrian's death.

"Can we stop fighting now?" Max asked, face softening. They could have this morning, at least. Some more time to live in this bubble of kindness.

Hadrian frowned, then nodded. "I just… I feel strongly for you, lad. More than I expected."

Max swallowed hard, past the lump that had returned to his throat. He felt the same—a sudden burst of need, mixed with something warmer, something deeper, that he'd never anticipated. He leaned forward and laid a gentle kiss on Hadrian's mouth. He hummed in satisfaction as Hadrian responded and reached to cradle his head. After a few long minutes, Max pulled back to meet those crystalline blue eyes with a soft smile. "I do too," he said gently. "Got any coffee?"

Hadrian blinked, then laughed. "Aye, lad. Let me up and I'll make you some. And none of that instant bollocks either."

He kept his promise, and a few minutes later, Max was sipping a mug of hot black coffee. Hadrian busied himself cutting up the leftover focaccia for a simple breakfast. When he was finished, Max nibbled at a slice, not really hungry, too heartsick to eat anything.

"You going to tell your cousin?" Hadrian said as he finished his coffee. "About…."

"He knows we've been seeing each other," Max said. "Oh. You mean, that I told you? Yeah, I guess so." He frowned, nerves running across his stomach. "I'm not looking forward to that conversation."

Hadrian nodded. "Need some backup?"

Max thought about it. He wanted to say yes, but remembered the promise he'd made to himself. "No," he said, after a moment. "I think this is something I need to do on my own. But—thank you."

"Thank me nothing," Hadrian said, rolling his eyes. "I'll be hearing about this, you watch. Give it a day or two before he's storming the pub, interrogating me like an overprotective father."

Max blushed. "Yeah, yeah."

"At least let me walk you to the tram," Hadrian said.

Max half smiled. "All right. But first…." He put down his coffee and walked over to straddle Hadrian's lap.

"If you insist," Hadrian murmured, as Max bent to press their lips together.

Later, Max dressed while Hadrian puttered around the kitchen, cleaning up after the night before and steadfastly refusing any help. "I'm a right bear about the kitchen. No one's to touch it but me." There was a simple pleasure in taking part in this small ritual, of being with him in even the most basic of elements, of dressing together, stealing a last sip of coffee, checking the weather. A normalness shared; mundane elevated. Later, he thought he'd look back at this moment as one of his favorites of their date. Maybe one of his favorite moments ever.

When they got outside, they found the day well started, the bright sun shining out of a blue sky, the wind tinged with the warm breath of coming spring. Around them, the air filled with a steady dripping sound as the long icicles dangling from the edges of Prague's old lovely buildings finally melted.

Soon they were crossing to the center of the street, to the little elevated platform that waited along the tram track. It was almost empty, giving them a small piece of privacy despite the open air. Max, spying his tram coming in the distance, turned to Hadrian. He had to swallow hard as the pain seared through his chest again. After this….

He'd have to be strong. Remember his resolve.

"Thank you for… well, everything," Max said, meeting Hadrian's eyes. He bit the inside of his lip to keep from crying out.

Hadrian furrowed his brow, watching him closely. "Don't do anything foolish, lad," he said, those blue eyes racing over Max's face. "Please."

Max took a deep breath, withstanding the scrutiny as best he could, trying to ignore the ache in his heart. He sighed as Hadrian pulled him close and kissed him hard, his hands running over his back, his hair. For his part Max melted into the kiss, trying to press it into his memory, knowing it was the only good-bye he'd ever get.

"Come see me tonight," Hadrian insisted as he pulled away. "We've got a party in the afternoon, but the bar will be open again at seven. You can keep me company, tell me how it goes with John."

"Sounds good," Max said, knowing it was a lie. He stepped away just as the tram pulled up in a spray of scattered slush, a great metal giant that hissed as its doors slid open. "Good-bye," Max called and gave Hadrian a small smile.

Hadrian just watched him, those blue eyes inscrutable.

Max stepped onto the mostly empty tram, grabbed a window seat, and watched Hadrian watch him as the tram pulled away.

The streets were busy today, as they usually were on a Saturday. People, loaded with packages or children, bustled around, weaving in and out of *potraviny* and restaurants. At each tram stop, more people flooded into the car, until Max was more than ready to get off. It was too crowded for him to be comfortable. He couldn't watch so many people at once.

His mind strayed, despite his anxiety, to the night before, to Hadrian… and there was the pain. Sitting there, he had to widen his eyes, to breathe deep to keep tears from escaping. He'd known Hadrian for such a short time. Why did it hurt so much to know this had been good-bye?

Because it had been the best night of his life, dramatic revelations aside. Because Hadrian was kind and good beneath his gruffness, and he cared for Max. Max felt like his heart was being ripped from his chest, slowly, one strand of muscle, one artery at a time.

The tram slowed and came to a stop a block away from his flat. Max hurried out the door, wiping angrily at his eyes. As he walked home, he thought about what to tell John. His cousin's opinion had come to mean a great deal to Max. He didn't want to lose the bond they'd slowly been forging since he'd first reached out.

Bracing himself for what was sure to be an uncomfortable conversation he was not in the mood for, he fit his key into the door of their building and stepped inside the dark, plastered foyer. He climbed the stairs that wound through the center of the building, and with each step, his heart felt a little heavier. At least John would have the satisfaction of knowing it was over—Max would never see Hadrian again.

To keep him safe, Max reminded himself, as he trudged up the stairs. He wiped his eyes, the movements fast, angry. Finally he reached the third floor and their apartment at the end of the hall. At first, struggling with his keys, with the tears in his eyes, he didn't look at the door. Then his heart froze.

It was standing open.

Just a crack, but enough to fill him with fear. John would never leave the door unlocked, let alone open. Karel, maybe, if he were feeling absentminded enough…. Max prayed that was the answer.

"Hello?" Max called as he stepped inside. The door creaked shut behind him. The apartment was unnaturally silent—a heavy, oppressive quiet that pushed down on Max like a living thing. There was a strange smell on the air, something artificial, like the acrid scent of permanent markers. Max wrinkled his nose, trying to fight his mounting anxiety as he stepped from the hall into the kitchen and didn't find anyone.

They must have gone out, he thought. Or maybe they were still sleeping—it was barely eleven.

His foot nudged something heavy. He looked down to see one of Karel's zombie mugs rolling in a puddle of cold coffee on the floor. His stomach turned over with a heavy lurch. Karel would never be so messy. Max bent to pick it up and placed it on the counter while his pulse pounded in his neck.

There was a quiet creak in the living room, the sound one made by shifted weight on the old floorboards in just the right spot. The pounding in Max's neck grew louder. He walked forward, toward the living room, dreading what he would find.

"Hello, Will."

Max froze in the doorway as that voice cut through the silence. His heart stopped as he recognized it. "Adelaide," he whispered, eyes closing instinctively, as if that would make her disappear. Hands shaking, he forced himself to look, to step into the living room, and felt his heart cry out as he saw Jean Claude's statuesque assistant sitting comfortably in his cousin's favorite chair. She was dressed almost as he'd last seen her—charcoal-gray pencil skirt, silk cream blouse, her suit jacket thrown over the arm of the chair. She was gazing at him with cool dark eyes that betrayed no emotion.

"You look surprised," she said, crossing her legs. "I wonder why."

"How did you find me?" Max asked. His legs shook. He felt like vomiting, like sobbing. It wasn't fair. Though he couldn't see it, he was sure she had a gun on her.

"Easy," she said, shrugging. "Did you think you could hide from us? Really, I thought you were smarter than that. I'm surprised you managed this long."

She shifted, and Max's stomach clenched. He tried to hold Hadrian in his mind, the way he'd felt pressed against Max's back, his arm around Max's waist, that safety, that… love.

"Please," Max said, hating the shaking in his voice but unable to stop it. He closed his eyes and thought of Hadrian. "Just… make it quick."

Adelaide tsked in annoyance.

The sound was so unexpected that Max's eyes flew open. He saw her lips twist in distaste as she adjusted the hem of her skirt.

"You misunderstand," she said, smoothing the fabric over her knee. "I'm not going to hurt you. Why would I? Jean Claude was quite clear about that."

Max took a step back. "Then why are you here?"

"Jean Claude merely wanted to know that you were safe, and that you hadn't misunderstood what happened before you left. You see, he loves you very much. You can't be surprised that he would worry about you."

A sudden rage burst through Max, burning away some of the fear. He straightened, felt his eyebrows snap down as his lips thinned. "Love me? He doesn't know the first thing about love."

Adelaide just watched him with those cool eyes. "Oh?"

"I want you to leave," Max said, riding that fury, letting it strengthen him. He nodded at the door, fists clenched. "You say you're just checking up on me? Fine. Go tell Jean Claude I'm fine, and he can fuck off my life."

"As you say." With a small sigh, she stood and walked over to the door of John's bedroom, her heels clicking on the hardwood. "But before I go, there is one thing."

Max felt his heart jump, the fury blanched in sudden, cold fear as Adelaide raised her hand and knocked. A moment later the door swung open to reveal John and Karel collapsed on their bed, hands tied, faces slack. Max stumbled forward, almost falling, as a terrible thought ran through him.

"Not dead," Adelaide said. "But sleeping. Certainly unable to move. My associate is quite deft with ties."

There was a small cough, and the little rat-faced man who'd asked him for directions to Foxrod stepped out from behind the door.

"You're not a student," Max said, too overwhelmed to be shocked any further.

The little man smiled. "No, afraid not," he said, in the blandest accent Max had ever heard, then shrugged. "You'll have to forgive my little deception. It was necessary. Now, we have a proposal to make." He nodded at Adelaide.

"You'll come with us," she said, sounding bored. "No fuss. No pain—your own free will, as Jean Claude would prefer. In return, we'll free your cousin and his lover. They won't have any lasting effects from our sleeping gas, and they can return to their lives just as they were."

Bitterness flooded Max's mouth. "My own free will, you say."

"Of course. Why would Jean Claude want anything else?" Adelaide stared him down. "He loves you. He only wishes that you love him in return."

"I assume, were my answer to be 'no,' that John and Karel would not do so well," Max said between clenched teeth.

In response, the little man shrugged. "Perhaps we'd have to pay another visit, later, when they weren't expecting company. Perhaps that visit would be more… damaging than this. I can't say."

With a feeling like he was drowning, Max thought it over, straining for loopholes, any way out of this. He found none. Gathering his courage, he straightened and took a deep breath. *At least they'd be safe.* Unbidden, Hadrian's blue eyes flashed through his memory. *And you,* he thought. *Hadrian, you'll be safe from me.*

"I'll go with you," Max said, with a voice like a dying man. "I'll go to Jean Claude. Just leave them alone."

The little rat-faced man beamed. Adelaide just nodded.

"Quickly, then," she said and strode toward the door as, behind her, the rat-faced man pulled out a knife and sliced off Karel and John's bonds.

Max watched, heart heavy, knowing he'd never see them again. "Good-bye," he whispered.

"Now" came Adelaide's imperious tone.

With a heart like lead, he turned and followed her out of the building. Outside, the air was cold. Max lifted his face to it and breathed deep, trying to remember the smells of Prague, a city he'd come to love.

"Our ride," Adelaide said, breaking his concentration. He turned and saw her holding open the door of a perfectly ordinary black car. Max slid inside as Adelaide closed the door behind him with a terribly final *thump*. Adelaide climbed into the driver's seat, the locks clicking into place as she pulled her own door shut.

"Where's the other guy?" Max said, fingers digging into the vinyl seat beneath him. "From the apartment. Is he following us?"

"Don't worry about him." There was a finality in her voice that sent ice ranging up Max's spine. She turned the car on and pulled away from the curb. "He has another chore to take care of. Speaking of, did you have a nice night?"

Fear cut Max's breathing short. "What? What do you…?"

"I wonder, was it worth his life? This lover of yours."

"No," Max whispered, his brain racing, putting together the pieces. Hadrian—they knew about Hadrian. And the rat-faced man was missing…. "No, he can't—"

"Did you really think Jean Claude would let you take another lover? Admittedly the first one—Christopher was his name, correct?— was more of a failed suitor, but that was enough for us."

Max's heart stopped in his throat. "You killed him." It wasn't a question.

"He was easy enough to take care of," Adelaide confirmed, sending ice stabbing through Max's chest. "An alley. Very neat but boring. Jean Claude has asked that this one receive more care. And you'll remember how fond he is of fire."

"You bastards," Max sobbed, darkness dropping down on him. "You said no one would be hurt if I came with you. You promised…!"

"John and Karel, yes. The others weren't mentioned. You should be more careful when making bargains."

Max, blind with fury, with terror, turned to the door and yanked at the handle, forgetting the locks had been engaged. When this failed, he threw himself at it, pummeling the hard metal. It didn't budge. Tears burned his cheeks as Hadrian's name thundered in his mind, filled his every sense. What had he done—God, what had he *done*—

"Don't hurt him. I'll do anything Jean Claude wants, anything—"

"Too late," Adelaide said. The car purred as she accelerated onto the highway. "Now get comfortable. We have a long drive before we get where we're going."

CHAPTER 27

"LATE!" IVAN bellowed as Hadrian hurried down the stairs, dodging a man carrying a case of wine and another lugging a heavy metal keg.

"I know, I know. I'm sorry, it won't happen again," he said, quickly unzipping his jacket and hurrying behind the bar, where Ivan stood with his inventory clipboard, carefully checking items off as they were delivered through to the storage room at the back of the kitchen. On the floor, Jitka was running from table to table, laying out purple tablecloths that she lined with soft tealights in charmingly rustic mason jars. Twinkling fairy lights had been strung along the ceiling and the usual lamps were dimmed to create a soft, candlelit atmosphere. The hearth fire was stacked with thick logs, waiting for a match to complete the picture.

"Humph," Ivan grunted, making a note as a small man with a pointed chin hoisted a keg of Staropramen over his shoulder and carried it into the kitchen. "You have not been late in four years, Hadrian. You pick today, when we have such a party to arrange?" He eyed Hadrian up and down. A small smile broke out on his face.

"What?" Hadrian asked. Vaclav wandered over and leaned against his legs. Absentminded, Hadrian reached out and rubbed the giant dog between his velvety ears.

"You had a date. A good date," Ivan said, poking him in the chest with the end of his pen.

"You're an old woman." Hadrian rolled his eyes, evading the question. A good date—had it been? Max's face, smiling in the morning sun, flashed through his mind, followed by the argument they'd not concluded to Hadrian's satisfaction. He knew now what Max's secrets were, was still processing everything Max had told him, including the fact that Max was not his real name. But what weighed on him most was the fear that Max would stay away, would decide it was, indeed, too dangerous to keep seeing Hadrian. The thought set acid churning in Hadrian's stomach.

He'd wait and see if Max showed up later. And if not, well, he knew where John lived. He wasn't letting Max go, not without a fight.

"You will tell me everything," Ivan said, then bellowed in Czech at a man carrying a box of imported beer with less care than he should have. Turning back, he finished, "But later. We have the lunch party, you remember? Mr. Matusek and his daughter's engagement?"

Hadrian nodded, rolling up his shirtsleeves. He had to banish Max from his mind, if only for a little while. "Okay. Where do you want me?"

Ivan nodded at a man lugging a box of beer bottles. "I have to go outside and check their truck. Last time they forgot to deliver three kegs. You go to the kitchen, organize the bottles, *ne*? And take Vaclav with you. He is getting beneath our legs, and I do not want anyone stepping on him."

"C'mere, boy." Hadrian patted his thigh, but Vaclav barely wagged his tail. Looking now, Hadrian could see some signs of stress in him—his ears drooped a bit and his posture was stiff. Maybe it would be best to get him away from all the hustle and bustle. "Let's go see what they've brought us, shall we?"

He went to step through the open kitchen door and found himself face to face with one of the deliverymen. "*Omlouvám se*," he said, stepping back.

The man shook his head and smiled. He was an ugly little man with an odd face—it was too pointed, the teeth just a little too large.

Hadrian didn't like the way the man looked at him as he stepped past, Vaclav padding at his side. But the kitchen was busy enough to make him forget the little man, what with the extra cooks and waiters Ivan had hired running about, filling the air with clattering pots and the savory smells of Ivan's comforting Czech recipes.

Behind the kitchen proper were brick walls that had been set into the earth. They sloped down, creating a long tunnel of a room brightly lit by high fluorescent lights along the curved ceiling. The appliances were a clash of modernity against the rough backdrop, all gleaming chrome and high-quality gas burners that could handle anything Ivan cared to cook. In the very back was a storage space with a rough dirt floor and shelves built into the brick walls. There, boxes of bottles were stacked between heavy metal kegs, filling the air with a cool mix of hops and damp earth.

"'Scuse us," Hadrian called, as he and Vaclav wound between men and women in white jackets. The cooks, all new to the restaurant, eyed Vaclav warily as he passed around them. Hadrian ignored them, waiting until they reached the comparatively quiet space at the back before kneeling and giving Vaclav a sympathetic wince. Both of them looked to the right, where a short leash had been hammered into the floor alongside Vaclav's food and water bowls.

Vaclav whined, a truly pitiful sound that made Hadrian feel like the world's biggest prat.

"Now, don't be mad at me, eh?" he said, reaching out to rub Vaclav's ear. Behind them, there was a heavy clang, and one of the chefs shouted something in Czech. "Boss's orders, and you'll be out and roaming again soon as the party's done."

Another whine, this time somehow sadder.

"C'mon, you big baby," Hadrian said, trying not to fall into the trap of those big doe eyes. He clicked the leash into place on Vaclav's collar. "I'll come by and pet you. And you'll have lots of company in the kitchen, all right?"

Vaclav gave him a look that said it was distinctly *not* all right. Feeling guilty, Hadrian turned away, setting to the work of sifting through the liquor deliveries. The noise and chaos of the kitchen increased around him as he organized the deliveries into pre- and postdinner drinks. The waiters would deal with serving the beer to the tables during the party. He would be strictly on bar duty, ready to serve any special drink orders.

Grunting, Hadrian hefted a box of specialty imports into his arms and stood. Vaclav whined at him again, then let out a little yip.

"Hush," Hadrian said, frowning. He saw Vaclav, contrary to calming down, had grown even tenser. He was shaking, his tail tucked low between his legs. He barked again, louder this time. Hadrian tried not to think about how it would disrupt things to have a barking dog in the kitchen. "What is the matter with you?" he asked, as Vaclav began to growl. They were starting to get odd looks from the kitchen staff now. "Calm yourself, eh?"

In response, Vaclav barked again. Louder. He pulled at his leash, leaning against it until the leather began to strain against the spike that tethered him to the ground.

Puzzled, Hadrian thought quickly. He had some dog biscuits stashed beneath the bar. Maybe they'd soothe him. It had to be the unusual activity in the kitchen that was winding him up. It must have been strange for a dog used to having the entire pub to roam in to be tied up.

Decision made, Hadrian hurried back through the kitchen, the box heavy in his arms. Vaclav's snarls followed in his wake. Outside, the pub had been utterly transformed. Everything glowed in the candlelight, giving a romantic air to the usually plain tables. Soft floral smells wafted from vases of roses placed at the center of the tables. In the background, orchestral music fell gently from speakers hidden in the four corners of the room.

It would have been perfect, if not for the loud bark that came from the open doors to his back.

Hadrian winced. Plopping the beer on the counter, he ducked underneath and nudged aside boxes of toothpicks and jars of olives, looking for the big red box of treats. "There you are," he said, finding it stuck behind some dust-covered tumblers. He was just standing when he heard Jitka calling to him. He looked over to see her standing by the stairs, looking harried with a broom in hand.

"Hadrian," she said. "Can you make fire?" She pointed over to the fireplace, where the logs had yet to be lit.

"Ah," Hadrian said, looking at the dog treats in his hand. "In a moment, Jitka."

"Please, they come soon and I must sweep stairs," she said, with a pleading frown.

Hadrian sighed and set the box on the counter. Vaclav would have to wait a few seconds.

Hurrying, he pulled a matchbook from his pocket—a leftover habit from his smoking days—and ran around the bar to the fireplace.

Vaclav's barking grew louder, more frantic, behind him.

As he pulled out a match, some part of his brain noted that the roses smelled strange here. A little too sweet, with a hint of something metallic. He made a note to check the vases after feeding Vaclav. Lighting the match was a practiced movement: close it between the packet, the starter strip, pull it away with a flick of the wrist.

The barking behind him reached a frenzied pitch as the little match sputtered into life.

"I'm coming Vaclav, Jesus," Hadrian muttered, before tossing the match onto the wood.

There was a silent rush, like all the wind being let out of a balloon. He heard someone scream behind him, but distant, like hearing through a tunnel. And then an invisible hand reached out like a freight train and thrust Hadrian into the air.

The world blurred. There was orange, and a blast of heat, but everything fell strangely silent.

He floated for a minute—longer—seconds, milliseconds—

Pain. He crashed into something hard, knocking the air from his lungs. He crumpled forward, the numbness lasting only a heartbeat before throbbing pain replaced it in every inch of his body.

His mind recovered before his body. *An explosion*, a voice was saying calmly in his head. *There was an explosion. Get up.*

Military training kicked in. Eyes still closed, his consciousness detached, he forced himself to step back from the pain, to catalogue it, mind racing along his legs, stomach, ribs. He took an experimental breath and choked on the inhale, his chest aching. But it was a dull pain, not the sharp jab he'd feared. His ribs might be bruised, but they weren't broken. The rest of him was a similarly dull ache. And there was something else. A smell that meant danger.

Get up, the voice said, as that smell grew stronger. *Get the hell up.*

Hadrian snapped his eyes open to see a wall of flame engulfing the room.

Black smoke billowed from the wreckage of the tables, their tangled purple tablecloths ablaze with flames that raced toward Hadrian and the bar. Workers were streaming up the stairs, panic on their faces as they covered their mouths from the smoke that floated above them. Hadrian saw Jitka among them, saw her mouth his name as she pushed uselessly against the tide. Then she was swept up the stairs with them.

He struggled to his feet. A ringing sound replaced the silence, soft but getting steadily louder. He wheezed, fighting to breathe through the smoke, and stumbled his way toward the stairs, where the last of the waitstaff had just disappeared. He was at the bottom, clutching the railing, when a new sound broke through the ringing in his ears.

A loud, panicked bark.

Cursing, Hadrian turned. The smoke was getting thicker by the minute, making a dense black layer in the air above him. Hadrian pulled his shirt over his mouth and ducked low, glancing at the fire as he ran to the kitchen. It was advancing quickly, the tongues almost within licking distance of his bar. He had seconds, barely.

Bursting through the open door, he found the emergency hoods Ivan had installed above the stoves working overtime. The air was a little clearer here. Vaclav, straining at his leash, gave a happy yip as Hadrian, coughing, stumbled over to him. With aching fingers Hadrian fumbled with his leash and pulled the great dog free. Instantly Vaclav was jumping on him, licking his face frantically.

"C'mon," Hadrian said, grabbing him by the collar.

Together they ran for the kitchen door. It had closed behind him, caught perhaps in a draft from the flames. Hadrian shoved it—and jammed his fingers against unyielding metal.

"The hell?" he growled, as Vaclav barked beside him.

He tried it again, first pushing with his hand, then his shoulder, then kicking the damn thing. Smoke was leaking beneath it, billowing up around him and Vaclav as the metal itself grew warm. Panic set in as he realized the horrible truth.

Someone had closed it and then wedged something against the door. It was a trap.

"I'm dangerous," Max had said the night before. *"He'll come after me, and you might get hurt...."*

Terror seized Hadrian as Vaclav danced around his feet. If Max's enemies had come for him—if they'd set this trap, and who else would?—then that meant they'd found Max.

He saw Max then, curled into himself in Hadrian's reading chair, despair written across his face.

"No, no, no!" he cursed. Frustrated and more frightened than he cared to admit, he turned sideways, again ramming his already battered shoulder into the metal. He bounced back, howling in pain, as Vaclav whined piteously.

Casting about, Hadrian grabbed a few discarded dishtowels and ran them under the tap, thankful the water was still working. He stuffed the damp rags into every crack and crevice in the door. It slowed the smoke but wouldn't keep it out for long. He pushed at the door again, more out of desperation than any hope it would work, and snatched his hand back with a yelp of pain. It was burning hot.

There was nothing left to do. They were well and truly trapped.

"Christ, Mary, and Joseph," he whispered, stepping away from the door. This wasn't how he wanted to die, not burned up in a coffin like this. There was too much left for him to do. And Max needed him. "Max... I...."

Furious barking broke through Hadrian's despair. Turning, he saw Vaclav scrambling up the boxes of alcohol at the back of the kitchen, his great white ears—now gray from the soot—pointed like a setter's. Frowning, Hadrian stared at him a long moment before breaking into a giant grin.

Vaclav's nose was pointing up, at a small depression in the ceiling, a hole that disappeared without any sight of its ending. A hole that led to a forgotten window, used in the past to deliver goods directly down to the kitchen.

"You fucking genius dog, you!" Hadrian shouted.

He reached Vaclav and began shoving boxes up against the wall, creating a kind of staircase. Scrambling up it, he stuck his head inside the hole, breath held lest he remembered wrong—but no. There, at the top and just big enough to fit a slim man, was the old glass window.

Standing on the boxes, Hadrian could just reach it if he stretched his arms out. He did so and felt his arm screaming in protest. "Yes!" he cried as his fingers brushed the glass. He stretched farther, jumping a little to push against it. It opened to the right with a squeal of rusty hinges, and—Hadrian crossed his fingers—stayed open. Hadrian gulped the fresh air gratefully that flowed down into the room, then climbed back to the ground.

"Hold still, you big mutt," he said, moving to the waiting dog. The smoke, drawn to the new exit, was getting thicker and making it hard to see. But Vaclav—clever, clever dog—barely moved as Hadrian wrapped his arms around his big barrel chest. Whining, the dog used his paws to scramble up the wall as Hadrian hoisted him higher, through the thickening smoke to the window outside.

"C'mon, mate—c'mon!" he gasped. He got Vaclav's head to the window. Then those strong paws found a purchase and, with a last grunt of effort from Hadrian, he popped free.

Hadrian fell back, coughing, his arms aching worse than he'd ever felt. He could no longer see the window above him, and even if he could, he doubted he had the strength to pull himself up. He wheezed, the world spinning as the smoke gathered around him. He bent over, hacking and coughing. Maybe it would be better if he just sat down, took a rest…. He was so tired….

He heard the voice again and realized it was Max's. *Get up, Hadrian. Get. Up.*

"I'm not dying," Hadrian growled. "Not… bloody… today!"

Adrenaline surged through him, banishing the haze in a wash of clarity he knew wouldn't last forever. Picking up a wooden crate, he added it to his pile and climbed up into the smoky darkness, pulling his shirt over his nose and trying to breathe as shallowly as possible. Unable to see, he reached, feeling until he found the edge of the window. He managed to get his arm out to the elbow, tried to find a purchase. His muscles quivered—it wasn't going to work. He was spent.

"Help! *Oy!* Help, someone, help!" he tried to shout, waving his arm around as fast as he could. The smoke grew thicker as it streamed past him into the outside air. Each breath was a struggle, and the world faded as the urge to fall backward into nothingness grew stronger.

Then a hand grabbed his forearm, pulling. Voices yelled his name as Vaclav barked in the distance. Hadrian gathered enough strength to kick at the walls as someone pulled, and then another pair of hands grabbed his free arm, pulling him up and through. He landed on the floor of the alleyway behind U Medvídků, the asphalt digging holes into his bruised skin as he gasped in the fresh, clean air. He didn't protest as he was dragged away from the smoke, out of the alley, and into the street beyond. There his rescuers let him crawl onto his knees, banging his back as he leaned forward and hacked black phlegm onto the street. The fresh air was almost too much, and his lungs ached as the coughs wracked his body. But it was a good pain. It meant he was alive.

"Hold on, Hadrian. You're okay," said a hoarse American accent beside his head.

Hadrian turned his head to see John kneeling beside him, Ivan standing just behind. Their faces were filthy with smoke. And then a very excited Vaclav was shoving forward and licking enthusiastically at Hadrian's face. Ivan pulled the dog gently away as Hadrian tried to get his breathing under control. "Jitka?" Hadrian gasped.

John reached out and helped steady him as he wobbled, dizzy from the smoke, the coughing. Now that he could breathe a little better, he realized his throat was on fire.

"We are all fine," Ivan said, voice hoarse. "I was outside when the bomb exploded. And Jitka is by the ambulances. You are lucky—Vaclav led us to you." He handed Hadrian an open water bottle, and Hadrian chugged half of it. It eased the pain in his throat, let him breathe without coughing.

"U Medvídků—it's ruined," Hadrian rasped, sitting a little taller. "I'm so sorry, Ivan."

Ivan shook his head. "It was just a building. It can be fixed. Not like my Vaclav," he said, patting the dog on the back. Vaclav whined and darted out of Ivan's grasp to lick at Hadrian's cheek. "You are hero. Thank you."

"Don't thank me," Hadrian said, his arm around the once-white dog. "It was a trap. Someone did this to kill me." He told them quickly about the door and how it had only been blocked once he'd gotten inside the kitchen.

Ivan stared at him from eyes like steel. "Why would someone do that?"

"Max," Hadrian whispered, meeting Ivan's gaze. "His ex-boyfriend is some kind of maniac."

"But to try to kill you…."

"Max warned me this might happen," Hadrian said. "Last night. He wanted to stop seeing me, said it was too dangerous. And now…. Jean Claude must be here. We've got to get Max someplace safe before—"

John stopped him with a hand on his arm.

Hadrian turned, saw the haunted look on John's face, and felt his heart constrict.

"He's gone," John said, grim. "Someone drugged us last night. Dropped a fucking canister of sleeping gas right outside our door. We woke up to find our flat empty. They took him."

Hadrian took a ragged breath and reached out to grip Vaclav's fur, taking what comfort he could from his steady warmth. This was Hadrian's worst fear realized. No—not the worst. There was still the chance that Max was alive. "Screw this. I don't like these games," Hadrian said, and spat a wad of something black from his throat. "We're going to get him back."

John met his eyes and nodded with a face like steel.

"Then you will all come stay with me," Ivan broke in, then held up a hand when Hadrian started to protest. "No—I do not understand everything, but it is clear that someone very powerful is after you. He will know where you live, and I want you safe." He clasped a hand on Hadrian's shoulder, making him wince. "You will go to the ambulance, yes? And then we will see to getting back the young man."

Hadrian nodded, resolve and rage whirling through him, giving him strength. He clenched his fist, gritting his teeth through the aching pain that was only just starting to hit him.

He would find Max or die trying.

CHAPTER 28

MAX PERCHED at the end of a plush king-sized bed, gazing through open balcony doors with disinterested eyes. Jean Claude had spared no expense in his kidnapping. Outside, Paris glittered in the dusk, her lights like warm stars beneath the fading periwinkle sky. Grand gardens mingled with the oldest buildings in the city before ending at the Eiffel Tower itself. Even as he watched, it blinked to life, a gentle explosion of gold sent to pierce the darkening night.

He'd always wanted to visit Paris. Now he might die with the best view in the city.

He and Adelaide had arrived at the elegant Le Royal Hôtel early that morning. Mute with grief and guilt, knowing John and Karel's lives depended on his obedience, he'd followed Adelaide carefully through the doors held open by a man in red velvet livery. He had a vague impression of marble, velvet, and gold as they walked through the lobby. Adelaide went on about the hotel's royal history and connections to Napoleon Bonaparte. As if it would impress him. As if he was supposed to care.

"And, of course, it is secured by Graywater," she added, nodding at a discreetly placed guard as they walked a red velvet carpet to the marble-ensconced elevators beyond the lobby.

He knew what she was really saying. This was a prison, more so than any real prison would have been. He was trapped.

She murmured something to the bellboy as they stepped into the mirrored elevator. Dozens of Max's reflections stared at him with hollow eyes as they began to rise. The journey upward carried them to the very top floor, where the doors opened silently onto a short white hallway with pale blue carpeting.

Adelaide led him to a carved walnut door at the other end of the hall. "Here you are," she said, fitting a gold key to the lock and opening the door for him. He stepped past her, shivering at the feel of her eyes on his back. It was like walking past a python at the zoo, but without the glass.

Inside, he had an impression of splendor. The first room was a sitting room, with walls papered in a powder-blue linen that must have been expensive. White plaster scrollwork separated them from the ceiling with delicate flowers, twisting vines, and other intricacies. The furniture was as impressive. He saw dark walnut wood, saffron-yellow cushions of crushed velvet, a marble-topped secretary in the corner, and a low glass table before an empty fireplace. To the left was a glass door that led to a wide balcony almost as large as the living room itself. On his right, an open door led to an equally grand and overwhelming bedroom. He could see another balcony entrance in there, this one with a view of the Eiffel Tower in the distance.

Max took it in, tasted money in the air, and knew he'd take Hadrian's attic apartment over this any day.

Thinking his name sent a violent pang through his chest. Max rubbed above his heart, willing his breathing to remain calm.

"The Imperial Suite," Adelaide said, snapping him back to the present. "Take some time to freshen up. Jean Claude won't arrive till later tonight, and I'm sure you'll have much to discuss."

"Jean Claude...?" Max's heard only his name. He stumbled forward, catching himself on a crushed velvet stool. "He's coming here?"

"Yes," Adelaide said, raising an eyebrow. "Of course. What did you expect?" She slipped out then, leaving him alone in the opulent cage.

Max made his way into the bedroom, not thinking, that blessed numbness guiding his movements. He'd barely been aware of the sun going down, the shadows lengthening around him. Only now that night was falling had he started to wake up. Staring out at the tower, his mind running in circles, he could come to only one conclusion.

"He wants to kill me himself."

He let it echo in the empty room. Hearing it out loud somehow made it more real.

He saw the gun again, the swift nonchalance of Jean Claude's movements as he drew and fired, and shivered.

Part of him almost wished Jean Claude would kill him. If he didn't, how the hell could Max live with this guilt? He was so tired of being afraid and running and losing the things that mattered most to him. At least his death would be an end. But when he thought of dying, he thought of Hadrian and knew he'd never want him to do that.

Hadrian....

Max rubbed his chest again, waiting for the numbness that had seized him since the car ride to dissipate. He was most likely dead by now. The fact whispered with cold starkness in his mind. Hadrian would have burned, maybe in his apartment, maybe at U Medvídků, or Čapeks, or—

The thought cut itself off, like a steel door slamming shut in his mind. Max took a ragged breath, wiping sweat from his forehead. "Get it under control," he whispered. Brutally he reinforced that steel door, shoving all thoughts of love and what he'd lost behind it. Instinctively he knew facing them would break him. And he refused to meet Jean Claude again on his knees like a broken doll. He'd die on his feet, dammit.

Numbness, cold and preserving, returned to let him think.

He had few choices. He could try to escape, maybe sneak outside, hit the streets, and disappear into the Paris underworld. But Jean Claude would come after John and Karel. Maybe even his distant family back home. No, escape wasn't an option.

So what was left?

Jean Claude was going to kill him. Max was confident in that. But to have tracked him down after so long and not done it right away meant something more ominous. Jean Claude was playing with his prey. Maybe he had a crueler way of finishing him off, something more painful than a quick bullet to the head.

Max was beginning to wish Adelaide had shot him in Prague and been done with it.

It was dark now, the tower even brighter against the pitch-black sky. Max looked at the tiny lights below and knew for every one there were countless people scrabbling anonymously through the city. He longed to join them, to be part of the faceless mass again. To be—

There was a scraping sound. A key turning in the lock. The click of the opening door echoed throughout the empty room.

Max froze. His veins ran cold, breath came quicker. He heard the door shut, and then footsteps, muffled in the carpet, filled his senses. He sat in that silent room and counted the seconds as his breathing reached a panicked fever pitch.

Jean Claude was here.

Let it be quick. Let me be wrong. Let it be a bullet to the head. Please.

A light flicked on, flooding the room with soft incandescence. Max blinked hard, shaking, unable to stop. The footsteps grew closer, then stopped just behind him. A hand, cold and strong, settled on the back of his neck.

No, he thought to himself, biting his lip to keep from screaming. *Don't look. The boogeyman isn't real. Bluebeard doesn't exist.* He closed his eyes, like it would keep Jean Claude at bay, and saw again his shop burning, the flames leaping to the sky. He heard Hadrian's dry chuckle, whispering out of the dark, waiting for Max to join him.

The hand tightened, forcing his eyes open.

"Hello, Will."

His heart skipped a beat at the sound of Jean Claude's silvery, low voice.

"No," he choked out and stood, shaking that hand off. Bracing himself, Max turned to see Jean Claude almost unchanged behind him. He was as powerfully lean as Max remembered, his black hair shot through with steel and curled in the fashion of a Roman general. He stared at Max with eyes the color of mercury, looking him up and down, reading, judging. As always, he was dressed in a suit built for the kill in dark gray, with snowy white cuffs peeking out at his wrists.

He was still handsome. Max had forgotten just how sleekly sexy he could be. But the hard-won knowledge of what he was capable of tempered any attraction he might have had. Everything about him screamed predator, danger. Now, knowing what he did, Max wondered how he'd ever come to love this monster disguised as a man.

The thought gave him courage. He took a deep breath, straightening his shoulders, and looked the monster in the eye. "I go by Max now," he said, hiding his shaking hands at his side.

"Yes, I'd heard," Jean Claude said after a moment. His vowels were long, his *R*s rolled with traces of his native French. "But Max is a lie, and I think we are past the point of lies."

"That's all you ever did to me," Max spat, anger fighting through the cold fog of fear. "Lie, and hurt."

"Lie? I never lied," Jean Claude said, still cool, still perfectly in control.

Max laughed bitterly. "You're a murderer and a smuggler, and God knows what else. You killed that man ten feet in front of me. In the apartment you wanted me to live in, for Christ's sake. You literally set fire to everything I loved. And…." *You said you loved me.* It hung on the air, an old pain Max hadn't known till that moment was still aching.

"I never lied to you," Jean Claude said again. "I told you I loved you, and I did not lie then. I do not lie now when I say that I still do." He smiled. "If I didn't, *cher*, you'd already be dead."

It was a cold slap in the face. Max recoiled, shocked at how easily Jean Claude said it.

"You're insane," Max whispered. "You killed…." He choked, unable to say his name out loud. "You don't know the first thing about love."

Jean Claude tilted his head, regarding him for a long moment, as Max shook in front of him. It was all Max could do to keep his head high. He'd made his promise—he wouldn't meet death on his knees.

"You are too skinny," Jean Claude finally said, shocking Max. "And whatever trash you're wearing should be burnt. I must go speak with Adelaide, and when I return, we will go to dinner."

"What?" Max said, taken aback by the quick change in subject. "Dinner?"

"Yes. It is night, and I am hungry. Surely even men on the run eat, *non*?" Jean Claude said, with a trace of cold humor.

"I'm not going to have dinner with you. You're a murderer. You're going to kill me!"

"Kill you?" Jean Claude lifted an eyebrow. "Why would I do that, after half a year wasted searching for you?"

Max stepped back, brow furrowed, his mind racing to keep up with what was happening. "Then what do you want?"

"Dinner, for the moment," Jean Claude said with a shrug. "And then… do not worry. You will know."

Loathing filled Max. He could only imagine what else Jean Claude would expect of him. "I'll scream," Max said, eyes narrowing. "I'll scream in the dining room, and all those people will know exactly what you are."

"No, I don't think you will," Jean Claude said with a small, thin smile. "I believe you struck a bargain with Adelaide before agreeing to return to me. *C'est vrai*? Remember, I do not forget a bargain."

He might as well have slapped him. The bargain—John and Karel's safety.

"So that's how it's going to be," Max said.

"Only if you choose," Jean Claude said. He reached out to lay a hand on Max's cheek, and Max winced, pulling back, then forced himself to be still. Slowly, those long, cold fingers traced the line of his cheekbone and gently grasped his chin. Jean Claude came forward, filling Max's senses with the subtle hint of his cologne as he leaned forward and pressed those patrician lips firmly to his.

All Max could do was hold still as Jean Claude took his mouth, tongue flicking out to explore old territory. With no warning, he bit down on Max's bottom lip hard enough to make Max whimper. Jean Claude sighed into his mouth, a sound that conveyed ownership and relief and possession all at once.

"This can be so easy, *cher*," he said, pulling back. He looked almost… tender. As if he really did love him. "If you let it."

A lump formed in Max's throat as Jean Claude let his hand fall away. He stood, silent, as Jean Claude watched him a long moment before nodding and turning to walk out the room.

As the door clicked shut behind him, Max lifted a trembling hand to his swollen lip. It stung beneath his fingers. The world around him narrowing to fear and danger, Max sat, wondering what on earth he was going to do.

CHAPTER 29

"*PRDEL,*" HADRIAN snarled, pulling back from Karel. He sat shirtless at Ivan's small kitchen table, a first-aid kit laid open at his elbows and Vaclav deeply asleep at his feet. Dark purple bruises ran down the front of his chest where the blast had slammed into him. The purple mixed with lurid blue and green on his right shoulder from his attempted escape from the kitchen, making his chest an almost artistic blend of angry colors. Added to that was a nasty gash above his right eye that was currently welling up with blood, threatening to fall.

Outside, the early evening had turned the world a dusky, beautiful blue. A perfect contrast to the horror of the day.

"You must sit still," Karel snapped. He held a peroxide-soaked cotton ball with a pair of tweezers. Blood stained it where he'd dabbed Hadrian's cut.

"Just slap a bandage on it. It's fine," Hadrian groaned. He fell quiet at the glare Karel sent his way, then hissed in pain as Karel poked at his cut again.

"There," Karel said, dropping the cotton onto the table and picking up a large butterfly bandage. He smoothed it over the cut, pulling the edges together. "You may need stitches. But we do not have time."

"Fine. Thank you," Hadrian said, grudging. He rotated his bad shoulder, wincing as it screamed in pain. He'd sprained it, but it would recover. He'd had worse in his day.

"You do not want stronger medicine?" Karel asked, frowning.

Hadrian shook his head. "Aspirin is fine. I can't afford to be woozy, not now. Every second we sit here, Max gets farther away."

Karel's mouth thinned. "I know. When I think about that… that… monster…." He turned away, taking a deep, shuddering breath. "Max is family now. I cannot see him hurt."

"We'll find him, Karel," Hadrian said, voice quiet. "I promise."

Karel nodded.

184

Just then, John walked into the kitchen, his cell phone pressed against his ear. "Thank you." Meeting Hadrian's eyes, he nodded. "Let me know if you hear anything else, okay, Susan?" He listened for another second before hanging up.

"Anything?" Hadrian asked.

"Jean Claude left New York three days ago," he said, looking grim. "Hopped his private jet in the middle of the night."

Hadrian pushed to his feet, ignoring Karel's protests. "Does she know where he went?"

"Barely even knows he left." John snorted. "This guy's got more secrecy around him than the president. Scrambled flight plans, no way to trace him. She checked with contacts in the NSA, FBI, Homeland Security. Either no one knows or they're keeping their mouths shut. But he's deep in with the French government—got more ties than in the States. Best guess says that's where he'll head."

"Let's go, then," Hadrian said. He was itching to be on the move, fighting back the thought that they might already be too late.

"Go where?" John asked, tone mocking. "France is a pretty big place, and we're not even sure he's there. You know something I don't?"

"John," Karel cautioned.

John shook his head.

"We can't just do nothing," Hadrian said. "He could be hurt, or...." He bit his lip, his jaw clenched tight, seeing the horrors he imagined mirrored in John's eyes.

"You think I don't want to drop everything, run, and get him back? He's my family." John's voice was dangerously quiet. "You've known him all of a month. You don't have the right."

"I'd think my commitment was clear at this point," Hadrian snapped back. They stared at each other, the air sharp with tension. "I saved his life. Almost lost mine for his. I...."

"You what?" John challenged when Hadrian fell suddenly quiet.

Hadrian's skin buzzed as the world spun around him. Did he? He knew now, that he'd do anything to get Max back. Knew he felt for him in a way he hadn't thought himself capable. Knew the only thing he wanted was another morning like that one, waking up with Max in his arms, kissing Max, loving....

The world zoomed into clearer focus as Hadrian realized what he had to say.

"I know you've been uncomfortable with my dating Max." There was something wrong about this—he should have told Max first—but it couldn't be helped. "I understand why. But there's something you need to know." He took a deep breath, not looking away from John's eyes. "I'm in love with him."

There was a small, happy noise from Karel they both ignored.

"It's only been a month," John said, not moving. "How can you be sure?"

"Sometimes you just know," Hadrian said, feeling it deep within himself, in some hidden, secret part. He loved Max. Simple as that.

John was silent, his gaze locked on Hadrian. The air crackled with tension, violence building up at the edges of the room. Then he sighed and looked at Karel, seeing something far away. The room seemed to relax as tension drained as quickly as it had come.

"I guess I can't argue with that," John finally said, turning back to Hadrian. "Does he love you back?"

Hadrian shrugged. "I don't know. Never got the chance to tell him—only just realized it myself. But it doesn't matter, does it? All I want is for him to be safe. That would be enough for me."

John let out a sigh and nodded. "Then we're going to need a plan."

"If you've finished with your peeing contest," Karel said, interrupting. They turned to see him watching them with a speculative eye.

"Pissing contest," John corrected, then winced as Karel glared at him.

Hadrian had to hide a small smile. For all John's commanding air, it was clear who had the final say between the two men.

"Finished?" Karel waited till John nodded before continuing. "The fire in U Medvídků was supposed to kill you, Hadrian. Do you agree?"

"Yeah. I'm guessing this Jean Claude doesn't take too kindly to rivals."

"Yes, that is clear." Karel nodded. "But the man who would kill you failed. And I do not think a man who can kidnap, drug, and murder will accept failure from his employees."

"You think he's going to try for me again," Hadrian said, following Karel's grim knowledge.

"I do not doubt that he will. It is likely that he is waiting for you at your flat, for you to return. And I do not think he will try fire again," Karel said, following some train of thought. "A man bent on murder, he will not do the same thing twice if he wants to remain quiet. He will try some other way."

"And if we know he's waiting for me…," Hadrian said.

"We can have a surprise waiting for him, *ne*? John, you have brought your pistol with you. And you have such a keen eye."

John was looking at Karel in a way that made Hadrian slightly uncomfortable. "When did you get so strategic?"

Karel shrugged. "I design video games, my mouse. Do you think it is all drawing zombies?" Fierceness came over him as he stood, looking from Hadrian to John. "Now, soldiers—go and trap this rat. I want our Max back where he belongs."

CHAPTER 30

AN HOUR later Hadrian was walking up to his building, trying to look tired and weak. It wasn't hard. His body throbbed, the aspirin barely dulling the pain that rode in waves through his muscles.

In his pocket he fingered the tiny Taser John had given him as insurance. It was Max's, found on his desk that morning. Hadrian sighed. It had barely been twenty-four hours since he'd gone to bed with Max and learned his secrets. Less than two since he'd realized, definitively, that he loved him. So much had happened. Max's smile in the sunlight seemed years away.

Gripping the Taser, he forced those thoughts from his mind and sharpened his senses. They'd only have one chance at this, if their guess was correct and the arsonist was still watching for him. He had to be sharp or the assassin might finish his job after all.

A deep breath filled his lungs with crisp spring air. He strained his ears as he stepped up to the building entrance and fit the key in the lock. No telltale click. He let out a sigh of relief. He hadn't really thought the front door would be wired with explosives.

"You with me?" Hadrian whispered. In his ear, his Bluetooth headset crackled.

"All set" came John's distant voice. "Be careful."

"I'm fond enough of my own skin, don't worry," Hadrian muttered.

Stepping into the dark hallway, he again stopped to listen. There was no sign of anything living, only the quiet creaks and moans of the old building settling around itself, with a few dim beams of moonlight splintering the black. Glancing toward the elevator, Hadrian shook his head and made his way to the stairs. It was a long, slow climb to the seventh floor, as he paused every few seconds to listen.

Carefully, he ran his fingers along the edges of the wood, ignoring the shooting pain in his shoulder as Karel's aspirin wore off. Nothing out of the ordinary. He reached for his door handle and put the key in slowly, carefully. When nothing clicked, he turned it, sending up a rare prayer that the fire starter hadn't tampered with his door.

Taking a deep breath, he ducked down and swung the door wide.

Something whizzed over his head, landing with a quiet thud in the wall behind him. He fell to the side, away from the door, holding his breath. John made a startled noise in his ear, then a blur of static crackled before the earpiece fell silent again.

Hadrian rubbed his chest where the bullet would have landed and gripped the Taser a little tighter. Someone shifted inside his apartment, sending the floorboards creaking. Hadrian held his breath, then tapped the tiny headset in his right ear.

A second later the sound of shattered glass echoed into the hall, followed by a grunt and the sound of something heavy falling to the ground.

Still cautious, knowing full well wounded men could operate a gun almost as well as whole ones, Hadrian peered around the doorjamb.

There was a small figure lying on the ground, his hand pressed to his right shoulder and a silenced handgun half a foot from his head. Glass glittered on the ground around him and a breeze blew through the broken window above Hadrian's bed. The pot Max had given him had been shattered, throwing dirt and shards of clay to mix on the floor with the moonlight.

Quick as a cat, Hadrian ran in, closing the door behind him. He kicked the gun away from the fallen man. A second later he knelt beside him, one hand over his mouth, the other holding his free arm down. "Move and you won't like the consequences," he growled. In the moonlight he could just make out frightened, beady eyes looking up at him from a small, pointed face. Reaching into his back pocket, he pulled out a length of cord, then grabbed the man by his good shoulder, forcing him to sit up. Hadrian ignored his cry of pain as he pulled his arms together and knotted them as tightly as he could.

There was a crackle at his ear, and John's voice filtered out. "You okay?"

"You got him in the shoulder. Clean shot," Hadrian said, yanking on the bonds to test them. They held.

John said something else, but the connection was too poor to understand him. Hadrian frowned. It had sounded like "...wasn't me."

"John? You there?"

The static suddenly cleared. "On my way over."

"Hurry up."

Hadrian stood, keeping his eyes trained on the man on the floor as he backed away and flicked on the light. Now he saw the stranger was blond and slim, and wearing a black sweater that glistened with blood. There was something ratlike and greedy about his face. He stared at Hadrian with narrowed eyes, his mouth half-open, panting.

"I've seen you before—in U Medvídků," Hadrian said, remembering. Anger boiled red-hot through his veins as he again saw the little man who had pushed past him out of the kitchen and realized it was the same face. "You started that bleeding fire!"

The man's eyes blanked and his mouth slammed shut. It took everything Hadrian had not to clock him, but he held himself back. Max was what mattered. If he killed him, they would lose their only lead.

Taking a deep breath, Hadrian focused, letting his rage simmer in the back of his mind. "What is your name?"

"Dead man," the other croaked, his eyes blank. "Or I will be soon if you don't do something about my shoulder."

Hadrian watched him and the growing stain of blood seeping into the wood beneath him. The man looked pale. Hadrian recognized the signs of major blood loss from his Air Force days—the man would be dead in an hour if they couldn't stop the bleeding. Gritting his teeth, Hadrian pulled off his shirt and ripped away the sleeves with a loud tearing noise. Wadding the chest into a cloth pad, he pressed it hard against the stranger's wound.

The man hissed in pain but didn't flinch.

"Hold still." Hadrian grabbed one of his discarded sleeves and used it to tie the pad into place, not bothering to be gentle. Stepping away, he looked down at his work. It was as crude as anything in the field, but it would keep him from bleeding to death at least. Just then, there was a quiet knock at the door. He checked the peephole, saw John's face looking grim, and relief swept through him as he reached for the handle.

But on opening the door, Hadrian got his second shock for the night. Standing beside John was a woman.

"What the hell?" Hadrian hissed, stepping into the darkened hall and pulling the door shut behind him.

In the light from the moon, Hadrian could see a young, amber-skinned woman, with round cheeks and dark brown hair pulled back into a severe ponytail. She wore black from head to toe, and had what looked to be a military-grade sniper rifle slung across her back. She also looked surprisingly familiar.

She eyed Hadrian up and down with cold, calculating eyes, then nodded.

"Hello," she said in an American accent, holding out a shiny metal badge. It was shaped like a shield against a dark green background, with gold swords crossed over bright white blades. Around the swords was an inscription in Latin that Hadrian didn't understand. "Maggie Singh. Reconnaissance Officer, Supreme Headquarters of the Allied Powers Europe. SHAPE, for short." She winced before tucking the shield back into her pants pocket. "Always hated that name. Sounds so old-fashioned. Like something you'd get in a comic book."

"SHAPE? Are you serious?"

He'd heard of them, of course. They had been founded about a year after the Korean War to coordinate NATO military forces in Europe. In the 1990s they'd been chopped up and put back together again in an attempt to streamline the organization. He'd heard chatter, in his UN days, that streamlining had meant going underground. There were a lot of rumors around SHAPE. None of them publicly verified.

Hadrian frowned at her, torn between shock and suspicion. Not for the first time since meeting Max, he felt like he'd waded in over his head. International smuggling rings, spy organizations, conspiracies, and plots within plots. He thought he'd left that world behind him. He just wanted Max back and safe.

After what Max had told him, it did make sense that some government organization was involved with him and Jean Claude. But there was something about her, something almost familiar…. The wheels turned in his head, slowly, till John helped him finish the leap.

"She's been on the course with Max. Another student—so we thought. Turns out we had a literal spy in our midst." He turned and glared at Maggie, who shrugged.

"You'll have to forgive my deception. The case we're building against Jean Claude is shaky, and he's got his fingers in all sorts of government pies. It was spy work on this one, or risk losing our chance at stopping him."

"Fat lot of good you've done so far," Hadrian snapped. "Where were you when he came to Prague and kidnapped Max? Busy teaching?"

"There were complications," Maggie said, her expression cool.

Hadrian met her eyes and read between the lines. Beside Maggie, he saw John stiffen. "Complications," he said, speaking slowly. It was a struggle to keep his voice low in the hallway. He wanted to scream. "Bullshit. I've met your type before, you skullduggery lot. Don't give two shillings for the people who get hurt in your little games. You used Max as bait."

"Yes. It was the only way. We know Max witnessed a shooting, but an eight-month-old possible homicide isn't enough to get someone as slippery as Jean Claude. We needed Jean Claude to commit a new crime, and we needed a witness. Max is the key."

"He's a bloody human being."

"And the only weakness Jean Claude has."

For a moment rage blinded Hadrian. He felt his fists clench, his heart surge. It took all his training to calm himself, to bring his breathing back to normal. It didn't dissipate his anger, though—just sent it to the back of his mind, waiting to be used.

"That means you need to get him back alive," John broke in, and Hadrian glanced over to see him glaring at Maggie. "Can you?"

"If we move fast, yes," Maggie said. "Jean Claude won't kill him. Not yet, anyway. If he wanted him dead, he'd have had his assistant shoot him here."

"And can you guarantee his safety after Jean Claude is arrested?" John went on, his voice dangerously even. "Can you protect him after that?"

Maggie turned to John, her shoulders stiff, then sighed. For a moment she slumped as her composure vanished. "Yes. I wouldn't have risked him this way if we couldn't. Believe it or not, I've grown close to Max. I had to risk him—I couldn't help it. But you have my guarantee that we'll do everything in our considerable power to keep him safe when this is done."

John turned to Hadrian. For his part Hadrian didn't trust Maggie as far as he could throw her, and the thought that she might have prevented Max's kidnapping made his blood boil. But he had to be practical, think of the now. What mattered was getting Max back.

"Then we're wasting time," Hadrian snapped, and John nodded.

"Agreed," Maggie said, stepping forward, some of her confidence returning. "And unless you'd like to lose more, I'd suggest you let me into your flat so I can interrogate our assassin before he bleeds to death."

"Not without us, you won't," Hadrian said, blocking her with an outstretched arm.

Maggie looked down at his arm, seeming to calculate her options, and Hadrian was happy to wait. Finally, she shrugged. "As long as you stay quiet."

Together they entered Hadrian's flat, the light too bright after the darkened hallway. The firebug hadn't moved from his spot on the floor. He watched them when they came in, his dead eyes glittering above a pointed nose.

"Hello," Maggie said, as Hadrian closed and locked the door behind them. He glanced at Maggie and was surprised to see that she looked calm. Cheerful, even. She set her gun on the ground, then slid down to sit on the floor in front of the bleeding man.

Tutting like a disappointed mother, she reached out and adjusted his bandage, not seeming to notice when he flinched away from her hands. "You'll live," she said with a small smile as she sat back. "I promise we'll get you some proper medical attention as soon as possible. My name is Maggie. I work with SHAPE. Do you know what that means?"

The arsonist didn't move.

"I'll take that as a no," she said when he didn't speak. "Not that I'm surprised. We mostly go after major criminals, not pond scum. International fraud. Illegal operations that threaten international security. We're the ones that show up and take you away and make sure no one knows where you've gone. Usually we'd let Interpol go after slimy little trash like you. But then you decided to swim with the big fish."

"I'm sure I don't know what you're talking about," the man said, breaking his silence. His lips pressed thinly together.

"Sure, I'll play that game," Maggie said, still sounding friendly. Hadrian could see her back, though, see how tense she was. "You got a name?"

The man tilted his head. "I've had a lot of names."

"Anything recent?"

"None you'd need to know."

"Who do you work for?"

"Myself. God. The lifestyle I always dreamed of," the man said. He grinned suddenly. "What else is there?"

"I'll tell you what I think," Maggie said, tilting her head, her smile widening. "I think you're a lowlife who has been promoted beyond his capabilities. I think Jean Claude uses you to handle his personal dirty work. You know that name, don't you?"

"I'm sorry to disappoint you," the man said, and coughed. "But I've never heard that name in my life."

Hadrian could feel his frustration bubbling over. "This is getting us nowhere," he growled. "We don't have time to screw around like this."

"The clock is always ticking for something."

Hadrian's fist curled. He wanted, very much, to punch the killer. But John's hand on his shoulder held him back.

"Okay," Maggie said with a small shrug. She reached into her pocket and pulled out a photo, then held it up to the assassin's face. Hadrian couldn't see what was in it, but as soon as he saw it, the assassin paled. "That's you stepping out of a Graywater vehicle," she said, her voice masterfully calm. "Now, isn't that Jean Claude's security company?"

"So what?" the other spat. "This proves nothing. You'll have to try harder than that."

"We'll see," Maggie said, her voice just this side of ominous. "I've a weapon here, and three witnesses who can testify that you attempted to murder this man. No matter what, you're going to jail. So don't think you're getting out of that."

He snorted. "If we're operating under the premise that my employer is big and powerful enough for SHAPE to get involved, do you really think I'll stay in prison for long? I'm too valuable."

"You *were* too valuable," Maggie said, nodding. "Maybe. But now you've failed to kill Hadrian twice. And it doesn't seem that Jean

Claude is very logical where he's involved, does it? Otherwise he'd never have sent you to kill him in the first place. And now we have evidence linking you to Graywater. Quite sloppy of you. That's the problem with small fish."

The man just stared back at her and didn't speak.

Maggie looked at him, sighed, and took a smartphone from her pocket. Hadrian's brow furrowed with confusion—what the hell was she doing? With a small moue of distaste, she held the phone in front of the man and snapped a picture, sending him blinking back from the sudden flash of light. Then, still looking unhappy, she began to text. "I think you're right, by the way," she said, as her fingers flew over the keyboard. "Jean Claude will get you out of jail. But I don't think he'll let you live to enjoy the fresh air."

"What are you doing?"

She paused with her finger poised over the Send button. "Just preparing to send a picture of you to my contact at the FBI, along with a copy of our vehicle shot. Tell me, how long do you think you'll have before Jean Claude finds out?"

The man, already pale from blood loss, turned shock white and his breathing grew labored. "He'll torture me if you send that."

Maggie leaned forward, eyes intent. "I'll delete this if you cooperate with us for real. I can make certain he never finds you. But if you won't speak, I'll drop you off on his doorstep myself."

Hadrian couldn't help but be a little impressed. He watched the arsonist stare at Maggie, his face pale, pupils dilated with fear.

"Winston Rafael," he finally spat. "And I say nothing else until I'm granted immunity for past crimes and complete anonymity and protection."

Maggie studied him a moment. "Done."

Hadrian started forward—this was the man who had tried to kill him twice! Again, John's hand at his shoulder stopped him. He turned to see John shaking his head. Annoyed, Hadrian shrugged John's hand off his shoulder.

"Now, then," Maggie said, settling back. "Where did they take Max?"

"Paris," Winston said.

"Paris is a big city."

195

"Le Royal Hotel," Winston sneered. "Crawling with Graywater guards, that place. Not that you'd get a warrant from the French, not with the clout he's got. Good luck stepping foot in there."

"Why does he want him?" Maggie went on calmly.

Winston's sneer widened. "What do you think? Hot little piece of ass like that ran away from me, I'd be in a punishing mood too."

It took everything Hadrian had not to run forward and strangle him. He took a deep breath, channeling his anger in a well-worn pattern, sending it to his feet, his hands, letting it awaken him—bring him to a higher awareness. Ready to fight, when the time came.

John, beside him, shook with anger. Hadrian saw his hand tightening at his side, but when he spoke, his voice was still soft and calm. "Maggie. How much time do we have?"

She nodded and relayed the question.

Winston shrugged. "I was told to rendezvous with them in Paris tomorrow. After that, I can't tell you."

"That's too soon," Hadrian said, his mind working a million miles a minute. It barely gave them time to get to Paris—and it was still longer than he wanted Max to be in the hands of that psychopath.

"We can make it. That's everything we need, I think." Maggie stood and stepped away from him. "Oh, one more thing. How do you communicate with Jean Claude?"

"Payphones. Burners. Anything that couldn't be traced—don't think you'll find anything on me, lady," Winston sneered.

"You tell him Hadrian was dead, yet?"

"Yes," Winston spat. "No other choice. Figured I'd finish the job tonight. Now let's talk pardon."

Maggie nodded, then smiled abruptly. "You've been very helpful, Winston. Thank you." She stretched, then made as if to leave.

"Where are you going?"

Maggie looked down at him. Now that the interrogation was over, cold fury came over her face. She radiated anger, controlled, stonelike, but rage nonetheless. "I'd really like to beat the shit out of you right now, firebug, but I know better than to hit a man who can't hit me back. Instead, I'm going to leave you here for my colleagues to clean up."

"What about my immunity? You said I'd be protected!"

Maggie shrugged and glanced at her watch. "You will, for now. Immunity, however—I don't remember saying anything about that." She turned her back on the cursing, snarling man and walked over to where Hadrian and John were standing. "Let's get going, gentlemen. I've got a lot of work to do and not much time to do it in."

Hadrian hesitated, glancing at his books, the shattered window, the man cursing him on the ground. Not the way he'd like to leave his apartment. He shook his head. Everything here was replaceable. Max wasn't.

"Don't worry," Maggie said, following his eyes to Winston. "My extraction team is already on its way. He'll be gone in an hour, tops."

"Good. Tell them not to touch my books," Hadrian growled.

She smiled. "If you're nice, I'll have them patch up the window too."

They left the flat, shutting the door on the cursing man behind them and moving in perfect silence. Outside, the quiet, chill night greeted them, the streets oppressive in their emptiness. Hadrian glanced at his watch as Maggie stepped lightly over the last step onto the snowy street. It was only 11:00 p.m. It seemed later.

"We've got to get to Paris," John said, as they paused in the street.

"*We?*" Maggie said, shaking her head. "I'm sorry, but I can't allow you to come with me. I have a team of agents on standby who are better trained for this kind of operation than you could ever be, ex-soldiers or no. And like it or not, you're both civilians now." Her eyes hardened. "This is not up for discussion."

John snorted. "Bullshit. You need us. And if you can't see why, then you're not a good enough anything to get Max back in one piece."

"Oh? Go ahead, then," Maggie said, voice dangerously low. "Enlighten me."

John turned to Hadrian, raising an eyebrow.

Hadrian nodded. He felt heady with battle readiness, his thoughts racing miles a minute. He'd felt this way before, in Kuwait, the Congo, like he could see a thousand possibilities before him, could follow the future to all its potential outcomes.

"You've got nothing to pin on Jean Claude, not yet," Hadrian said. "You need Max for that. And if Jean Claude gets word you're coming for them, he'll be out of Paris and rid of Max before we've got a hope of finding him alive."

"Still don't see how I need you."

"You've got about thirty-six hours to rescue Max and arrest Jean Claude. Which means you don't have time to launch a full-scale mission—you're going on your own, with a few other agents, as you said. But once you get there, assuming all goes well, you'll still have to get Max to cooperate with you. You think that's likely?"

Maggie frowned, then opened her mouth wide.

Hadrian cut her off. "The answer is no. He's been betrayed by too many people pretending to be who they weren't. He's already afraid of the FBI, Interpol. Why is he going to think you're anything but another mind fuck from Jean Claude? Or, for that matter, say he does believe you. Will he think you can keep the people he loves safe?" Hadrian shook his head. "I've met Jean Claude's type before. They don't screw around. If he just wanted Max quiet, Max would've been shot in the street. No, Jean Claude wants Max's cooperation. Which means he's also threatening John. Maybe Karel. And Max probably thinks I'm dead."

He met Maggie's eyes and held them, blue against oak brown. "So he won't leave Jean Claude if he thinks John and Karel will be in danger, and he won't trust you to tell him they're safe. It's got to be me or John, plain and simple. We're your only chance of getting Max out of there."

Maggie studied him a long moment. "Hadrian Walls, eh?" she finally said. "I've seen your military records, of course. Thought they were exaggerating. Guess they weren't." She sighed, then threw up her hands. "Fine. It's unorthodox, but so's everything about this. As of right now, you're both temporary SHAPE deputies. But you damn well better do what I say."

John and Hadrian exchanged a look. Grim purpose passed through them. They nodded.

"Now," Maggie said, eyes glinting. "Let's go stop this bastard."

CHAPTER 31

MAX TOOK a deep breath, hoping it would calm the trembling in his hands. It was no use. The best he could do was to stick them behind his back and straighten his shoulders.

This time he wasn't acting for just Jean Claude. Before him was Le Royal's elegant ballroom, full of rich luxuries framed by floor-to-ceiling glass windows with a perfect view of the glittering Eiffel Tower. The floor was a creamy marble, echoing the lobby, the walls more cream, more gold. Milling inside, eating *confit de canard* off bone-china plates and sipping champagne, were the kind of people who noticed every person who walks into the room. He couldn't have any of them commenting upon him, seeing the rage that wanted to burst out of him like a wild tiger, the fear that wrapped around his throat.

Jean Claude had been very clear about what would happen if he were to make a scene of any kind.

Adelaide, dressed elegantly in cream-colored satin that flattered her Amazonian build, turned to face Max. Her graceful features stood out above the low neckline of her dress, but did nothing to hide the coldness in her eyes. "He is waiting for you," she said, eyeing him up and down. Max felt his fists clench as she nodded in apparent satisfaction. "You are much cleaner now. Good."

"White never suited me," Max gritted out between his teeth.

Adelaide pursed her lips. "You're wrong. Jean Claude has excellent taste."

Max swallowed hard, remembering how he'd ended up in the revolting costume. After Jean Claude had left his room, Max had found a Burberry suit bag waiting for him in the living room and a note suggesting he try it on. He'd taken one look at the note and shredded it with nimble fingers before dumping the bag unceremoniously on the ground.

Adelaide had walked in to see him still in his jeans and sweater and shook her head. When Max didn't move, she'd shrugged and picked up her phone. "One call." The threat was clear.

"You'd kill them over a suit?" Max had asked through clenched teeth.

"That is your decision."

Of course there was only one choice.

His lip had throbbed as he buttoned the steel gray shirt Jean Claude had left him, the cufflinks held together with small silver bars. Then the white suit itself. Hateful as it was, Max knew it suited him exceptionally well, highlighting the olive undertones of his skin and his dark, curling hair. That made it worse. Disgust filled him as he thought of dressing up to please such a monster.

Now, standing on the edge of the ballroom, that feeling came back tenfold as he realized Jean Claude had guaranteed that everyone would be staring at him. Inside, all the elegant people were dressed in blues and blacks. A room full of bruises. And him, the white sacrifice, virginal, sure to attract their eyes—eyes that would further force him to play the part he'd been assigned.

Jean Claude was flaunting him, and at the same time, guaranteeing a room full of witnesses would confirm Max was here of his own volition. He was that confident in his scheming and his control over Max.

Adelaide gestured to the far side of the ballroom, where a table had been set flush against the large windows. It was made private by a display of weeping plants and a carefully placed Japanese folding screen. Those seated within could observe the room while maintaining an elegant anonymity.

Max took a deep breath and began winding his way through the tables, ignoring the curious stares that followed him. It seemed to take forever for him to reach Jean Claude, and with every step, he grew a little more nauseated.

Jean Claude was staring out the window when Max walked in, which gave Max a moment to hide his surprise. He was wearing a suit the exact same shade of gray as Max's shirt, with a silk button-down in the white of Max's suit. He'd set them to matching. Made it clear, even at this level, that he was in control.

Anger surged through Max, along with a bitter frustration at his inability to do anything.

"William," Jean Claude said, turning. There was something in his eye—something almost like affection. A hint of what they had been, before. "Sit, please."

Max nodded stiffly, his old name stinging his ears. He pulled out a chair from beneath the intimately small table and tucked his legs beneath the draping white linen that covered it. Before him, a china plate, gilded at the edges with gold leaf, sat nestled between dozens of forks, spoons, and knives. To steady himself, Max picked up the glass of water beside his plate and took a long sip. He was braced for Jean Claude to come over, to be forced to submit to him again.

Jean Claude, however, made no move to approach him, instead watching him from across the table with a speculative gleam. "You look very elegant, *cher*. Burberry suits you."

Max set down his glass and forced his hands into his lap. "Almost as much as the 'murderous bastard' look suits you."

Jean Claude shook his head and sighed, as though Max were a particularly unruly child. "This view is too elegant for such language. Have some manners."

Max's retort was swallowed as a waiter coughed discreetly at the edge of their table. He had a small cart with him, on which were a bottle of wine and two crystal glasses. Jean Claude waved him over and said something in French too quickly for Max to understand. The waiter nodded, set the glasses before them, then returned a moment later to pour a deep red wine into each. It flowed smoothly, the liquid like bloody silk.

When the waiter had gone, Jean Claude lifted his glass and held it in the air. "To lovers reunited."

Max, with teeth clenched, didn't move. Jean Claude kept his eyes on Max as he drank, long and slow, his exposed throat bobbing with a sensual elegance that Max dimly remembered loving a long time ago. Now it repulsed him. The blood-colored wine, the forced expense of it all. Like watching a vampire feed.

When Jean Claude set the glass down, his thin lips were stained dark red.

"Aren't you worried about having me in public?" Max exploded, unable to take the silent cat and mouse. "Someone will come looking for me, and now all these people have seen me."

"Why would I be worried?" Jean Claude's tone was irritatingly nonchalant. He reached for the leather-bound menu in front of them and glanced through it.

"You kidnapped me," Max hissed.

"Please. You're here entirely of your own volition," Jean Claude said, raising an eyebrow.

"My own—you threatened my cousin's life," he snapped. "What choice did I have?"

Something dangerous flashed in Jean Claude's eyes, sending a shiver down Max's spine. "Be careful, *cher*. I don't remember you being stupid. You will have realized by now that if you were to look for any evidence supporting what you say, you'd find nothing. Nor would anyone believe such nonsense." He looked away, and Max felt like he'd been released. He sat back, shaking slightly, appalled at the power this man still had over him.

His brutally efficient assessment stung, all the more painful because he was saying what Max had thought only moments before. It was a perfect trap, a kidnapping with all the gloss of voluntary association. He bit the inside of his lip to keep his mind sharp, then took another sip of water to hide the despair that threatened to overwhelm him.

Curiosity came then, fighting through the despair. There was a question he needed answered—a question he'd had in the back of his head for almost a year now.

"I almost think you did this on purpose," Max said. In his mind, he saw again the day of the shooting, the look on Jean Claude's face when he realized he'd been seen. "Letting me escape, I mean. I've thought about it a lot. You could have called down to the lobby, had someone there detain me. The doorman, for Christ's sake. Or even when I was alone in the city, I think you could have found me. Why didn't you? Why did you let me go?"

Jean Claude stared at him. "I wanted to give you a chance to return to me," he finally said. There was hurt in his voice. A thin strand of pain Max almost missed. "After... I thought you would come back. For the sake of our love, if nothing else. I certainly didn't think you foolish enough to run away to Europe, try to hide from me."

"You murdered someone!"

"Yes. I did. He was a liability, and he deserved worse." Jean Claude lifted an eyebrow. "In my business, one must make sacrifices. I could have made you understand, if you'd come back to me as you were supposed to."

Max fell back, his chest constricting as though a band were tied around it. What was Jean Claude saying? Power, or control, had gone to his head until he'd forgotten how real people worked.

"So my shop, was that one of your 'sacrifices'?" Max's voice fell to a whisper. He felt tears coming to his eyes and bit his lip to hold them back. The world blurred behind his glasses. "You destroyed everything I had. How could you do that and think I would ever let you touch me again?"

Jean Claude leaned forward. A spark of anger set his eyes blazing. "You betrayed me," he said. "I was forced to do that when your stubbornness kept you from coming home, like an angry child. Willfulness gets punished, William. I cannot tolerate it. You are mine, and you ought to have learned the lesson by now."

Max took a deep breath, fighting his fear. The way Jean Claude was speaking was frightening. He seemed disappointed rather than angry, like Max was a pet he intended to punish and keep for a very long time.

Like he thought Max was coming home with him.

With a deep, steadying sigh, Jean Claude sat back. Some of his cool returned as he smoothed a hand through his dark hair. "I did not want to do it, but you forced my hand. I can't trust you anymore, *cher*. I must do these things for your own good, as well as mine."

It was the first time he'd spoken of the danger Max being alive was putting him in. Max jumped on the chance. "Then you should have killed me upstairs!" Max felt a hint of hysteria rising in him and squashed it down mercilessly, knowing he couldn't afford the luxury. "Like you killed my store, and my life, and...."

Hadrian. His jaw clamped shut. Pain—hot and livid—ran through him, the grief he was not yet willing to set free. He couldn't, not if he was going to keep some semblance of control.

203

"For what it is worth, I am sorry to have caused you pain," Jean Claude said softly. "But it was unavoidable. You are so stubborn, my William. Why didn't you come back to me? Let me explain, before all this unhappiness?" He reached across the table and pulled Max's hand, limp and unmoving, into his. It was too much like Hadrian had touched him, so recently.

Max snatched his hand back.

Whatever kindness had come over Jean Claude fled. His eyes flashed. "If that is how you insist on acting, there will be more pain. I will not stop so long as you insist on disobeying me. And believe me when I say that more will die, if necessary."

Max shook. "Just kill me, then. Please—if you ever did love me—end this."

Steel closed over Jean Claude's face. He shook his head and raised a hand for the waiter to return. "That is precisely why I cannot."

Max was mute as the waiter came and took Jean Claude's order. He listened without hearing as Jean Claude spoke of other things, all of them inconsequential. Some changes he'd made to the apartment back in America. The weather in New York. Max let his eyes drift to the tower outside, focusing on the way her lights seemed to dance against the night sky, letting them blot out the terrifying truth that was slowly forming at the edge of his thoughts.

Longing, sharp and dull as an old blade, hit him in the stomach. He wanted Hadrian so bad it hurt. Max closed his eyes and let himself fall back into memory, finding his way into Hadrian's bed, just that morning, waking up and feeling safe and loved and whole....

He opened his eyes again as a waiter set a plate in front of him, along with a heavy steak knife. Max looked down to see rare filet mignon, perfectly centered on a plate of exquisitely fragile china. The sight of it turned his stomach.

"Eat," Jean Claude said, picking up his steak knife and delicately carving into his meat. "You'll never taste meat this fine again."

"Shockingly, I'm not hungry," Max retorted. His eyes roved over his food, coming to rest on the knife beside his plate. An idea began forming. "Is it required for this charade?"

Jean Claude watched him with those cold gray eyes. There was a sense that Max had finally crossed a line. A danger, hot and present, that hadn't been there before.

Good. Enough playing pretend.

"Things will be different now," Jean Claude said, his voice tight. He paused to take a bite of steak that dripped blood onto his plate. "We will return to New York tomorrow night, but I'm afraid it will be some time before I can trust you again. In that period, you'll stay with Adelaide or me at all moments. You can take some work from me. I know you need to keep occupied, and I'll not deny you the chance to exercise your talents. I have a new manuscript collection from Afghanistan that needs looking after." He paused to sip at his wine, letting his words sink in.

"Afghanistan? A manuscript collection?" Max said, putting the pieces together. Panic at this new evil jumped to the edge of his fingers, brought sweat rising to the skin of his neck. "You want me to help you with your smuggling. I won't do it."

"Yes, you will," Jean Claude said calmly. "Please don't make me repeat myself. You will do as I say and you will be grateful for it, and at night you will come to my bed and make love to me and you will like it. And you will never leave me again."

It was like a slap of cold water. To hear it said like that, so brazenly....

"You want a slave."

"No. I want you. And I'll do what it takes to secure your cooperation," Jean Claude snapped.

"I'll kill myself first," Max spat, panic flooding him. He couldn't go with Jean Claude, couldn't be his slave, wouldn't let him... let him.... "I'll—"

He jumped when Jean Claude slammed his fist onto the table, sending flatware scattering and overturning Max's untouched wine. Red seeped across the table, filling the air with its heady, fermented smells. Thinking quickly, Max grabbed a thick cloth napkin and began wiping at the tablecloth.

"Leave it," Jean Claude said evenly.

Max stiffened, then pulled the dirty napkin back onto his lap. He kept his eyes locked on Jean Claude's, away from the table—and the steak knife he'd pulled into his sleeve under cover of the spill. As Jean Claude looked away, nostrils flaring, Max shifted and tucked the knife into his waist. His jacket slid over the handle, hiding it.

"It's your fault we're in this mess," Jean Claude said, as Max returned his hands to the tabletop. "Your reckless impetuousness."

"You can't control me," Max spat through his clenched jaw. "I am my own man. I won't be your slave."

"I don't want a slave. I want my lover back. But if you won't cooperate, a slave you'll be in the meantime." He closed his eyes as if in pain and shook his head.

A moment later Adelaide appeared at the edge of the table.

"Take him back," he said to her. "And lock the damn door. I'll be in later."

Adelaide nodded and waited elegantly for Max to rise.

Max didn't move. He couldn't. He looked at Jean Claude, at what stretched before him… a life locked away in his flat, with a monster he could never love again, a monster that'd killed….

"Hadrian," Max whispered. His name was like a stone dropping. Everything—the room, the dangerous woman at his back, the monster across the table—fell away in Hadrian's wake. Hadrian was dead, and his killer wanted to keep Max like a pet.

Max's eyes welled. He didn't bother to dry them. Instead, he met Jean Claude's eyes and held them, forcing him to see, to acknowledge him.

Something tightened around Jean Claude's mouth, perhaps guilt.

"You say you don't want a slave, but that's all you're going to get," Max finally said quietly. He felt the knife at his waist like a promise. "If you do this to me, one of us will be dead before a month's end. I promise you."

Jean Claude's mouth tightened. "Take him back," he said.

Max jumped a little as Adelaide grabbed his bicep in a clawlike grip. He shook her off and straightened himself with as much dignity as he could find. Then, shoulders rigid, he followed her out of the ballroom and away from Jean Claude.

CHAPTER 32

ONCE THEY'D agreed to work together, Maggie wasted no time in contacting her people and putting plans in motion. First they had to make sure Karel was safe. Maggie drove them back to Ivan's flat, where Karel and Vaclav greeted them anxiously. He went over John with concerned hands before doing the same to Hadrian, only then realizing there was a third member of their party. Vaclav sniffed her shoes experimentally before letting her pet him with a cautious wag of his tail.

"It's a long story," John said, forestalling any questions. "She's Maggie. Pretend student at Foxrod, real-life member of the Allied forces. A group called SHAPE."

"Undercover investigator," Maggie said, with a hint of cheer. She shook Karel's hand.

"You will help us to retrieve Max?"

She nodded.

"Good. Then come inside."

Karel was quickly brought up to speed while Maggie contacted her team from Ivan's living room. Hadrian paced as John talked, trying to keep an ear on whatever Maggie was saying. He couldn't make out much and was relieved when she hung up and joined them in the kitchen.

"I've got a team ready to take us to Charles de Gaulle Airport. We've got to operate small, though. Can't take the risk of the gendarme knowing we're in town or we'll spook Jean Claude early. We'll take a private jet. One of SHAPE's small holdings."

"Fine," Hadrian said. Vaclav pressed himself against Hadrian's legs with a worried whine, undoubtedly sensing his stress. Hadrian reached down and gave him a distracted ruffle. A vicious headache was beginning to pound at the back of his brain. He knew from experience that it would only get worse as time went on.

"We take off in two hours," Maggie said. She looked around and saw the tired faces. "Airport is about forty-five minutes from here, so that gives us a bit of time to rest. I'd suggest you nap, but I don't think you'd listen," she said, forestalling Hadrian's protest. "A sit down, and a cup of coffee might do you good, though. In the meantime, I've some more things to arrange. Where's the chef?"

"Ivan?" Karel said. "He's at the restaurant still. The emergency crews are still working and he did not want to leave them."

Maggie nodded. "I'll have someone keep an eye on him too. Excuse me." She stepped out of the room, leaving the three of them alone.

Hadrian saw the look Karel gave John and knew they'd want to speak in private. They'd agreed on the way to the flat that Karel would have to be moved to one of SHAPE's safe houses until Jean Claude had been arrested. It was too dangerous to leave him here, not if they wanted to rescue Max without any more bloodshed.

He saw John bracing himself for this conversation and tactfully made himself scarce.

Wandering into the hall away from their tense voices, Vaclav at his heels, he took stock of Ivan's apartment. It hadn't changed much since Hadrian had stayed here all those years ago. Still very much a bachelor's pad, plaster walls and the old oak floor spotted with white clumps of Vaclav's hair, and very little in the way of decoration. Ivan had poured himself into the pub. That was where he really lived.

Hadrian's temples throbbed, reminding him that sitting down for a bit might not be a bad idea. He turned into Ivan's small, comfortably furnished sitting room. A ratty couch—overstuffed, sagging, and covered in cranberry plaid—took an entire wall. Hadrian eased himself down onto it, pulling a mustard-yellow cushion beneath his head.

Vaclav whined and settled next to the couch, his head on Hadrian's chest.

"There you go, boy. It'll be all right," Hadrian murmured, and stroked Vaclav's still-sooty fur. "What a handsome fellow you are."

In response, Vaclav licked the palm of his hand, then gave a wide doggy yawn. Turning once, he lay down on the floor next to Hadrian and closed his eyes.

"Good idea," Hadrian said, and followed suit.

It seemed like he'd barely fallen asleep before John was at his shoulder, shaking him awake. Max's face, soft in Hadrian's dreamscape, faded as Hadrian opened his eyes to see John holding out a cup of coffee.

"That wasn't an hour," Hadrian complained. He sat up, took the coffee and gulped half of it down before his tongue could register the heat. At least his headache was gone.

"More like twenty minutes. Maggie got a call," John said. "Transit's ready early. One of her people is coming to pick Karel up, but we've got to leave now."

"Karel take it okay?"

John sighed, rubbing a hand down his face. "Well enough. He tried to fight it, but agreed when I pointed out that he'd have to keep Vaclav with him."

Hadrian nodded, knowing Karel's fondness for the dog. He swung his legs to the side and set his unfinished coffee on the floor. "Then let's go."

A few minutes and one teary good-bye later found them racing through the streets of Prague in the dark, the lights from the buildings a golden haze against the unreal feeling of the early morning. Hadrian cracked his window, letting the rush of cool night air wash over his face, centering him. Beside him, John was similarly taciturn, staring out into the night with an uneasy frown.

Soon they traded the city proper, with her ornate buildings and the castle upon the hill, for the highway. Countryside stretched black around them. They drove for almost an hour before Maggie's headlights slid across a sign in the dark. She slowed and turned the car off the highway and onto a rural dirt road that stretched into what Hadrian had assumed were fields. Then they passed beneath a bank of trees and emerged into a wide field lit by low floodlights. A long stretch of dirt had been cleared to make a rough runway. At one end a small prop plane, just big enough for a handful of people and painted jet-black, waited beside a metal shack.

A woman and a man, both dressed in more black, could be seen waiting by the side of the plane. As they pulled closer, Hadrian saw the woman wore a pilot's headgear. She was tapping her foot against the ground impatiently. The man, dark-skinned and smiling, seemed calmer.

Maggie pulled up to the side of the shack and hopped out, and Hadrian and John followed her. "Got my bird ready, Charlotte?" she asked, walking up to the woman.

"*Ja,*" Charlotte said, then scowled. She spoke with a heavy German accent. "I am not happy still, Agent Singh. They are civilians."

"Good thing it's not your call, then. Bernard?"

"*Oui, madame.* Everything is ready." The man stepped aside, nodding respectfully.

"You brought the gear I requested?"

The man—Bernard, Hadrian reminded himself—looked over at the two men waiting behind Maggie and grinned. "*Mais oui, madame.* It is inside."

Charlotte harrumphed and turned to climb up the short ramp.

Hadrian raised an eyebrow. "Not the social type, I see."

Bernard grinned wider, flashing perfect white teeth. "She takes some getting used to. But she will get you to Paris in one piece."

"Great."

Inside, a half-dozen seats were pressed to the sides of the narrow plane. It was simple, functional. Hadrian and John took seats together. A quiet roar sprang to life as Charlotte started the plane, and Hadrian sent a wistful look toward the cockpit. He remembered how it felt to have an engine come to life under him. It had been ten years, but he never really forgot.

"You miss flying?" John asked, voice low.

"Sometimes," Hadrian said. For a moment he was soaring again, the clouds a luminous floor beneath him, the sky an endless sea above. Then he thought of the wars, the death. The vision soured. "Not always."

Just then, Maggie climbed inside with Bernard at her heels, the door slamming shut behind them. She sat across from them and fastened her seat belt as the propellers roared to life outside the plane. Bernard moved to sit beside her, his posture relaxed, expression serene. He wore black stealth gear, like Maggie, and like her, it fit him well.

"What's the plan?" Hadrian half shouted over the noise. There was a lurch, and the plane began sliding backward.

"Charlotte'll get us to Paris in two hours," Maggie shouted back. "We've got transport waiting for us at the airstrip."

"And then?"

Bernard lifted his hand and made a fist. "We get him back. And crush *la Bête* for good."

Hadrian watched as his expression morphed from still and serene to anger. "What'd he do to you?" Hadrian half shouted.

Bernard shook his head. "Do I need a reason to hate an evil man?" He shook his head. "Besides, he is an embarrassment to my country."

"Right." Hadrian sat back, feeling the plane turn and move forward. Out the window, he could see the runway lights moving slowly, then faster past them as the plane picked up speed. There was a bump, and they were airborne. The noise quieted as they entered the atmosphere and the world outside fell away.

"Now, listen up," Maggie said and leaned forward. "Here's what we'll do…."

CHAPTER 33

MAX WAS dreaming. There was a cabin in the woods, and Hadrian was sitting beside him in front of a fire, one arm wrapped around his shoulders, the other gently entwined with his right hand. They were safe. They were warm. They—

His eyes opened. It took Max a moment to remember why he was sleeping beneath a softly blurred Baroque canopy.

Cool blue light filtered through the window, lightening everything yet giving the world a sense of the unreal. A gray day that had started without him. When he breathed, his chest felt heavy, and he remembered Hadrian was dead.

Shifting, he reached beneath his pillow to feel the heavy wooden handle of the steak knife he'd smuggled out of dinner the night before. He would use it today. He could not leave with Jean Claude, no matter the threats to his family.

The night before he'd braced himself for Jean Claude to appear again, to make good on his promise that Max would… well. He'd held the knife at the ready, prepared, or so he thought, to attack when Jean Claude appeared. But he'd never come, and Max had finally fallen asleep from sheer exhaustion sometime in the early morning.

He took a breath, opening his eyes farther, and looked outside to see storm clouds filling the sky, turning everything as dim and empty as he felt. It was a good day for death. The thought was melodramatic, but Max embraced it. *Good.* He felt damn melodramatic.

Preoccupied with these dark thoughts, it took him a moment to feel the presence in his room. When he did, he froze, his hand still gripping the knife handle.

"You are awake," said a familiar voice.

Max slipped his hand out from beneath the pillow and turned to find Adelaide sitting beside his bed. Groping at the bedside table for his glasses, he slipped them on to see she wore an elegant summer dress, the print floral and pink, as bright as she was cold. Reflexively, he pulled the sheets closer, then sat up.

"It is late," she went on. "Two in the afternoon."

"You watch people in their sleep now?" Max forced himself to sound brave while shivers of fear crawled up his spine. She'd always given him the creeps, even when he'd first started dating Jean Claude and thought she was just an assistant. Of course, now he had good reason to fear her.

"I've been thinking." She was so still, he wasn't entirely sure she was breathing. "Jean Claude made a mistake bringing you here."

"Yeah?"

"I would have shot you in Prague. Made a clean break of this mess."

Ice filled Max's veins. She shifted her position, and he saw something black and heavy in her lap. "Is that why you're here?" Max asked. Exhaustion dragged at him. He was so tired. "If you're going to shoot me, shoot me."

She watched him another moment. "No," she finally said, sounding almost thoughtful. "It would be easier, but I won't do it. I also won't take that knife from you."

Max's heart stopped. "Knife? What are you—?"

"The one under your pillow. You took it from the table last night. Jean Claude would have seen it if he hadn't been so distracted," Adelaide finished. "You're far from subtle."

Max's thoughts raced as his pulse slowly calmed down. She knew about the knife, but she was acting so strangely. Why was she watching him sleep? If she wasn't going to kill him, what did she want?

"Why not take it from me?" Max said, voice even despite the trembling in his arm. "I'm going to try to kill him, you know. I won't let him touch me."

The look Adelaide gave him was almost pitying. "You couldn't hurt him with that if you wanted to. He knows how to handle a knife. Besides—you're not a killer."

The words stung, but he knew they were true. "Then why…?"

"I told you. It would be better if you were dead. For everyone, I mean," she finished. "A knife to the wrist is neater than a bullet." She stood and walked to the door, the gun hanging heavy from her hand, leaving Max shocked into silence. Then she stopped, as if remembering something. "Jean Claude won't be back till this evening," she said, face impassive once more. "After that we're leaving for New York. Security will be much tighter there. So take today to do whatever you need to, in privacy. I'll keep the guards in the hall."

She left as if nothing had passed between them at all.

Max was a shaking, sweaty mess. As soon as he heard the door shut, he gasped, panic sending him shuddering in the wake of her words. His body shook with it. This evening—and now he knew for sure. His life had a time limit on it. He would not let Jean Claude take him anywhere.

His hands still shaking, he reached beneath his pillow and pulled out the knife. It was sharp, heavy. The best quality, meant for making fast work of thick meat. He lifted the blade to his wrist and imagined what it would take to plunge it in.

Then his eyes burned. He felt tears well up, not of sadness but of rage. He realized, in that moment, that he did not want to die like this.

He would not give Adelaide the satisfaction. He wouldn't use it on himself.

But Jean Claude....

Max pushed the knife away from himself, let the light play off the blade. He gripped the handle tight, thinking of what he might be capable of, if pushed.

God knew he'd been pushed enough.

The loss of Hadrian ate at him like a black hole. He loved him. He knew it, now that it was too late to tell him. And Jean Claude had taken that away from him, like he'd taken so many other things.

A cold resolve hardened around Max's heart as he gripped the knife. Adelaide was only half-right. Maybe he wasn't a killer, but he was a very angry man, and that might just be enough. He would wait for Jean Claude and be ready. One way or another, it would end tonight.

CHAPTER 34

HADRIAN, WITH a blonde and voluptuous version of Maggie on his arm, stepped out into the Paris evening. He grunted uncomfortably under the streetlights and reached up to yank at his neck where Maggie had insisted he wear a bowtie. It was the last piece of a tuxedo ensemble that made him feel ridiculous. Maggie, on the other hand, was a picture of elegance in an understated black dress and deceptively sturdy heels that suited her beautifully. Above them, the first stars twinkled in the periwinkle sky, watching over the City of Light. The street itself was crowded. Cars zoomed over the cobblestones, and pedestrians, mostly clad in fine evening wear, dominated the sidewalks.

They paused on the sidewalk, waiting for the traffic to slow. Across from them, Le Royal gleamed in the night, spilling gold into the street, its front gardens lit with fairy lights and carefully placed lanterns. It wasn't a tall building by Parisian standards, with only seven floors. But it was wide and stately, the architecture turn-of-the-century French and dripping with class. The hotel dominated the block in the way that all old, rich things do—subtly, but with unmistakable grandeur.

Hadrian took this in with a scowl, then reached up to scratch his cheek.

"Watch it," Maggie hissed, as his hand brushed his face. "You'll screw up your makeup."

Hadrian rolled his eyes but lowered his hand. Maggie had spent the better part of the afternoon working laboriously to change Hadrian's appearance. When she'd finished, he'd lost his sharp cheekbones, and his eyes had been changed from blue to brown. A wig that gave him a ponytail completed the disguise. "I didn't sign up to be your Barbie doll," Hadrian said. "Look like an idiot."

"A rich idiot," Maggie corrected. "One who won't be noticed having dinner in a place like Le Royal. Would you rather Jean Claude and his cronies spot you and have Max killed?"

"Obviously not," Hadrian snapped.

"Then shut the hell up and stop making me regret bringing you on this mission," she said, tightening her grip on his arm.

He sighed, wishing John was going in with him. He still didn't trust Maggie. But since Jean Claude thought John was alive and Hadrian dead, it had been clear that only Hadrian could enter the hotel with Maggie without putting himself in danger of being spotted. The makeup was an insurance plan, as was John's gun, tucked discreetly into the waistband of Hadrian's trousers where his jacket would hide the bulge.

Charlotte and Bernard had already left to begin their part. They'd been dressed as sharply as he was, her in a wool shift dress and fur coat, him in a suit that had to have cost more than Hadrian's apartment. They'd been spared the goofy makeup, though that hadn't taken the scowl off Charlotte's face. Small suitcases were all they'd needed to complete their cover as wealthy tourists, checking into Le Royal for a night of Parisian beauty.

"John's in position," Maggie said, tapping the microphone she'd disguised as a diamond earring in her right ear. Hadrian glanced behind them to the small pension where they'd taken a room. John was waiting on the third floor, a long-view camera in hand pointed at the front door of the hotel. Earlier it had been Charlotte on duty with the camera. She'd been the one to see Jean Claude leave that afternoon, and no one had spotted him since.

"He'll let us know if Jean Claude returns. If we can find Max and extract him before then, we'll save ourselves a lot of heartache. And if we find Adelaide, she'll lead us to him. Remember: Max is the priority tonight."

"He damn well better be," Hadrian added grimly.

Maggie nodded. Taking advantage of a gap in traffic, they hurried across the street. "I know this is deeply personal for you. But try not to get me killed, all right?"

"I'll do my best."

The gardens were empty, save for a nodding doorman who held open the large, double-door entrance to the hotel. Stepping past him into the foyer of Le Royal, Hadrian was blinded by opulence. The lobby soared overhead, with walls painted a pristine white edged with cream marble and gold trim. Waterfall chandeliers sent light sparkling through the lobby, flickering off red velvet carpets and the gleaming red uniforms of the hotel staff. It didn't escape him, however, that some of the "staff" was stiffer and more alert looking than the average bellboy. He noted their placements—undoubtedly security—as he and Maggie bypassed the check-in desk.

Beyond the lobby, the hotel split in two directions. On the left stood a bank of elevators and a grand staircase that swept upward into the hotel. On the right was a marble arch that led to a ballroom filled with dinner tables. At the back of the ballroom, floor-to-ceiling windows showed off the Eiffel Tower to grand effect. It was a romantic room, but Hadrian, again, felt uncomfortable. There was too much money. He felt the wealth like an itch against his skin just as his wig scratched at his scalp.

They turned right and paused just inside the arch, waiting to be served. Maggie had used SHAPE's influence to get them a reservation under assumed names, in keeping with their cover. So far no one had taken a second look at them. Hadrian bit his cheek, thinking maybe the wig had been a good idea after all.

"Remember," Maggie said, as she stood peering at the Eiffel Tower with appropriate disinterest. "Keep your eyes peeled. You remember what they look like? It's possible that Jean Claude snuck in the back."

Maggie had shown him photographs of their targets on the plane. He'd been taken aback by Jean Claude, his haughty profile. He'd hoped for something ugly. Hadn't been prepared for the handsome photograph Maggie had handed him, or the visceral hate that swept through him when he looked at those cold eyes.

The other photograph had been of a tall, broad-shouldered woman with a beautiful face. Jean Claude's assistant, a woman named Adelaide, who was as cold-blooded as her employer. According to Maggie, she was the one who'd drugged John and Karel and done the actual kidnapping.

Hadrian nodded, seeing both their faces in the back of his mind.

"Good," Maggie said and nodded to the waiter approaching them. She gave their fake names, and they followed the waiter to a table at the edge of the dining area. They had a good view of the rest of the room. As of yet, it was relatively empty, but there were a few tables of guests dressed as they were and more were coming in behind them.

"*Que désirez-vous, mademoiselle?*" the waiter asked.

217

Maggie responded in perfect French. They began a conversation that Hadrian, whose French had been limited to curse words learned from other UN soldiers, quickly tuned out. Instead, he turned his attention to the dining room, subtly surveying it as best as he could.

It was filling up quickly, in twos and threes and a few larger parties. The volume in the room grew higher, filling the air with light chatter and the chink of silverware against china plates. As Maggie's voice died down and the waiter wandered away, Hadrian let his mind grow still. It was an exercise in instinct, letting the subconscious see what his conscious mind could not. He panned the room, scanning faces, waiting for that little tug of something that seemed off.

"Hadrian—do you see her?" Maggie suddenly said. She nodded subtly at the entrance to the ballroom, and Hadrian turned as if he were looking for the waiter.

There. He recognized the statuesque brunette by her long hair, the cold expression on her face. Adelaide stood near the entranceway, surveying the ballroom with apparent disinterest. She wore a vibrant red dress that only emphasized the cold distance on her face.

From the corner of his eye, Hadrian saw Maggie gently brush her ear. "Charlotte, we've got eyes on A. No sign of the Beast. Hit communication."

"They're in position," she said, to Hadrian this time. "Ready to go on our word."

A man dressed all in black came up to Adelaide. Hadrian pegged him as security, judging from his wide shoulders and the nondescript suit he wore. He leaned into Adelaide and whispered something in her ear. Her expression never changed, but her body stiffened. Nodding, she lifted something square and black to her mouth. A walkie-talkie. She spoke into it, then frowned down at the device.

"Charlotte's frequency jammer worked, which should keep the gendarmes out of our hair," Maggie said, watching from the corner of her eye as Adelaide slowly lowered the walkie-talkie, her face like stone. She whirled, turning away and striding quickly from the ballroom, the bodyguard at her side.

"You ready?" Maggie asked, glancing at him.

Hadrian took a deep breath. They were so close. They didn't have room for anything to go wrong. "Now or never," he said, clenching his fist to hide its shaking.

Maggie smiled as if he'd said something funny and brushed her ear again. "Clear the building, Charlotte."

There was a second of calm before the fire alarms screeched to life. A faint smell of smoke filtered into the air—Bernard's handywork, done with a smoke bomb dropped into the main air vent. Hadrian had a visceral memory of the U Medvídků fire, of being trapped in the kitchen, before shaking his head with a violent jerk and hurrying to his feet.

It was amazing how quickly even the most civilized situation could turn ugly, Hadrian thought. Around them, panicked people had already begun scrambling for the exit, creating a bottleneck of expensive silks and furs that clogged the entrance to the ballroom. Maggie and Hadrian waded into the chaos as the loud clangs overhead bounced across the massive room, shaking the glasses left abandoned on the tables. Finally they fought their way past elbows and stomping feet to the hall outside. There, more people were running down the main staircase and pouring out of the halls, their expressions alternating between panic and annoyance. Hadrian was glad for his height as he strained to see over their heads, searching for Adelaide.

"Where the hell is she?" Maggie hissed.

Hadrian scanned the sea of people, not finding anyone tall enough to be her. Then he caught a flash of brown hair and red silk at the top of the grand staircase, moving against the tide of escaping people.

"There—the stairs," Hadrian said, grabbing Maggie's arm.

"Move it before we lose her again!"

Together they fought their way through the distracted crowd. Hadrian prayed his disguise would hold as they moved past scared men and women, ducking behind them to avoid the gaze of the hotel staff trying desperately to coordinate the evacuation.

Finally they reached the top of the staircase, where the stream of people finally trickled to a halt. The alarms still raged, pounding against his eardrums. Here in the halls, blinking blue and red lights strobed across the doors and carpet, adding visual confusion to the disorienting noise. Hadrian shook it off as they turned left into a long hallway, at the end of which were a mirrored wall and a pair of elevators, one of whose doors were just closing. They hurried down the hall, watching the numbers tick above the elevator doors, going up to the seventh and final floor.

"That's where they have him," Maggie shouted over the noise. Her face turned blue as an alarm light rolled across her.

Hadrian was already jamming on the Up button. A few seconds later, the elevator beside them opened. They stepped inside a largely silent room, which was disorienting after the explosion of sound and color in the hallway, and Hadrian found himself fighting a spurt of dizziness.

"Remember—we want things quiet until the last possible moment," Maggie said as the doors slid closed. The elevator whirred smoothly to life, the rich design barely registering any movement. If not for the numbers ticking up on the elevator's console, Hadrian wouldn't have known they were moving.

"I know," Hadrian growled.

Suddenly the elevator stopped, lurching to a halt at floor six. "She's jammed the elevators," Maggie cursed, leaning on the Door Closed button. "I was hoping we'd have more time before she could gather her security team.... Shit. They'll be waiting for us. You ready for that?"

Hadrian nodded and pulled out John's gun as Maggie did the same with hers without letting go of the elevator button.

"Charlotte," she said into the air. "You got eyes on the exits?" She nodded, then looked at Hadrian with a sigh of relief. "They haven't left. Great. Be ready for my signal. And try not to get shot on me, okay? I don't want to think about the incident report if I lose a civvie in this."

Hadrian took a deep breath, battle-calmness coming over him. His hands were steady on the trigger as he moved to the left of the doors. Finally, something he was good at.

Maggie gave him one last look, nodded, then released her hold on the button before ducking to the right. The elevator doors sprung open with a ping.

"Freeze!" said a loud, authoritative voice.

Maggie shifted position on her gun, gripping the barrel so the handle pointed outward. "Don't shoot," she called out, shifting the gun into view of the open doorway.

"Come out" called a different voice—a woman's.

Maggie carefully sidled into view, her hands in the air. She stepped into the hall, and he braced himself for a gunshot. None came.

"The other one too," said the same woman.

Hadrian bit his lip. Fighting his instincts, he put his hands and the gun behind his head and stepped out to join Maggie. In the hall, a half a dozen gun barrels pointed at them, all held by men and women with blank faces and dark suits.

At the other end of the hall, Adelaide stood, arms akimbo, her expression still cold. "I believe we have arrested some terrorists," she said. "Don't move, or we're within our legal rights to shoot. Fatally."

Hadrian's belly clenched, the tension in the air sending sweat dripping down his face. This was it.

Beside him, Maggie bent slightly at the knees, bracing herself, and he did the same. "It's too bad you're in the kidnapping business," Maggie suddenly said, smiling at Adelaide across the sea of guns. Hadrian felt a begrudging wave of admiration for her cheek as Adelaide moved her dead eyes to Maggie. "I didn't want to do this, you know. It's a really nice building."

Adelaide's expression never changed. She started to say something, but before she could speak, Maggie leaned her head against her shoulder.

"Charlotte," she said, voice calm. Then she threw herself to the floor, Hadrian milliseconds behind her, as an explosion rocked the hallway.

CHAPTER 35

MAX SAT at the end of his bed, the knife beside him.

It was dark outside. His second night in Paris. A bitter chuckle burst from his lips. Unbidden, a conversation with Hadrian popped into his mind, the remembered voice like splintered glass.

"Where would you go? Someplace you haven't been," Hadrian had said. They'd been in a coffee shop, the table small enough that their knees brushed.

Max had gripped his tea and smiled as he answered truthfully. "Paris. My father spent a year there in college, and he talked about it all the time. Well, the food, really. I want to eat French food in France, and Paris seems the place to do it."

Hadrian laughed. "I don't know what answer I was expecting, but that's the best motivation I've heard yet."

Max had rolled his eyes, then let the topic drop. He'd thought, at the time, that he'd never get to Paris, not with Jean Claude hunting for him.

Now… well, he wasn't sure if this was true irony or not, but it felt that way. When he'd dreamed of it, Paris had been a place of lights and beauty, delicate foods, and silken wine. Sitting there, discussing it with Hadrian, he'd allowed himself the fantasy of the two of them together in the City of Light. Too late now. Much, much too late.

He blinked slowly and looked down at his hands. The time for daydreaming was over. He had to steel himself for what was coming. Clenching his fists, he thought of everything Jean Claude had taken from him. His name. His life. His business. What he had left of his father.

And—more than anything—Hadrian. There would be no Paris trip for the two of them, and Jean Claude was to blame.

It was night now, almost time for Jean Claude to return. He'd expected Adelaide to come before this, to check and see if he was still alive, and to confiscate the knife if he was. But she'd never shown. Max wasn't sure what that meant, but he did know two very important things. Jean Claude would be coming—and Max still had his weapon. Grabbing the knife in both hands, he took in one last look of the view from his bedroom. The Eiffel Tower, turning gold as the dark fell and her lights bloomed, really was a beautiful sight. Max took a deep breath, soaking the tower in, before turning his back to the bedroom.

Walking through the darkened living room, he hurried to the door of the suite and crouched beside it. His hands were slick with sweat, and he had to wipe them on his jeans a few times before he could grip the handle without dropping the knife. In his mind he made a mantra of all the wrongs Jean Claude had done to him and repeated it in a loop, over and over again. Giving himself strength.

His name. His work. Hadrian. His name. His work. Hadr—

He lost his place as the room suddenly erupted in sound. A harsh, screeching noise that had to be the building's fire alarm was pulsing through his ears. He cried out, covering them as he tried the door handle. It was locked, of course. Max bit his lip, then glanced at the balcony doors open at the other end of the room. He caught a whiff of smoke, and a wave of panic ran through him. He'd prepared himself for death at Jean Claude's hands, or so he thought. But a fire?

"Shit."

Letting the knife rest at his side, Max hurried to the balcony and threw open the doors before running to the waist-high railing at the balcony's edge. The noise from the alarm was louder outside as it blared from every open window in the building. He could see flashing strobe lights from lower floors and a growing group of people gathering in the lawn below.

Clearly people were evacuating. Except for him, of course.

"You lousy asshole!" Max cursed, not sure who exactly was his target—Adelaide, Jean Claude, life in general. He ran back inside, grabbed the phone, and held it up to his ear. Beneath the screeches, he couldn't hear anything. He pressed a few buttons, realized it was dead, and dropped it to the ground. He rubbed his temples, trying to think. Maybe if he got the bed sheets and tied them together—Jean Claude wasn't such a bastard that he'd leave Max to burn to death—was he?

Max reevaluated that thought. Maybe this was Jean Claude's way of punishing him for everything. He'd decided to kill him after all.

Without warning the room shook beneath him, knocking him to the ground as an explosion rocked the building and sent pictures crashing to the floor. A glass vase shattered as it fell from the mantle above the fireplace, sending shards of glass through the room. The alarms abruptly stopped as the shaking slowed, leaving Max in a dizzying silence. He struggled to stand, pushing himself to his feet, the knife still, miraculously, in hand. As he did so, he heard a steady *pop pop pop* drift its way into the quiet. Muffled screams followed. They seemed to be coming from below his room.

His fear blended with confusion as he froze and listened carefully. More gunfire, lots of it. Another explosion, quieter this time. Shouting.

Had a war broken out in the hotel? Another shadow company come to fight Jean Claude? Or some kind of terrorist plot?

It would be just his luck, to be kidnapped and land in an unrelated war zone.

There was another noise beneath the gunfire, this one closer. A door banged open in the hall and footsteps sounded, someone big pounding along the floor, coming closer. Max blanched and considered hiding. He'd seen footage of ISIS terrorists in hotels and schools, and it wasn't exactly how he wanted to die. But then he remembered his resolve and why he was standing by the door in the first place. It might be a terrorist—or it might be Jean Claude coming to take him away from the hotel.

"Hadrian," Max said aloud. It filled him with strength, even as his heart sped up and fear threatened to freeze him in place. Bracing himself, Max gripped his knife and prepared to attack.

The door flung open, and an unfamiliar man burst inside. Max didn't give him a chance to strike first. He howled and leapt at the stranger, knife raised above his head and ready to slash. The other man was quick. He ducked neatly to the side, and Max slammed into the wall shoulder-first. The knife clattered to the floor.

Pain registered as a distant, dull throb as Max pushed himself to his feet. The stranger hadn't moved and was staring at him with hands raised. His mouth was open, as if he were talking, but Max couldn't hear him over the roaring of his own blood. It wasn't Jean Claude, but that didn't mean anything. It could be a henchman, someone worse, and he was coming closer.

"You're not taking me to New York," Max cried, scrabbling for the knife. Again, he charged, his reason lost in desperation.

The stranger—and there was something familiar about him, but then, Max didn't know anyone with such an ugly ponytail—caught his wrist, twisting his hand to send the knife flying.

Before Max knew what was happening, he was on the floor, his cheek pressed to the hardwood and a knee pushing with surprisingly gentle force into his back. He listened to muffled gunshots from the floor below, panting hard.

"Now," said the voice, and this was familiar too. Painfully so. "I'm going to stand up, and then you're going to stand and not attack me, all right?"

Max said nothing, his mind working to understand what was happening. That voice was so familiar. Why was it familiar?

"All right, lad?" the man asked again.

"Don't call me that," Max snapped, not realizing what he was doing. He pushed up against the ground, but found it useless under the weight of the man's knee. "Don't...."

"Max," the voice said again. There was a ripping noise, and something dark and hairy fell to the floor by Max's face. The weight lifted from his back, but still Max couldn't move. Something strange was happening. "Stand up, love. Look at me."

An icy hand gripped Max's heart. He thought he... but it was impossible. A trick too painful to believe. And yet he had to see for himself.

Bracing himself against the ground, Max pushed up onto his knees, then stood. Then, tearing the Band-Aid off, he turned, ready to confront....

"Hadrian," Max whispered.

The ponytail was gone, revealing his familiar shorn hair. There was something strange about the face, but Max could see the edges of makeup, could see Hadrian emerging from whatever he'd smeared onto himself.

"No," Max said, shaking his head. "This is a trick. Something Jean Claude cooked up. Your eyes are wrong," he said, and backed away, shaking his head.

Maybe-Hadrian cursed, then fumbled at his eyes. When he looked up again, they were a familiar ice-blue. He hurried forward, grabbed the tops of Max's arms, and gave him a little shake. "It's me. I'm real. I swear it."

"No," Max moaned. He didn't realize he was crying until he felt the tears drip from his chin. "You're dead. The fire—Jean Claude had you killed...."

Hadrian smiled, keeping his blue eyes fixed on Max. "Didn't take. I'm tougher than all that, lad."

"I...." Max lifted a hand, ran it down Hadrian's cheek, and felt the stubble he remembered, the sharp contours of his cheekbones emerging from beneath his makeup. "Why did you have a ponytail?"

Hadrian barked a laugh, a short, harsh sound. "I had to have a disguise. Apparently, 'ponytailed ponce' was the only one in my size."

And suddenly Max believed him. Choking back a sob, he threw his arms around Hadrian's neck and kissed him with everything he had. Hadrian answered in kind, pulling him flush against him, crushing his lips with his own. Max delighted in it—in Hadrian's hard body, the smooth muscles holding him tight, the shorn hair he couldn't stop running his hands over. He kissed Hadrian until he really knew he was alive, kissed him because he couldn't say the thousands of things he wanted to. How afraid he'd been. How much he needed him.

Then Max pulled back and met Hadrian's eyes. "I love you," he blurted out. "I know it's been so fast and you probably want nothing to do with me and you almost died but, Christ, I've got to tell you. I love you, Hadrian." He gasped, then fell silent as words abruptly failed him.

A slow smile spread over Hadrian's face, sending Max's heart fluttering. "I love you too."

Another round of gunfire burst through the air, shocking them back into reality.

Hadrian grabbed Max's hand and tugged him toward the door. "C'mon. It's a long story, but I've got a secret agent downstairs and a few others waiting for us. They'll get you out of here, take us someplace safe...."

Max started to go with him, then pulled back, stricken with horror, as he remembered what Jean Claude had said to him. "I can't," Max said, face going white. "Jean Claude... he'll kill John if I leave. Karel too."

Hadrian shook his head, smiling harder. "No, lad, that's the thing—they're safe. Karel's in a safe house as we speak, and John's across the road, waiting with our getaway car. He's got nothing left on you. I promise. You're safe now."

Max still shook his head. "But he'll come after me. Who are you working with, the FBI? Interpol? He's got people everywhere." Cold fear sent Max shivering, cutting through any relief he'd felt. "And he'll kill you, Hadrian. Once he knows you're alive…. God, he'll really kill you this time. I can't believe you came here. You've got to get away!" Max felt sobs building in his chest. He let Hadrian pull him to him, let Hadrian hold him tight, as all the fear of the last few days threatened to take him over.

"Here's the thing," Hadrian said, his voice low in Max's ear. "I don't believe that's true. You've friends now, friends higher than the FBI, than Interpol. And they need you alive." He pulled back slightly and cradled Max's head in his hands. "You'll need to testify, lad. And we'll probably have to go into hiding for some time."

"We'll?" Max asked, raising an eyebrow.

Hadrian nodded. "I'm not leaving your side again. Not so long as you'll have me. And I'll help you through this, and at the end, you'll be safe."

Max took a deep breath and looked into Hadrian's blue eyes. Did he trust him? Did he believe what Hadrian was saying?

Max let out a breath and felt his entire body relax. He did.

"Okay," Max said, surprising himself with the strength in his voice. Fear melted away in the face of Hadrian's confidence, and Max felt his spine stiffen. "Then get me the hell out of here so we can skewer the bastard."

Hadrian grinned and did a little fake bow. "If you'll follow me—"

There was a sharp *pop*. Hadrian looked down at his chest, confused. Max followed his gaze. There, just below his breastbone on the right side, a dark stain was spreading. There was another *pop*, and Hadrian's shoulder jerked forward.

"Lad, run—" he choked out before collapsing face-forward onto the ground.

Leaving Jean Claude standing in the doorway, chest heaving, handgun pointed straight at Max.

"No!" Max shouted, falling to his knees beside Hadrian. He sobbed, tears flowing freely, as he pressed down on Hadrian's wounds, putting pressure on them. Hadrian was choking, his chest heaving as he tried to breathe and coughed up blood instead. Red spread along Max's hands. He pulled off his sweater and held the wool to Hadrian's chest, ignoring the demon that stood in the door and stared at him.

"Leave him," Jean Claude said, his voice rich with disdain. "He will be dead in minutes. You can do nothing else."

"You piece of shit," Max hissed, his eyes not leaving Hadrian's blue ones. Hadrian was staring up at him, his mouth trying to form words. Failing. Max could only sob and try to press harder on his wounds, knowing it was no good. There was too much blood.

"Come with me now. Or I will shoot you too."

"Go ahead!" Max spat. He looked at Jean Claude, his teeth bared. "Do it. Kill me!"

There was a deadness in Jean Claude's eyes. A kind of removed madness. "You'd like that. But then… no." He shook his head. "No, *cher*. I'll not give up on you so easily." With a small sigh, he turned the gun from Max to point at Hadrian. "Come away from him or I'll shoot him again. Perhaps it would be kinder—like putting down a dog."

"No," Max sobbed. Shaking, he ran a bloody hand down Hadrian's face, willing him to live, somehow. "I'll come with you. Don't hurt him."

Hadrian tried to grab his hand as he stood. It took everything Max had to pull away and leave him bleeding on the floor. He stood, and Jean Claude came farther into the room, walking toward the balcony.

"Come," Jean Claude said again, pausing.

Max sent one last look at Hadrian. There were feet running toward the room from down the hall. He looked up and saw a woman dressed in black, her face bruised. Another woman and a man, both wearing torn resort wear, followed on her heels.

"Max!" the woman cried, and Max did a double take.

"Maggie?" he called, shocked to see his classmate running toward him, gun in hand.

She barreled into the room before stopping to raise her gun, taking aim at Jean Claude. "You're under arrest for kidnapping, attempted murder, and conspiracy to commit theft. Put your weapons down and raise your hands above your head. Comply now or I have the authority to shoot."

Jean Claude sneered. With snakelike quickness, he reached out and pulled Max flush against his chest. At the same time, he brought his gun up and pressed it into Max's temple. "What rock did you crawl out of to threaten me?" he snapped. His grip on Max's shoulder was painful. Despite the drama, Max couldn't tear his eyes away from Hadrian on the ground. The man with Maggie was kneeling over him, applying pressure to his wounds, but the blood was still seeping onto the ground around him.

"Follow and I shoot him."

Jean Claude began walking backward, dragging an unresisting Max with him. The balcony doors at their back were propped open, and Max met Maggie's eyes as they stepped outside together. They blazed with helpless anger.

The night air cooled Max's cheeks. He could hear shouting and more crashes from inside the building. In the distance, wailing sirens grew louder as they approached the hotel. "What are you doing?" Max half shouted, as Jean Claude yanked him around the corner, away from the room and closer to the edge of the balcony. It was a wide space, meant for meals and lounging. The tower rose majestically in the distance, blotting out the rest of the sky.

"Waiting for our transport," Jean Claude said, his grip tightening on Max's arm. There was a whirring sound, and Max looked up to see a helicopter approaching from the distance.

"They'll arrest you," Max said, desperate. "You've got witnesses now, and you shot someone in public. You can't get away!"

Jean Claude snorted. "Why? Because I escaped a deliberate terrorist attack and defended my life against a dangerous man who set off bombs in my hotel? Whoever that bitch is working for is not going to risk exposing their agents to a trial. They can pin no crime on me, not without you." His hand tightened.

"Then you should kill me," Max said.

"I told you before. I love you, more than anything in this world." Jean Claude pulled Max to him, smashed his lips onto Max's mouth, and forced Max's open, his tongue an invader, dominating. It was too close to

Hadrian's last kiss, too close to that brief moment of hope. Max bit down hard, tasting blood before Jean Claude threw him back with a cry of pain.

"You—how could you?" Jean Claude snarled, his voice thickening as his tongue swelled.

Max spat Jean Claude's blood onto the ground. "Fuck you."

Something like sorrow came over Jean Claude's face, cut through with rage. He held up his gun and pointed it at Max. "Fine, *cher*. I tried." Tears ran down his face. "Good-bye."

Max snapped. He looked down the barrel of the gun and thought of Hadrian bleeding inside. His vision clouded with anger. Jean Claude would get away with it, get away with so many sins.

With a scream of raw, primal pain, Max launched himself at Jean Claude, grabbing him around the middle. They teetered there, at the edge of the roof, for just a moment. Then, with a roaring sound screaming in Max's ears, they went over the edge.

CHAPTER 36

HOSPITALS, JOHN reflected, were the same everywhere you went. Of course, the field hospital in Iraq, a glorified tent set up in the middle of the desert, had been a bit draftier. But the principals remained: uncomfortable seating, sterile white halls, doctors and nurses rushing past with exhaustion in their eyes.

He shifted on the hard chair outside Max's room, wishing more than anything to be home. He bent forward, letting his head drop into his hands. He couldn't escape the antiseptic smell that permeated the air, the soft beeping of machines from the open door beside him. Only the fact that the announcements were in French told him they were still in Paris.

A gentle hand landed on his shoulder. He sat up to see Karel, a cup of coffee in hand.

"It is not bad," Karel said, holding it out to John. "We have worse at our offices."

John nodded his thanks, took the cardboard cup, brought it to his mouth, and drank deeply. It was bitter, in just the right way for the mood he was in.

Karel looked past John, through the thick glass into the small private room where Max lay hooked up to about a million beeping machines. "Any change?"

John shook his head. "Doctor said it might be a few days. Could be today. You never know with these kinds of things." He sighed, a heavy sound full of regret. He couldn't help but blame himself for this. He kept running scenarios in his head. If only he'd gone in too, instead of waiting outside. If he'd been more alert in the first place, when that scumbag had drugged him and Karel. If….

Karel looked down at him, eyes narrowed. "This is not your fault, John," he said, reminding John just how perceptive he could be. It was wonderful, and highly annoying.

"I could've done more," John said, taking another sip of coffee.

In response, Karel sat beside him and took his hand.

John tightened their fingers together. Even now, deep in his self-loathing, he was glad to have Karel's hand in his.

He'd never forget the nightmare of their supposed rescue. He'd watched through his camera as the fire alarms in Le Royal had gone off, sending people flooding into the streets. At that point things had been going according to plan, but then—boom. The explosions were his first hint that something had gone wrong. It had taken everything he had not to run inside after them, but he'd had his job: watch for Jean Claude and call them on the special, jammer-safe phone Maggie had handed him. He'd had to bite his lip as the sound of gunfire echoed into the street, mixing with screams of hotel guests and passersby alike, the growing sirens of approaching police cars.

He'd waited an agonizing hour before getting the call from Maggie. She'd been in an ambulance, paramedics shouting in the background, and told him to get to the hospital, Hôtel-Dieu, as fast as he could.

"Max—is he...?" John had asked. His heart stopped as Maggie paused.

"No, but... it will be close, John. Just come as quickly as you can."

He'd sped off into the night, racing down the street into Paris proper before he could find a cab that would take him to the hospital. Once there, Maggie had met him in the emergency room, her gun still hot in her hand, her dress torn and smudged with smoke. She'd told him everything while simultaneously flashing her SHAPE badge at everything that moved. How Hadrian had been shot twice in the chest. How Max had gone over the edge, taking Jean Claude with him.

Now, he rehearsed the litany of injuries in his head. Broken knee and arm on his right side. Shattered femur on the left. Six broken ribs. A concussion. Max had been in a medically induced coma for the past week, and only this morning had the doctors pulled him out of it, letting him return to a more natural sleep.

He was supposed to have been safe with them. Now....

"John," Karel said, squeezing his hand.

John looked up and saw Maggie pushing a wheelchair down the hall. In the chair sat Hadrian, looking strange and uncomfortable in a pale hospital gown, his throat bruised from where they'd had to insert a breathing tube after his lung collapsed. He pulled an IV along with him, and white bandages peeked out from the gaping chest of his gown.

"Hadrian," John said, standing. "How're you doing?"

Hadrian scowled. "Feel like shit, what do you think? Look like a right idiot in this thing too," he said, plucking disdainfully at his gown. His voice was rough, still weak from the breathing tube.

"You'd look worse in a coffin," Maggie said frankly.

Hadrian scowled up at her. "Don't you have better things to do than push me around all day?"

"Nope. How many times do I have to tell you that I'm responsible for your security now? You're not getting rid of me anytime soon."

"Just great," Hadrian grumped. Then his face softened, and he looked toward Max's room. "Any changes…?"

John shook his head. "Doctor says it could be any moment now, or it might take another week. There's a lot of healing to do."

Hadrian nodded, his blue eyes troubled. "Well, if you don't mind, I'll go sit with him for a bit. Keep him company, like."

"Of course," John said. He stepped aside as Hadrian pushed himself to his feet, reaching to help steady him. Hadrian waved off help and managed to stand up straight enough.

"Careful," Maggie said, eyeing him up and down. "You did get shot in the chest. Twice. And also flatlined in the ambulance. Twice."

Hadrian rolled his eyes. "Been through worse. 'Scuse me."

John watched as he walked, semisteadily, into Max's room. He didn't miss how much Hadrian had to lean on his IV pole, but he said nothing. He'd been in Hadrian's position before and remembered how much he'd hated the coddling, the worry. He'd give Hadrian space.

"How about we go get some food," Maggie said, raising an eyebrow. "You two look like you could use the break. And, frankly, I'm starving."

John hesitated, not wanting to leave Max and Hadrian alone.

Maggie must have read his worry because she waved at the ends of the hall to where Charlotte and Bernard were standing with forced casualness. "SHAPE's got this on lockdown. They'll be safe. I promise."

Karel squeezed his hand, and with a last look back, John nodded and followed Maggie down the hall.

CHAPTER 37

MAX'S FATHER stood in their kitchen in New York City, a pot on the stove. He was stirring it with a wooden spoon, sending strong earthy flavors rising into the air. His beef stew.

No, Max's mind insisted. It was goulash.

His father turned, smiled at him, but didn't speak a word. Instead, he picked up a bowl, ladled the goulash into it, and added three dumplings from a pan next to the stove.

Max took it to the table and sat. There was a newspaper beside his seat, open to the obituary pages. He picked it up and scanned through the lists of the dead before coming upon a familiar name.

William Mracek (1987-2015)
William was found dead in his apartment.
He was the successful owner of Book Life,
a book repair shop located in the East Village.
He is survived by no one.

Max stopped reading, setting the newspaper down. It didn't seem to matter. Instead, he turned to his goulash and scooped up the fragrant broth, bringing it to his mouth. Only, when he went to taste it, there was nothing.

A noise at the edge of his consciousness was trying to break through. Max shook his head, as he would if a fly were buzzing about his ears. It didn't go away, but got louder. A persistent beeping, like the heartbeat of a machine.

His father patted him on the shoulder and walked out of the kitchen. Max watched him move away as the beeping grew louder.

Beep…. Beep…. Beep….

He tried to eat more goulash, but the room was growing darker, turning black. Soon, all he could see was his hand in front of his face, and then not even that.

He was lost in an ocean of black. Drowning in it.

A light in the distance—small, red, like the flare of a buoy, marking the edge of the bay. It pulled at Max, and he let it tug him forward, following that blinking light.

There was a gasp. He realized it was him. Slowly, carefully, he opened his eyes.

His first impression was a blur of white. It took him a long moment to filter out what he was seeing. A white-tiled ceiling and the long fluorescent bulbs used in offices and hospitals. A persistent beeping over a quiet thrum, like a machine breathing. The red light was on top of a metal box across from him, some kind of machine.

There was a curious floating sensation to his body, and his skin felt distant, removed. He had a moment of panic as he tried to move his limbs and failed, sending some machine beeping wildly.

"Shh, you're fine," said an urgent voice at his side.

Max felt a hand on his cheek and turned his head to meet Hadrian's deep blue eyes. Everything was blurry, which only added to the floating feeling.

"Stay calm. You've been asleep for a few days," Hadrian went on.

Max concentrated on Hadrian's thumb where it stroked his skin, letting it soothe him. Something came back to him then. Hadrian had been on the ground, there had been blood....

"You're...."

"I'm all right, lad," Hadrian soothed. He smiled, that wisecracking, crooked grin that Max loved. "Twice thought dead, didn't hold either time. Told you I was tough."

"Oh," Max said and leaned into Hadrian's hand. His skin felt warm, good. "The hospital gown makes your skin look green." His words sounded syrupy to his ears and his voice was hoarse. "Am I floating?"

Hadrian snorted. "Now, how'd you end up with all the good drugs, when I've got two holes in my chest?"

"I've never done drugs before. Kind of like it."

"Careful with that, lad."

"Shh," Max said. "Let me have this. It's been a long day. Month? Year?" He rolled his eyes, taking in the blurry outline of Hadrian. He was in a large armchair, pulled up to Max's bedside. His long body, usually so powerful, looked frail. But he was alive. "Still handsome," Max murmured. The grogginess was fading now. The floating persisted, but it was distant. He could feel his mind begin to work. "Why can't I move my arms and legs?"

Hadrian nodded at his body, then stroked his cheek again.

Max looked down to see his legs propped up in the air, wrapped in heavy plaster casts. His right arm was the same. Only his left arm was free. He raised it experimentally, pleased to see his fingers wiggling. "That's a lot of plaster."

"You did fall off a roof, love."

Max's heart doubled in his chest. "I like it when you call me that."

Hadrian blushed. "Yeah, yeah."

"It's nice," Max insisted. He thought another moment, then frowned. "Where are my glasses?"

Hadrian winced. "They broke, Max. When you…. Well, how much do you remember?"

Max frowned, forcing his mind to go back. Prague came first—he'd been coming home, found the door to the apartment open. There was a knife on the floor, and in the living room….

Everything rushed back.

Jean Claude's face, his cold eyes and hard smile, as he told him what he wanted. The knife. Attacking Hadrian by accident—the brief moment of joy as he realized he was alive, only to see him shot dead by that murderous bastard.

And then the roof.

Max inhaled sharply in remembered fear. It chased away whatever grogginess had been left in him. He again tasted Jean Claude's blood, felt the fear and adrenaline pump through him as he threw himself at Jean Claude. They'd tumbled into the open air, wind smacking their faces as they tumbled down, and then….

Pain. A great deal of pain.

"You've got to stay calm," Hadrian said, cutting through the memory. "Please, Max. Take a deep breath."

Max did as he asked and felt the fear fade slowly.

"I'm going to call the nurse," Hadrian said, reaching for a button. "You just woke up. This is too much for you—"

"No," Max said, his voice hoarse in his own ears. "Please. Tell me what happened."

Hadrian's blurry eyes met his. Max stared into them, willing him to understand. Finally, Hadrian nodded.

"Well—and this is all hearsay, mind you, as I was bleeding out on the floor. You two went over pretty quickly. Maggie found you afterward, got you to a hospital."

"Maggie?" Her face came back to him, her eyes wide as she ran into the room. "What was she doing there?"

Hadrian rolled his eyes. "Turns out she's some kind of super spy for an international organization called SHAPE. She's been watching you since you ran away from Jean Claude."

"She... what? *Maggie*?" Max asked, incredulous. "Midwestern, English teacher Maggie is a spy? But... we went drinking together!"

Hadrian shrugged. "In all this mess, is that the thing you have the most trouble believing?"

Max thought about it, then nodded for Hadrian to continue. He'd have to digest that later. And he and Maggie needed to have a very serious talk. "So Maggie found me, and what then?"

"We both came here," Hadrian went on quietly. "You almost died, you know. Not many people survive a seven-story fall. If it hadn't been for a few bushes at the bottom...."

"But I didn't die. We didn't," Max said, wishing he could touch Hadrian. He leaned into his hand again, hoping it would be enough.

Hadrian nodded. When he spoke, his voice was hoarse. "There was one other piece of good luck. Jean Claude—they think he broke your fall. Apparently you were on top of him when they found you."

Max took a deep breath to steady himself. "Is he...?"

Hadrian shook his head. "No, but it might have been a mercy if he were. He's paralyzed from the neck down. He can still talk, his mind is fine, but everything else... gone. The good news is, Maggie was able to fast-track a warrant to search his business offices here without the local government's interference. SHAPE has got enough to link him and Graywater to a dozen smuggling operations in the past ten years, international ones. That will keep the local governments from interfering.

And that's not even looking at murder charges. There's some chance he might be tried for committing war crimes...." He stopped.

Max was shaking his head, overwhelmed at everything Hadrian was saying. "And Adelaide?"

Here Hadrian paused. "She got away in the fighting. But they're looking for her. Won't be long till they find her either. You're in the clear, Max. Maggie says you'll have to testify, but... he can't come after you anymore."

Max felt his head spinning. Jail, war crimes. Jean Claude would be put away. Max was free. Of course, he was unhappy Adelaide had escaped. She'd made her feelings clear, after all, and Max didn't think he'd ever forget the way she'd looked at him when she told him to commit suicide. She was loyal to Jean Claude in a way he'd never encountered before.

He took a deep breath and let it out slowly as he pushed Adelaide from his mind. There was enough to worry about for now. Maybe—just this once—he'd trust to luck.

"Does that mean I'm safe?"

Hadrian nodded. "You could even return to New York, if you wanted," he said softly. "Take back your real name. Forget this all ever happened."

Max's eyes widened. Return to New York? Maybe he could claim the insurance money on his studio, if it wasn't too late... he still had his reputation in the book-repair community, he could see his apartment again... the streets of New York....

He felt Hadrian's tension beside him and smiled.

No, not anymore. If there was one thing he'd realized in the midst of all this chaos, it was that New York wasn't his home. Prague—with John and Karel, and Hadrian—that was home. He was building a new life there, and it was a good one. And now there was no more need to hide. He looked at Hadrian, really looked at him for the first time since he'd woken up, and saw a future he didn't mind walking into.

"Think my visa's still good?" Max finally said, eyes roving over Hadrian's stoic face. "I was thinking of setting up shop here, actually. Once I can move again."

Slowly, Hadrian broke into a grin. "I'm sure SHAPE can do that much. After all, they owe you."

"Yeah," Max said. He turned his head to nuzzle Hadrian's hand. "They really do."

There was a noise then, and Max turned his head to see John standing at the door, Karel just behind him. The next few moments were a quiet mix of gentle hugs and reassurances, a family reunited. Max felt loved, warm. The whole time, Hadrian by his side, he felt his choice had been confirmed.

He was home. He was with family. *His* family. And nothing would take him away from them ever again.

EPILOGUE

Later

THE EVENING air was cool, filled with the quiet sounds of crickets and night animals waking up to begin their days. Dusk had faded to the dark palette of the night sky, sprinkled throughout with distant silver stars. Here, just before the mountains of Český ráj, the darkness was unspoiled by electric lights. They had a pure view of the night, lined below by the edges of the great mountains and the forest before them.

Hadrian would never get tired of the view.

He sat back in the cushioned loveseat he'd dragged outside Ivan's cottage, letting the crackling fire pit warm his feet as he folded his hands across his taut waist. Behind him, quiet music drifted into the night, punctuated by happy laughter and occasionally singing. Cups clinked and plates were scraped. It was a happy, joyous noise.

Hadrian sighed. They'd all needed this night.

The hospital in Paris had kept them for an agonizing month of steadily increasing boredom. But it had taken that long just for Max's injuries to stabilize, for his legs and arm to begin to heal. Even when they'd been released and returned to Prague in special SHAPE ambulances, it had been another month before either Hadrian or Max had recovered enough to comfortably leave John and Karel's apartment. It was only now, deep into May, that Hadrian felt he was totally healed. Max was still hobbling along, stuck with a cane even though his casts had been removed.

The cane hadn't stopped Ivan from declaring a party absolutely, 100 percent necessary. Ivan had rushed to Hadrian's side as soon as he returned to Prague. During his recovery, he had kept both Hadrian and Max sane with delicious food and charming company. The visits from Vaclav hadn't hurt either.

Thinking of Ivan turned his thoughts to the odd family he'd somehow gathered around himself. Before Hadrian had stepped outside, John and Maggie had begun what promised to be a very competitive arm-wrestling competition. Karel and Ivan, out of loyalty, had bet on John, but everyone else—Donovan, Jitka, even Max—had put their money on the highly trained, highly armed Maggie. She was still living in Prague, though she'd dropped the pretense of being an English teacher and instead moved into the flat underneath Hadrian.

"Easier to keep an eye on you two before we go to trial," she'd said when he'd found out about the move. "Oh, relax. I'm not spying on you… that much." Maggie added with a wink when Hadrian had angrily protested.

Grudgingly, if tortured, he'd have to admit it wasn't that bad having her there. He'd been nervous to return to his flat, though the glass had been neatly repaired and the blood cleaned by SHAPE. There was a foul taste in the air that only grew worse when Max started sleeping over. Having Maggie beneath him helped remove some of that fear. It meant that he had help keeping Max safe. They were allies, much as he disliked her.

She sometimes brought up cookies. That helped too.

Hadrian's shoulder protested as he shifted in his seat, but he ignored it. It still hurt sometimes, especially in the damp. He wasn't sure if the pain would ever go away, but found he didn't care. It served as a reminder to hold on to what he loved. Of how easily it could slip away.

Hadrian's brooding was interrupted by the door opening behind him, letting out a swell of laughter and music before banging shut again. Lopsided footsteps treaded the grass, and Hadrian smiled as he recognized the limp as Max's. He was barefoot, Hadrian's city boy. Couldn't keep his shoes on once they stepped outside of Prague. He'd told Hadrian that he liked the way the earth felt beneath his feet.

It was just another one of the many things Hadrian was discovering about him.

"You've been out here awhile," Max said, moving gently beside him.

Hadrian side-eyed him and caught Max's wince. "Leg bothering you?"

"Just stiff," Max said, leaning into his side.

Hadrian lifted his arm and wrapped it around Max's shoulders. "So, how badly did John lose?" Hadrian said with a small smile. He'd bet on Maggie, just to annoy John. While John's animosity toward him had largely faded, there was still a level of discomfort that Hadrian couldn't help but poke at now and again.

Max winced.

"That bad, eh?" Hadrian laughed. He squeezed Max a little tighter. It was still such a novelty to put his arm around him, to feel him warm and safe against him.

"Let's just say that we should buy him dinner next time we go out."

"Fair enough. Like those new glasses," Hadrian added, as Max sighed and leaned his head on his shoulder. He did too. They were different from the silver he remembered. A thicker black metal that added a touch of sophistication to Max's look. They suited him.

"Still can't believe I had those plastic pieces of junk for so long," Max said, his forehead wrinkling in disgust. The emergency backup glasses the hospital had provided for him had been a recycled pair left over from the communist occupation. They had not been flattering, to say the least. "It was nice of the hospital to give them to me, sure, but…. Christ. How ugly can something get?"

Hadrian, wisely, said nothing.

Max fell silent, and Hadrian let the night sounds and the fire wind their way around them. Max felt good against him, solid and safe. He still couldn't believe how lucky he'd gotten. That day he'd found Max in Čapeks, his face blushing like a child caught stealing a cookie, was one of the best days in his life.

And speaking of Čapeks….

Hadrian shifted, rubbing his hand up and down Max's shoulder a moment. Nerves fluttered in his belly, but he plunged ahead. He had something to give Max, and now was as good a time as any. "You still planning on teaching when we get back to the city?"

Between their injuries and the general need to recuperate, Max hadn't been working since he'd returned to Prague. But lately he'd been growing restless, ready to get back to the normal pattern of life. The question now was, what did that mean?

"I don't know," Max said with a sigh. "Teaching is fine. I'm good at it. It pays enough, barely. But…."

"It's not what you're meant to be doing," Hadrian finished when Max fell silent.

"No," Max said. "It's not. I miss working with my hands. I miss repairing books and making new ones. I was good at that, dammit. But I just don't have the money to set up a shop in Prague, and building your reputation in the community takes so long. I'll have to teach for a few years while I set that up, I guess." He shifted, then turned a half smile to Hadrian. "Still, I can do it now. That's more than I'd ever expected. It might be hard, but it's worth it. It's just… going to take a while."

"Hmm. Well, maybe," Hadrian said, shifting uncomfortably.

"What do you mean?" Max asked, eyebrows furrowed behind his glasses.

"Ah—I've done something, lad. Try not to hate me too much. I was hoping it would be a surprise, but…. You know I know you're independent and I respect the hell out of you, right?" Hadrian fumbled. He was more nervous than he'd anticipated.

Max sat up and turned to face Hadrian fully. His expression was guarded. "Just tell me, Hadrian."

Hadrian puffed out his cheeks, then exhaled. "Well. You remember in Čapek's, the book repair room? Thing is, the guy who usually does their repairs injured his hand a while back. They weren't sure how long it would take to recover. But I was in there last week, talking to Andrea, and it turns out the damage is permanent. He can't come back to the shop. And I happened to mention that I know a top-class book-restorer who's looking for work, and…."

"And?"

"Well, I showed her that *Robot* book you made me. She liked it."

That was an understatement. Andrea had been very impressed with Max's work—more so when Hadrian explained to her that he'd done it in a bedroom, not a workshop, with a handful of basic tools.

Hadrian took a deep breath and met Max's eyes. "So, if you want, you've got a job there. Andrea will give you run of the workshop, in exchange for a 20 percent take on your commissions and first priority to any jobs that come through the shop. I told her you'd have to work out the final details, though. But the offer is there."

For a moment Max didn't move, and Hadrian forgot how to breathe. Then he stood, climbed into Hadrian's lap, and took his face in both his hands. "Thank you," Max said. "You grumpy, sexy bastard... thank you. God, I love you."

Max kissed him, and Hadrian brought his hands up to pull him tighter against his chest. The butterflies in his gut soared, but in the best way.

After a while, Max pulled his head back, still grinning and beautifully flushed in the light from the fire. "I mean it, you know. I really love you. Scares me sometimes."

"I love you too," Hadrian said, bringing his thumb up to trace Max's smile. He felt his heart skip in his chest, knew he'd never get tired of that feeling. "We can be scared together. If that's all right with you."

"I think we'll be just fine," Max said. "After all, you got shot for me. And I fell off a building with an evil international smuggler. Can't get much scarier than that, right?"

"Right," Hadrian said. "Now, shut up and kiss me."

Smiling, Max crashed his lips down onto Hadrian's.

Around them, the night quietly went on, the party behind them continuing to fill the air with laughter and hope. Hadrian twisted his hands tighter in Max's jacket, pulling him closer, knowing he would never let him go.

Together they waited out the dawn.

H. E. KOLLEF is an author and aspiring librarian. She was born in New Jersey, spent her early twenties writing and teaching English in the Czech Republic and Korea, and is currently attempting an MSc in Library Science in the UK. It is possible that she was bitten by a peculiar bug as a child, one that encouraged wandering feet and a tumbling mind. Her favorite city is Prague and she recommends it to everyone she meets, especially if she thinks they'd enjoy romance, hearty beer, and snowy walks along the winding Vltava river.

Her latest project is H. E.'s first foray into the world of romance novels; it is a contemporary thriller; there are explosions. You can learn more about it, along with her previously published work, at HannahKollef.com.

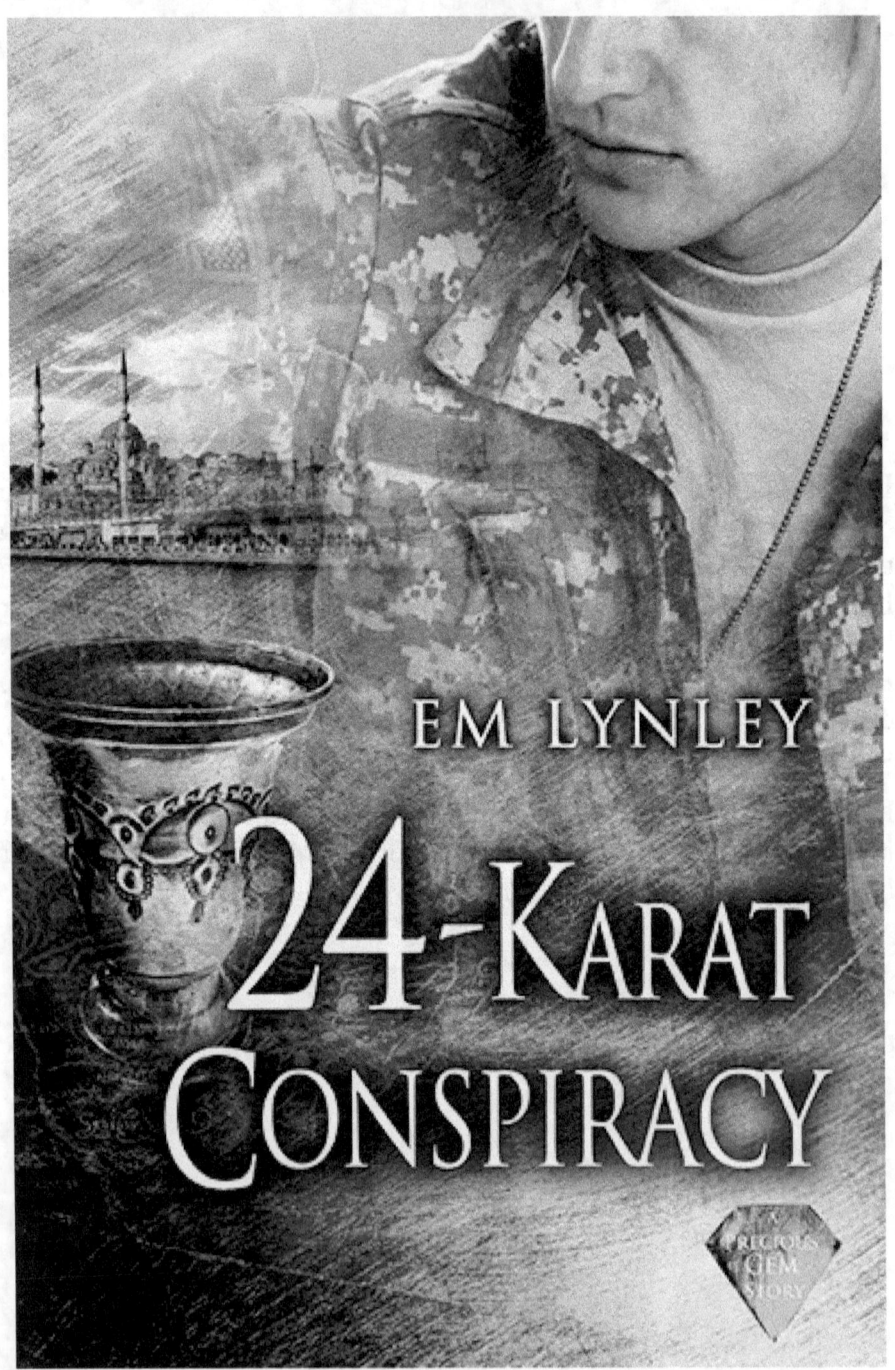

Maggie Kavanagh

Blind Spot

Also from Dreamspinner Press

www.dreamspinnerpress.com

Miller's Creek

R.G. GREEN

PAINFUL
LESSONS

S.C. WYNNE

www.ingramcontent.com/pod-product-compliance
Lightning Source LLC
Chambersburg PA
CBHW051632260626
47170CB00004B/1149